A Piece of Heaven

Abeni Kahmila

Shades of Yellow Publishing
Blue Springs, Missouri

Cover concept by: Vance Ashworth

Cover designed by: CreationsbyDonna@gmail.com

Layout and Interior designed by:
Interiorbookdesigns.com

ISBN 978-0-9914734-0-3

Library of Congress Control Number: 2014903297

Published by:
Shades of Yellow Publishing
Blue Springs, Missouri
www.shadesofyellowpublishing.com

This book is dedicated to anyone that has a dream. It doesn't matter who you are, it doesn't matter what your circumstance in life is at this point, you can still make your dreams come true.

Acknowledgments

I would like to thank God for watching, protecting, and guiding me throughout my journey. Thank you for the opportunity to have witnessed things that at the moment seemed like the worst thing ever, but in the end there were important lessons that I needed in order to grow into the woman I am today. Thank you for sending your guardian angels and spirit guides to watch over me during my writing process. I am forever grateful.

Thank you to my family and friends that supported me along the way, even if it was to simply looking at my fan page and offering feedback.

A special thanks to my beautiful children, Jordan and Ayah. I am thankful that I am your mother. Jordan, thank you for telling me that you believe in me. You will never know how much that meant to me. I know that I am inspiring you to great things along your journey, and I can't wait to see you evolve in a grown man. Sometimes I can't believe that you're sixteen now. When I think about the fact that I was pregnant with you when I was your age, I feel emotional. We have grown up together and made hard times, good times. We've struggled together, we laughed together, and we've argued together, but if there is one thing that I know for sure it's that we have always stuck together. You are my first love. Raising you has been a learning experience for us both. Thank you for loving me. You know how important the feeling of love is to me, and you are so good at showing love. Always remain positive and look at the bright side. Remember, it's not the problem, it is the way you handle the problem that matters.

Ayah, my sassy mini me. Thank you for sharing your time while I finished writing. You have been such a blessing in my life because when you were born I felt inspired again. I knew that you would be watching me, and it was important for me to give you something positive to watch. Thank you for being who you are. You're something special, your light shines bright anywhere you go. You'll always be blessed because you have an understanding about love, and inner peace at an early age. Keep meditating and you will always have love and inner peace.

To my Nephew Jelani, you are so special. You have so much charisma, and confidence. Next to your mother, I am your number one fan. Keep being you, and don't let anyone change who you are. Never forget, you have the power to determine who you become. Don't ever let haters rob you of your joy. You were born to be different, embrace it.

To Crystal, I would be typing all day if I mentioned all the things we've been through together. We have truly had our share of laughing, and crying but we have always had each other's backs no matter how much we can get on each other's nerves at times. To Brittan, I just love you to pieces. You are so sweet and genuine. I look to you for that calm, cool attitude laced with just the right amount of sassiness. It has been so fun getting to know you, thank you for loving my brother the way you do.

To both Crystal and Brittan, thanks so much for reading page after page, and offering honest, constructive feedback. I chose to have you two read because I feel like I can trust you. There are not enough words to express how much you both mean to me. I have been blessed enough to have you two as sisters whether we share blood or not.

To my Mother for teaching so much about life, I will keep your lessons with me forever.

To my Aunt Dolly for always being supportive of me and whatever I was going through, not only my book.

To Lyric Xpression for your beautiful spirit and powerful poetry. I can't thank you enough for putting me in contact with Glenda at Pink Kiss Publishing.

A special thanks to Glenda Wallace, thank you for your patience, your time, your support, your advice, your professionalism, etc. I am so thankful for your position in my life. Special thanks to Donna Osborn Clark with Creations by Donna for my book cover. I am so happy to have had the chance to work with you.

Special thanks to my brother, Vance Ashworth for all of your work on my book cover as well as the brainstorming, creative direction, and assistance with picking out the initial picture for the cover. I don't know what I would have done without your help because I didn't know where to start. We make a great team, its great exchanging ideas with a fellow artist that understands the vision that I had.

Chapter 1

If you looked at my life and seen what I've seen…

It was another Saturday night in my house, and I was bored as hell. I lie on the small bed in my room listening to my mother, Sharon, complain about how fucked up her life was. She was in the hallway right outside of my room, I could hear her clearly. She was literally kicking her bedroom door and screaming loudly saying that she was going to kill herself once and for all. As I listened to the banging from my room, I wondered if she had shoes on both feet, or if she only had one shoe on like the last time. I could hear her calling herself stupid bitches and whores. I hated when she threw tantrums like that, I always felt like I was going to have a panic attack when they occurred.

Listening to music was my only escape from the craziness my mother caused in the house on any given day. I would stay in my room and zone out to my music for hours at a time. It seemed like our house was always loud and chaotic. I was sixteen years old, but I felt years older. I carried the stress of thinking I was going to one day come home and find my mother dead from suicide since that seemed to be her favorite thing to say. Nothing made my mother happy, so the household walked on eggshells due to trying aimlessly not to upset her.

My mother constantly complained about money and bills. Her complaints had me stressed to the point where I was afraid to ask for anything, even things that I knew I needed. It seemed like there was never any money to buy things we needed or wanted. The one thing my mother did buy me was a pager. I loved it because I finally had something that the other kids at school had. She didn't buy the pager for me to fit in, though. She bought it so that when I even thought about leaving she could page me and remind me that I was on punishment. It seemed like she made up reasons for punishment as needed. I don't ever recall being asked how my grades were. I never got punished for things like grades. I got punished for being fed up with her bullshit. I could always feel my outbursts coming on because my heart would start to beat fast and I felt like I was suffocating. Some days these feelings would come at the moment I saw her car pull into the driveway. There wasn't ever a day when I lived with my mother that I was happy to see her walk in from work. I had a hard time understanding how every day could be a bad day. I understood that in life there would be bad days, but not every day. Some people appreciate life and all of its beauty. While I realize that I am one of those people, I also realize that my mother was not. There would always be a conflict between us for that reason.

My mother's life was exhausting to watch. I had seen my mother move on after years of being physically and mentally beaten by my father. After leaving my father, I watched her go from being independent and feeling like she didn't want or need a man. From there, she began settling. As pretty as I felt she was, my mother fell for an overweight, unattractive man named Dale with low self-esteem. This man was too insecure to ever let her leave his side unless it was for work. My mother seemed to equate Dale's insecurity with love. If he became jealous, in her mind, he cared. I guess it was okay that she went to work, since he didn't. Although he was consistent in stopping into her job ever so often without calling to make sure she was there.

My mother was a petite woman with what anyone would say was a perfect figure. She was definitely well proportioned at thirty-five years old. It bothered me to watch her wear clothing that hid her curves because Dale always got upset and accused her of cheating on him if she wore anything that was the least bit sexy. She never wore makeup because Dale didn't like makeup. He believed that by her wearing makeup she was trying to look pretty for someone else. Their relationship was the reason I planned to stay single forever. If this was how men were, I wanted no parts of them.

My mother had always had low self-esteem. That's what her siblings always said anyway. They made it seem as though she had talked about committing suicide even before my older sister was born. My dad told me that when they first started dating she always called herself ugly and stupid. He also said he became frustrated after a while because any compliment he gave her was turned around into something negative. At first, he thought her insecurities were cute because he could build her confidence. After a while he started wondering if something was really wrong. My mother never wanted him out of her sight. If he was away hanging out with his friends he had to be prepared to come home to a fight with my mother. I refused to believe that she thought so low of herself that she would put her insecurities on display to her man.

Whenever I asked my mother about her childhood, or past relationship, or anything about herself in general, she would get frustrated and change the subject. I went into my adulthood not really knowing who my mother was. One of the other things that my dad told me was that even though my mother talked about killing herself, she hadn't ever actually attempted following through with it when they were together. He believed my mother simply needed attention, and that was the only way she felt she could get it. I really didn't care what her reasoning or logic was. I was just sick of her saying she was going to kill herself. It was not uncommon for her to say that shit every day. I had tried for years to help her in the best way that I could, yet she always made me feel like my best wasn't good enough. I would listen to her and give her advice, though at some point, I became frustrated and disappointed in her. It took me years to learn that there was no help I could give her. I found that she had to learn to help herself. My mother never understood that happiness is a choice. It hurt me tremendously to watch her live her life never being totally happy.

On really bad days where any signs of happiness were nonexistent, it seemed like she would take her frustrations out on me. It was like when she felt the world kicked her ass, she would come home and kick mine. It wasn't always physical, though that would have been nice. It was most often mental abuse which seemed to hurt worse than any amount of physical pain. One of the things she frequently said was that she wished she could snap her fingers and we would all disappear. We knew she wasn't speaking of Dale when she said that. She made it clear that Dale was the only one she really wanted in her life at the time. The only time she realized that she had children was when Dale finally left her years later. I can still hear her voice in my head yelling, "WHY SHOULD I HAVE TO LEAVE MY MAN FOR Y'ALL?" She was only talking about her children and she made that clear by staring directly at us when she said it.

My mother made it known that she felt her children had ruined her life. For the life of me I couldn't figure out what would make someone say such awful things to her children. When she said things like that I felt the pain in my chest. I knew that we all got on her nerves, but I also realized that I got on her nerves more than my sister and brother because I was always mouthing off. I lost respect for mother as a child because she brought chaos wherever she went. She told me quite often that I reminded her of my father. My mother had always compared me to my father, yet she never had anything good to say about him. I was good at provoking her, but I knew not to say shit when she was going off on one of her rants. I was sure if I did say anything she would yell and say things to make me feel even worse than I already did. I would hide out in my room, or whatever room she wasn't in.

My mother was a master at belittling people. While others said I was so pretty, she made me feel so ugly. I believed I was unattractive for years, and why wouldn't I? The woman that birthed me gave me no validation in regards to being pretty. Sometimes, it wasn't the screaming or the awful things she said that got to me. It was the way she looked at me. The look on her face made me feel worse than shit on the bottom of her shoe. I avoided mirrors for years because I didn't like what I saw, and I didn't understand what other people saw. I thought my slanted eyes made me look like a Chinese girl and I wasn't proud of my dark chocolate skin. When I did get compliments on my tall slender body, I would downplay them. My mother was always praising my sister for her light skin, but never complimented me on my dark skin. I found this to be odd because my mother had the same dark skin that I had.

Chapter 2

Who can I run to when I need love?

I didn't understand why she chose to pick at mostly me all those years. As I got older and asked questions, I learned from my uncles and aunts that my mother had always hated being the only dark skinned child my grandmother had. She believed that was the reason my grandmother treated her differently from her other children. I also learned that my mother knew not to pick on my older sister, since Angel was my grandmother's first granddaughter. Angel was light-skinned like her father. This meant that even though it was clear that my grandmother hated me because she hated my father, she loved and protected Angel. My mother learned as a teenage unwed mother, living with her mother, not to fuck with my sister. My mother almost never got angry with my brother, Leonard Jr. She was loving and patient with him in a way that only a loving mother could be. My younger brother was the product of her love for my father, so there was no way she would ever treat him badly. My mother always reminded me that Leonard Jr. was planned; I was not. She reminded me of this as well. Despite the fact that I felt like my mother was always trying to force Leonard to choose sides, he and I were always very close. Leonard wasn't as close to Angel as he was to me, but they were close enough. Closer than Angel and I would ever be.

Angel hadn't lived with us for about a year by the time I was sixteen. My sister was eighteen years old, but acted like she was younger. She loved telling people how mature she was for her age, but she rarely showed it. She rented an apartment about ten minutes away from my mother's house with her best friend. I was thankful for the fact that Angel didn't live with us anymore. I couldn't stand her, and the feeling was mutual. When my mother wasn't around harassing me or provoking me, it was my sister. I doubt Angel ever realized how much it hurt that she was always making fun of me. Instead of helping me with my shortcomings, my sister laughed at them. She seemed to get a thrill out of saying mean things in an effort to hurt me. Sometimes, I wondered if Angel was as crazy as my mother. The main thing she said to make me cry was saying my father was a "crack head". I honestly had no idea that my father was on drugs of any kind until Angel told me. I was about ten years old, and that shit hit me like a ton of bricks. I knew my mother would not do anything to my sister for saying those hurtful things about my father but I told her anyway.

When Angel initially told me that awful news I wasn't bothered by it because I knew it wasn't true. I also knew my father had my back, and although he wasn't Angel's father, I believed that when he spoke, she would listen. So I told her that I was going to call my daddy right then and tell him what she said. I had tears in my eyes because my feelings were so hurt that she could even think to say something so mean. I grabbed the phone, and she stood right behind me with her hands on her skinny hips.

My sister stood in the kitchen and rolled her green eyes as she spoke to me. "Heaven, do you really think I care if you call your daddy on me? He's just a stupid crack head. What can he do to me?"

I put the phone down and decided against the call altogether. I cried even harder. I didn't respond to Angel, I left her standing in the kitchen with an evil stare on her beautiful face. I simply walked past her and into the living room where my mother was sitting watching TV and smoking a cigarette.

When I went to tell my mother this vicious lie told to me, my mother said, "Honestly, Heaven, why are you making this such a big deal? I thought you knew ya daddy was a crack head."

I was standing in front of her as she sat on the couch with Dale. I said, "No! I didn't know that! How would I have known? Nobody told me anything!" I was pouting like a toddler, even though I was ten years old at the time.

My mother looked at me as though I was exhausting her. It was clear that she was trying to be patient. She took a long pull off of her cigarette and exhaled toward the sky, as though she were being considerate of me by not blowing smoke in my face. After her long pause, she replied, "Well now you know. Ain't no sense in cryin' over spilled milk. It is what it is."

I stormed off and slammed the door to my room.

My mother yelled at me as I ran up the stairs, "Don't you slam doors in my god damn house! You don't pay no bills here god dammit!"

I never forgot that night. Up until that point, I wasn't sure what a crack head was, but I was sure that it wasn't a good thing. I had seen kids at school get into fights when someone jokingly called them or their family member a crack head.

Angel followed me upstairs to our room after I talked to my mother. She was bothering me and she knew it.

I sat on my bed watching her sit in front of her dresser brushing her hair. The smirk on her face was undeniable. Aside from the talk about suicide that my mother did, Angel and Mother were a lot alike. They actually looked a lot alike as well. The difference was that Angel was lighter and had long brown hair. Both of them were shorter than me, and had nice figures. Personally, I couldn't stand being around either of them because they bored me to pieces. They were always flattering each other and saying how beautiful the other was. When Angel lived with us she spent most of her time in the bathroom mirror or in front of her dresser mirror acting like she was posing for pictures, or brushing her hair. She was always inconsiderate about taking showers, too. Angel couldn't care less about how long her shower lasted or that she used all the hot water. I really believed that I didn't fit in at my mother's house and that my living conditions were awful. I wished my father wasn't strung out on drugs almost every day of my life.

Chapter 3

I decided to hop out of the bed and make a move since my mother had pulled one of her usual moves. After her tantrum, she ran out of the house, got into her car and sped off saying she wasn't going to come back. These were the best days for me, because it meant that I was able to break out of prison, if only for one night. The consequence the next day would be worth it. As usual, Dale sat on the couch looking stupid in the face. It made me laugh that she affected him this way. It wasn't an "I feel sorry for you" look. It was more like a "this bitch is crazy and I don't know what to do" look. This was a normal day in our house, and it was sickening to say the least. It felt like the moment I walked in from school my mood changed. I didn't understand positive and negative energy at the time, but I did know that I felt safe only in my room. I got the vibe that I was an intruder anywhere else in the house. I had made my room as comfortable and cozy as possible, since that was where I spent most of my time. I rarely saw roaches in my room, which was odd since roaches seemed to be everywhere else in the house. I was able to keep it clean and situated just how I liked it also. It was always quiet, and that was something I cherished since my mother was always beating the doors until they had holes in them, or breaking dishes, or pulling out her hair and yelling "FUCK YOU, BITCH" to herself. I was able to tune at least some of the noise out with my stereo that I had gotten for Christmas the previous year.

I felt like I lived in a madhouse and it was survival of the fittest. We were almost always hungry, since there was rarely an abundance of food in the house. I found that to be sad because my mother worked two jobs for as long as I could remember. It didn't make sense to me that we always had to do without. My mother was always defensive when I asked about money, but I suspected she worked so much because Dale didn't work enough. I would be defensive too if I had a worthless man living off of me. That would never be me. I would be single before I worked like a damn slave and I had a man living with me. It bothered me to see him laid up on the couch watching TV, and drinking a beer on a day-to-day basis, like he didn't have a care in the world. He lacked the sense of pride that I felt a man should have. Dale had pride, but he didn't have the right kind of pride. The *right* kind of pride is working to make an honest living in order to provide for your family so that they don't do without. My mother made it okay for Dale to be mediocre. Despite how often my mother and sister complimented each other, she believed she couldn't do any better than Dale. Watching the relationship they had made me feel like I didn't ever want to be in one.

I had a nice long nap, and I knew it was time for me to step out for a while. I was staring into my closet at my clothes while I grooved to the radio. I wanted to leave the house since my mother wasn't there. I knew when she came home she would blow my pager up, but I didn't care about that. I just wouldn't answer her page. The problem was that I had nowhere to go. My two friends, Tandra and Zandra, who were twin sisters, were my age and they were stuck at home too, so kicking it with them wasn't an option. Just when I was about to give up any hope of leaving the house, my cousin, Misa, called. Misa was eighteen years old which was the same age as my sister. Misa and Angel didn't get along, for some reason. My sister was always rude to Misa. I loved Misa so much because she was always more like a sister to me than Angel.

Misa was heavyset, but not what I would consider fat. She was what we call "thick" in the black community. Misa wore her hair short, and kept it colored honey blonde. She had always been so pretty to me and had a smile that could light up any room. Misa was always telling me how pretty I was, and she seemed to genuinely believe that. I didn't see how she could think I was so pretty, especially in comparison to how pretty she was. She was light-skinned, with a cute round face. Misa was always fun to be around, too. She had this personality where she could get along with most anyone. She was always telling jokes, or giving me advice about "these niggas" as she would say. Misa was a bad influence in a lot of ways, but I didn't realize that then. All I knew was that despite the fact that she had heard through the family grapevine that I was this awful, mean, and fast slut, she fucked with me. My mother was really good at talking to her three sisters, mostly lying about things that I had done. She had them all thinking I was the spawn of Satan by the time she got done talking to them. For years I cried because I cared about the way my family viewed me. After a while I stopped giving a fuck. When I saw my mother around her family – or other people that knew her – she came off like a saint. I would think I was a liar and a slut too, if I heard my mother's description of myself. Behind closed doors, I would question my mother as to why she lied about things I had done.

She would look at me like I was wrong for asking and simply say, "Well, you might as well have said the things that I said you said." The Sharon that we saw in the house was different from the Sharon that others saw. When I told her that might as well and actually doing, are two different things, she got upset with me. At some point, I learned that when my mother told people those crazy lies, she truly believed them.

I sat on the edge of my bed listening to Misa on the phone talk about how she was bored too. Her tone was hype which was usual. She asked me what was up with me for the night. She had her mother's car and was about to leave her mother's house in North Kansas City to come to South Kansas City where I lived to pick me up. I had twenty minutes to get ready. Before we hung up I told her she had to hurry up in case my mother came home.

After I hung up with her, I took a shower in case I ended up fucking that night. I was a virgin, but I was tired of being a virgin. Both of my best friends had already had sex. They made me feel like I was missing something. I took extra time cleaning my pussy, and smelling the towel to make sure I was fresh. My biggest fear was someone saying they fucked me and my pussy stunk. I went back into my room and put on my Fruit of the Loom panties. I didn't have any sexy underwear and that pissed me off. I wore my black bodysuit with my hunter green jeans and black Jodeci boots to go with it. I knew the outfit was outdated and played out, but I didn't have anything else. It was one of the few outfits I had that made me feel like I looked older than my age. I wore my long jet black hair in a wrap. I thought I looked okay, but I needed makeup. I would get eyeliner for my lips and eyes and red lipstick for my lips once I was with Misa.

When Misa pulled up and honked exactly twenty minutes later, I was grabbing my purse to leave. My little brother, Leonard, came out of his room and told me that he was telling our mother. He assured me that I would get into trouble. Leonard was always my sidekick, and even though he said he would tell on me, I knew he wouldn't. My brother had gotten his ass beat for lying to my mother to keep me out of trouble. Those were the few times he got into trouble for having my back. I knew he simply didn't want me to leave with Misa out of concern. I loved him a lot and appreciated the love he gave me, but I had to get out. I wasn't a dummy, contrary to what my mother and sister thought. I knew I would be in trouble when I came back, I simply didn't give a fuck. I had gotten to the point where I got a kick out of upsetting the household. My logic was that mother called me bad, so I would show her bad.

As soon as I opened the car door to my Aunt Trina's '92 Toyota Camry all I smelled was weed smoke. Misa was already as high as a kite. I heard "I Got 5 on It" blasting from the radio. She passed the blunt to me as she pulled off bobbing her head to the music. I hit the blunt a couple of times and passed it back. We were talking and laughing hysterically over the music while I looked in the mirror trying to put on eyeliner and lipstick. I was admiring myself in the mirror because I believed I was my sexiest when I was high. I didn't ask where we were going because it didn't matter. I was just happy to be out of the house.

We were on the highway headed "down north." She lived in the suburbs, and at the time, South KC was considered the suburbs as well. For us, going to the city was exciting. We were riding around looking for something to get into when my pager went off. I checked the number and it was Joey. I had met Joey on one of the nights that I had snuck out with Misa. We didn't get to talk as often as I would have liked in the two week time span that I had known him. In fact, we had only talked on the phone twice and once in person the first time we met in the Burger King parking lot. I thought he was really cute, mainly because he was light-skinned, had a gold tooth, and his Nautica jacket made me think he had money. At that time, that was the perfect package for me. Tonight would be the second time we saw each other. I told Misa that he was paging me, so she pulled over into Paul's Liquor Store parking lot so I could use a pay phone. We were in a rough neighborhood, but I wasn't scared at all. I was almost too excited about all the boys that looked different from the boys at my school to be afraid. That thuggish shit drove me crazy, and from what I saw, they were rugged and didn't have a fear in the world. I dialed Joey's number. When he answered, I asked who paged, knowing it was him since I recognized the number. He told me he wanted me to come through and chill with him. I told him I would and that I had my cousin with me.

We went to his shabby apartment that was in a terrible looking neighborhood. I wasn't afraid at Paul's Liquor Store, but for some reason, I was afraid here. There were people standing outside looking spooked like zombies, there were also people casually serving them whatever drug they needed.

Misa and I put our game faces on and walked past them. We passed two girls outside yelling and screaming at each other about who fucked whose man. A small child that looked to be no more than three years old sat on the porch of the complex watching. The argument between the two young women didn't really scare me since I felt like I knew how to defend myself, and their argument over their boyfriend had nothing to do with me.

When we walked into the hallway, the smell of piss and old garbage seemed to smack us right in the face. Joey eventually met us in the stinky hallway. He was calm and cool as he walked up and asked us what was up. He didn't seem to be phased by his surroundings. He looked nice in his plaid shirt, with denim jeans that fit him perfectly. He had his braided belt tied so that the end hung out from underneath his shirt. He was wearing dark brown Timberland boots and I could tell they were expensive.

Misa walked in front of me as we followed Joey to his apartment. She had a strong personality and always had to lead. I didn't mind because I didn't have a strong personality and I hated leading, I was a better follower. After he opened the door to his place, he let Misa walk past him to get in. Then he blocked the door so I couldn't walk in without touching him. He stood in the doorway smiling at me while he looked me up and down. He asked me why I looked so nervous. I lied and said I wasn't. He coolly shrugged, then moved aside so that I was able to walk into the apartment.

When we walked into his apartment, I was surprised to find that it was clean. After all, he was a male and I thought they were all messy. The couch was old and worn out, the kitchen table was just as old and only had three chairs that didn't match. There was a big ass stereo in the corner of the living room. He was blasting "Po' Pimp" as though he didn't have neighbors. Joey and his younger brother, Kev, shared the apartment he lived in. Kev was very quiet, almost to the point of weirdness. He didn't speak to me and I didn't speak to him when I walked in and sat down. We were sitting on the couch listening to music while Misa stared at Kev like he was a piece of meat. I knew based on her track record that she would fuck him that night. Joey and Kev were sitting across from us in dining room chairs that they brought into the living room. Misa was dancing harder to the music than she needed to, so that her breasts would bounce. I wasn't sure if she was trying to fuck the chair, or show Kev that she was interested. Kev watched the show that Misa was putting on and didn't try to hide it. I knew Joey was trying to play it off, but he was looking too.

At some point, we started drinking Alize and Sprite, and I started feeling more relaxed. Joey started flirting more, and smiling at me. I had a buzz from the liquor and I was feeling more confident. I began to flirt back with him. I lied to him and told him that I was seventeen, so I was trying to act the same way I thought a seventeen year old would act. I assumed seventeen year olds were wiser, and were surely having sex. I had no idea whether or not I was saying or doing the right thing. I was trying not to act nervous, since I knew that most seventeen year olds probably weren't nervous around boys. Joey was twenty years old and I assumed that he wouldn't entertain me if he knew the truth.

Chapter 4

Just bring the weed, we got the drinks you need…

After a while, Kev and Misa left the room. Joey got up and turned the music down. There was a rap song playing that I thought was more than disrespectful. The rapper was saying, "Bitches ain't shit but hoes and tricks," and I found that to be disgusting. I was mad at myself for thinking it was catchy and that I liked the beat. Despite the cool beat, I felt like the music was still too loud, but I was going with the flow so I didn't say anything about it.

Joey seemed so confident, like there wasn't a nervous bone in his body. He sat down right next to me on the couch. He sipped his drink while watching me. He asked me if I was cool, and I told him I was as I sipped my drink as well. In all actuality, I wasn't cool. I was nervous as hell. I knew that I liked him and I wanted him to like me, too. We sat and talked. I was shocked at how normal he seemed. I thought he would be too cool to lighten up and laugh, but I was wrong. If he told me once that I was pretty and sexy, he told me twenty times. The more we vibed, the more I was feeling him. The more alcohol I drank, the more chilled out I became. I took a joint out of my purse that Misa had given me before we walked in and asked if he wanted to smoke with me.

He chuckled. "You don't seem like the type to smoke."

I asked, "What do you mean by that? What does a weed smoker look or act like?"

He explained that I went to a "white" school and the girls were the prissy, stuck-up type and they normally didn't "get down like that". His comments hurt my feelings. I didn't see myself as prissy or stuck-up at all. His ignorant comments irritated me, so I rolled my eyes at him and lit the joint.

After I hit it a couple of times, I watched him watch me. I asked if he was going to smoke it or not. He took a few pulls then asked if I was mad at him for saying those things about what type of person I could have been. I told him I wasn't and I busted out laughing hysterically. I couldn't stop laughing because all of a sudden, I found it to be hilarious that he would think I was stuck-up. Joey sat on the couch and watched me, then laughed a little. His laugh was nothing like mine. I had my head in my lap to hide my face because I was laughing so hard.

Joey said, "You got you a buzz, huh? That was some fire shit you brought, huh?" The look in his eyes grossed me out for some reason because he looked horny, like he could jump my bones at any given moment. I did try to contain myself and become at least somewhat serious in an effort not to look like a child. I was ashamed because I had only had a few pulls from the joint and I was behaving like I was at Def Comedy Jam. Once I pulled myself together, we relaxed on the couch with laid-back grins on our faces.

After a while, he asked if he could kiss me. I told him yes. I had never tongue kissed before, but I was about to learn. I didn't bother to tell him that I had never tongue kissed before. His lips were soft and thick, I felt myself becoming turned on. I wasn't a pro at kissing by any means, but somehow I knew he was in his comfort zone. I was judging by the way my body felt. He was slowly swirling his tongue in my mouth. He stopped and looked me in my face and asked if I was cool. I told him I was, so he got up and turned all the lights off in the place. The only lighting was from the stereo.

As he walked back towards the couch, I saw that he had unbuttoned his pants. I also noticed that his dick was hard. I was turned on and ready to see how far things would go for the remainder of the night. I was hoping that we could speed things up a bit. I heard moaning coming from the only bedroom in the house and I was becoming envious. Misa and Kev were in the room fucking, and I wanted to be doing the same.

Joey came back to the couch after turning off the lights and started kissing me again, while attempting to undo my bra. When I realized that he was struggling with my bra, I helped him by unsnapping it. He lifted my shirt up and starting sucking on my breasts. I tilted my head back and moaned softly. I had never felt anything like what I was feeling. Eventually, I laid my head on the arm of the couch. He scooted my body down so that I lay on the seat of the couch and started unbuttoning my shirt. After he unbuttoned my shirt, I took it off along with my bra and tossed them onto the chair across from us. He climbed on top of me and slow grinded on me while he sucked on my neck. I had my hands on his head as I awkwardly nibbled on his ear. He made his way to my breasts again and kissed them. I was rubbing his head like it was a crystal ball and I was a fortune teller. He stopped teasing my breasts and looked up at me and laughed. I still had my hands on his head when he said, "Will you stop that? That doesn't even feel good." I moved my hands fast and rested them at my sides. Before I could think of a reply he said, "You ready for me?" I knew we were done making out when he asked if I was ready for him. I was ready, and I told him just that. He was on top of me as he unbuttoned my jeans and I rubbed his dick through his boxer shorts. He stood up and pulled his jeans down to his ankles, but he didn't take them off. He also left his shirt on. His dick popped out of his boxers like it was trapped and was finally set free. I couldn't help but stare, though I tried not to. Joey watched me watch his big ass dick. I got up and took my jeans and grandma panties off. I was totally naked as he sat on the couch and admired my body, but he never took his clothes all the way off. We were kissing, but at that point, it was bullshit kissing because we both knew what time it was. I was finally going to enjoy the feeling that my friends had experienced.

Joey tried to finger me, and it hurt like hell. I kept squirming, and fidgeting. He was confused and asked if I was a virgin. I assured him that I had been with my ex for three years and we had sex all the time. Joey either believed my lie about having had a boyfriend, or he didn't give a fuck one way or the other. He had started trying to finger me with two fingers then went to one. I grabbed the couch and squeezed the sheet that covered the couch because of the pain I felt. He was finally able to get his finger in, it felt awful. It seemed like all he was doing was using his finger to explore, like he was learning too. He was on top of me at first then he stopped fingering me and sat next to me. I didn't know what he was going to say. He kissed me on my cheek and smiled at me. His smile suggested that he was trying to come off as patient, but that wasn't the case. He told me that he knew I was a virgin. I kept up my lie and said I wasn't. He challenged me and told me that since I wasn't a virgin it shouldn't be shit to fuck him right then. I was almost turned off by that comment. I felt like he was bullshitting me, I thought we both knew what we wanted. What difference did it make if I was a virgin anyway?

Joey pulled a condom from the pocket of his jeans, then sat on the couch and put it on. I noticed it was a Magnum, I guessed that meant he really did have a big dick. Sometimes, when I eavesdropped on the conversation the boys had in school, they said they only wore Magnum condoms because they couldn't fit regular sized condoms.

After the condom was on him, he climbed on top of me and attempted to put his dick in. His dick wouldn't go in because of my moving and squirming. The room became hot all of a sudden, even Joey was sweating. He started off pumping softly then as he realized he wasn't making progress, he started pumping more aggressively.

I was literally in tears because of the pain, he couldn't tell because it was dark in the room. I let my tears roll down my face, and sniffled ever so often. I couldn't believe this was the feeling I had been chasing, this was what my best friend, Tandra, said made her irritable if she didn't have it. The tip of his penis was barely in my vagina. I felt a throbbing sensation, and not a good one.

Neither of us was saying a word, he was determined to get that cum off for the night. Finally, after one good thrust, his penis was inside of me. I felt a slight pop, and then he kept pumping. I felt like I was in hell, the pain never stopped the entire time. I felt like I had a cramp right on my pelvic wall. He rudely told me to open my legs, so I did.

After about six pumps, Joey busted a nut. I was sure that he had busted because his lower body shook and he started moving differently. When he was done, his body collapsed on top of me. I laid there feeling more emotional than I had ever felt in my life. I wanted to cry. After about a minute he got up, pulled his pants up and told me that I could go into his bathroom and wash up. I got up and grabbed my clothes and went into the small bathroom.

Chapter 5

All I wanted was a little love....

The closet in my room was bigger than the bathroom in their apartment. I saw a folded towel sitting on the sink, so I wet it and used his soap to clean myself. As I wiped my throbbing vagina, I felt pain. I looked at the towel and saw blood. I didn't panic because my friends had already told me what to expect. I finished cleaning myself and looked in the mirror to fix my hair. I stopped messing with my hair and studied my reflection in the mirror. I didn't like who I saw. I understood at that very moment what I had done. I had given away the most precious gift I could ever give a man. I had given Joey my virginity. I had laid on a couch with a man I barely knew, and got fucked while listening to some gutter ass rap music. This was not how it was supposed to happen. What the fuck was I thinking?

As much as I didn't want to, I went back into the living room where Joey was sitting on the couch. Before I walked into the living room I snuck and put my ear to the door where Misa was with Joey's brother. I didn't hear anything but snoring, and that pissed me off. I was ready to go home, or at least get the fuck out of there.

We sat listening to music without saying a word to each other. Joey's head was leaned back on the couch and his hands were behind his neck. He was rapping along with his music, while bobbing his head. He had his legs stretched out and crossed. This dude was obviously on chill mode.

I didn't recall falling asleep, I just remember waking up. Joey and I were sleeping on the couch that we fucked on. It was a small couch so we were cramped. He slept behind me with his arms wrapped around my waist. I kept hearing my pager go off. I knew it had to be my mother. I knew I wasn't going to return the page, but I jumped up in panic because I knew I had fucked up. I looked out the window and it was broad daylight. I hadn't planned on spending the night. When I got up, Joey slowly woke up and told me to calm my ass down, then he turned over and went back to sleep. I completely ignored him and went and banged on the door to Kev's room.

Misa came to the door like I was bothering her. She didn't say shit, she just rolled her eyes and walked past me to the bathroom and closed the door.

I went and put my shoes on in the living room and ran my fingers through my hair to at least attempt to fix it.

Joey was up by this time, he stretched while he told me to chill out. After all, it couldn't be that big of a deal that I had left my mother's house without permission then stayed out all night.

Misa calmly came out of the bathroom, no rush whatsoever. She casually told me that my mother had been paging her back-to-back as well. The fact that my mother was paging her seemed to irritate her. She told me that she wasn't going to call her back. She asked if I was ready without looking at me. Of course I was ready. What kind of fucking question was that?

I gave Joey a hug when we left, only because he asked, not because I wanted to. I felt hatred toward him and I hoped I never saw him again in life. I blamed him for me losing my virginity.

Misa didn't bother to give Kev a hug, and he didn't bother to get up to see us out.

On the ride to my house, I asked Misa what they did in Kev's room. She laughed and asked me what I thought they did. When I told her I thought they did the same thing Joey and I did she looked alarmed. She stopped smiling and looked at me in a strange way. We rode in silence for about five minutes. Then she asked me if we used a condom, and I told her that we did. We rode the rest of the way to my house in awkward silence. She acted like she couldn't believe this happened. I wasn't sure what she thought would go on when she gave me a joint and left me alone in the room with Joey. I had never seen her look so serious in my life.

When we got to my mother's house, Misa practically sped off as soon as the car door opened. I didn't see my mother's green Camry parked in the driveway. I figured she was at her second job since she normally worked the entire day on the weekends. She had worked part-time for years. I was relieved that she wasn't home. I planned to soak in a hot bath because my pussy was still hurting.

When I walked into the house the first person I saw was Leonard. He came out of his room and told me that my mother was pissed and I was in big trouble. I already knew that, so I became defensive with him. I demanded that he get the fuck out of my face. I wasn't in the mood to hear that, I needed to get my ass in the tub. Leonard told me that our mother had been calling my friends' parents to find me. How embarrassing was that? I didn't want my friends in my business unless it was me that put them in it.

I left Leonard standing in the hallway and walked past my mother and Dale's room. As usual, Dale was laid across the bed looking fat and lazy watching TV. When he saw me his face looked as if he had seen a ghost. I laughed to myself at him, because I knew he wouldn't say anything to me. He would get up and call my mother at work and alert her of my arrival. I went into my room and grabbed clean underwear, sweats and a t-shirt to put on after my bath. I went into the bathroom, ran my bath water and added plenty of bubble bath and olive oil to the water. I sat on the stool as I waited for the tub to fill up, looking through the numbers in my pager. I wanted to see if Joey would page me to say something. I'm not sure what I wanted him to say, but I guess it didn't matter anyway. He didn't page me, and why would he? The chase was over. Joey had gotten from me what I could never give another man again. I pondered the thought as my eyes started to water. I decided right then that whatever happened with Joey and I that night didn't happen at all. It was my word against his and he couldn't prove shit. I wanted the chance to lose my virginity again. The next time would be done the right way. The only pages I had were from the twins' phone number and my mother. My mother had paged me about twenty times in a row. She would put "911" at the end of our home number to signify an emergency. I would deal with my mother and her emergency later. I got into the tub and enjoyed the hot water. I could barely clean myself since between my legs was still hurting.

Chapter 6

I'm gonna knock you out...

After my hot bath, tired wasn't the word for how I felt. I went into my room and turned on my radio. I planned to lay there and zone out listening to the music. Instead, I ended up falling asleep for what seemed like hours. When I woke up it was dark outside. I'm not sure when my mother walked into my room, but I felt someone staring at me while I slept. I sat up sleepy-eyed in my bed and looked at her. I wasn't sure what to say, I was trying to figure out what her next move would be.

She turned the light on as soon as I sat up. I noticed she had on a t-shirt with leggings and a pair of tennis shoes. My mother also had a belt in her hand. I already knew that it was about to be a bad night because I was not about to get hit with a belt. I was sick of that shit. Why was it always me getting my ass beat when I was wrong and not my brother? I lost count of how many times I had asked my mother to talk to me and tell me what I did to upset her like she did with Leonard. It bothered me immensely that she felt that she had the right to hit me with a belt when she was mad. I took it as disrespect. She taught me early on that when someone puts their hands on me to hit them back. Was she supposed to be exempt from what she taught me?

"Where the fuck you been all night?" my mother asked.

I told her I had been with Misa all night. She asked me again where I had been. Her tone was downright nasty. The truth was that at this point it didn't matter where I had been, she was clearly heated. Now I was on the defense, so I told her again, rudely, that I had been with Misa. I was defensive because I despised being cursed at. It made me lose respect for her and I wanted to talk to her the same way she thought she could talk to me. After the second time that I told her where I had been, she stood there with a look of hate in her eyes. My mother told me to stand up. Reluctantly, I did as she asked. As I stood in front of her, she told me that she was giving me one more chance to tell her where I had been all night. There was no way that I was going to tell her exactly where I had been.

My heart was pumping from fear but I couldn't let her know that. I felt like it would be flattering for her to know that I was afraid of her. I learned at an early age not to let her know that she had gotten to me. I taught myself the "never let them see you sweat" rule after years of dealing with my mother taking advantage of the fact that I feared her.

I vividly recall her coming in from work in one of her fucked up moods. She walked into the house and slammed the front door behind her. She started complaining about life and how she regretted coming home to the same shit every day. My mother felt like she should have kept driving and end up in the middle of nowhere. She said anything would be better than coming home to her children who were always in her face stressing her out. She changed her clothes then came into my room. She never felt she had to knock in a respectful manner since it was her house. My mother typically either beat at the door with her fist, or if it was cracked she would kick it open like she was trying to knock it off the hinges. I normally jumped in panic because I knew she was looking for trouble. I was eleven years old at the time, but age didn't matter to her.

That particular day, she beat at the door with her fist. I got up and opened it immediately. I didn't say anything when I opened the door. I just stood and stared at her. My mother had a wild look in her eyes. The crazy look in her eyes was replaced quickly with a look of amusement. She was amused by my fear. She told me to come into the living room with her. Her tone was downright nasty and she had a belt in her hand. We walked from my room to the living room where Dale was standing looking like a guard dog. He had a smug look on his face and he didn't blink as he stared at me. My mother asked me why had I lost my house key. She also asked me what I would have done if Dale wasn't home. Dale didn't say shit; he just stared at me like he was loving every minute of my mother behaving this way. I was more hurt by the fact that I felt like my mother was acting out to prove something to Dale. My voice was shaking as I answered my mother. I was trying not to say the wrong thing because I didn't want to get a whooping. I hated the way I felt when I was hit with a belt. The physical pain was nothing since she was a small woman and her hits weren't hard at all. It was the emotional aspect of being hit that got to me. The fact that when she saw tears, she felt that she had won. I told her that I would have gone across the street to my friend's house if Dale wasn't home. That answer wasn't good enough for her. She yelled at the top of her lungs that it was the most stupid thing I could have said. My mother made it clear that she didn't understand how that made sense when she paid her hard earned money for me to have a house key. She told me to bend over and put my hands on the arms of the couch and not to move. I did as she said in tears, but I begged her not to hit me. She assured me that it was too late to beg since I had already lost my key and I had to suffer the consequence. It was fucked up in my opinion because I had only lost my key to get in the house that one time. My mother made it clear that my role was to see that Leonard got in after school every day. God forbid he had to stand outside in the cold, or be too hot in the summer dealing with my shit.

I was bent over waiting for the thick leather belt that she nicknamed "the motivator" to hit my ass. When the belt did hit my ass, I screamed out in horror. My feelings were hurt more than anything. I simply made a mistake, but in our house there were no mistakes. I begged and pleaded for her to stop the entire five minutes that she hit me with the belt. I didn't try to turn around, or move from my position at the end of the cheap baby blue couch in our living room. The more I begged her to stop the harder she hit me, so I just stopped and cried as I listened to her. She was telling me between hits all that could have gone wrong as a result of me losing my house key. The main thing was Leonard being locked out behind my irresponsibility.

I felt like I was having a pissing contest with my mother in my room the night I returned home from hanging out with Misa. I knew I was wrong for sneaking out, and not calling her to let her know I was alive as well as other things. I told myself on the car ride home with Misa that I would take whatever punishment my mother had for me, excluding a physical beating. I felt like my mother was aware of my mindset as far as being hit with a belt. She was trying to see how far she could go before I lost control of my temper. We stood staring at each other and she said, "So you're not going to tell me where you were all night, Heaven? Is this the way you want it?" Her look was supposed to be a warning, but I felt like calling her bluff that night.

I chose not to say anything, I was curious as to how far she planned to go as well. I simply stood there and looked at her as if to say "do your worst", I was tired of playing this game with my mother.

Before I could even think about saying anything, my mother slapped me across the face with The Motivator. There was no hit on my ass that could compare to the way my face was throbbing in pain. I immediately reacted violently because I was so angry. I felt too angry at the time to deal with the fact that my feelings were hurt by her behavior. I yelled at my mother as loud as I could that I hated her, and I called her a stupid bitch. As I yelled at her, I rushed at her and punched her in the stomach. I was ready for a fight after years of taking her verbal and mental abuse. I was fed up with her transferring her negative energy to me and everyone else. When I punched her in the stomach I felt a sense of relief, I felt like she deserved to have her ass beat by me. I was pissed when Dale ran into the room and pulled me away from her and threw me onto my bed as though I were a rag doll.

My mother stood in the middle of the floor in my room in a state of shock. I honestly don't think she ever thought that I would put my hands on her. Dale had been in their room sitting on the edge of the bed listening the whole time. When he ran into my room he was only wearing a pair of briefs, and the smell of his body was nauseating. When Dale threw me on the bed, I went into attack mode. He was trying to pin me down but I refused to let him, I kicked him repeatedly and spit in his face as I called him a pussy. For me it wasn't really about me staying out all night. It was more about me being sick of those two.

My mother stood there as he manhandled me all over my twin bed with her arms folded as though she was satisfied. He was finally able to grab hold of my wrists and pin me down. His big body was on top of mine and his breath was only comparable to death, it smelled awful. As I tried to wiggle myself from his firm grasp, he moved faster so that I couldn't move. He was telling me how disrespectful I was and that I was going to pay for my behavior.

I wasn't really concerned about Dale, the fact was I hated him and we both knew it. I wanted more of my mother and I was determined to get to her because I wanted to kick her ass. I felt like she deserved an ass kicking more than anyone. Her ass kicking would be for talking against my father to me, for upholding my brother constantly, for making me feel stupid at every opportunity she got, for lying on me to her sisters, for allowing Dale to put his hands on me tonight, and ultimately, not making me feel like she loved me. It was on. The anger that I felt in my heart fueled my desire to get Dale off of my small body. I used my long legs to kick him in the stomach since he had me on my back. He let out a loud grunt as he rolled off of me. I jumped up and came at my mother again. I felt powerful since I thought I saw fear in her eyes. My mother dropped The Motivator when she realized I was coming to attack her. I felt a level of rage I hadn't ever felt before.

Unfortunately for me, the fear that I thought I sensed in my mother wasn't actually fear at all. There wasn't a morsel of her that was afraid of me. I was planning to come in for another punch in her stomach but she caught my fist in her hand. I didn't want to let her know that I was shocked at her being so quick. I thought she was too old to be fighting and I had planned to use that to my advantage. I knew she had her share of fights growing up, but I didn't suspect she still had any real fight in her. She pushed me like she was fighting a grown woman, not her child. She asked me if I was feeling froggish, and she begged me to leap if I was. Despite the fact that her tone and her stance were defensive, I still came back at her after she pushed me.

Dale was standing in the doorway holding his stomach and yelling at my mother. He was telling her that I needed my ass beat, and fast.

My mother didn't respond to Dale as she pushed me into a corner where I had my stereo sitting.

I fell into it backwards and knocked it over. I no longer wanted to fight my mother, so I sat in the corner and covered my face hoping she would feel sympathy for me and go away. She didn't. I wouldn't look up at her as she stood in front of me and yelled like a mad woman for me to look up at her. She kept telling me that since I thought I was so tough she wanted me to prove it. I didn't want to prove anything anymore. I was comfortable taking the loss. My mother pulled me up by my arms then pushed me into the wall. I yelled at her, "Leave me the fuck alone!"

She said, "Or what?" as she slapped me upside the head and grabbed my hair. She didn't let go until she shoved me into the wall once more.

I was again fed up and gathered more courage to defend myself. I ran head first into her stomach while telling her how much I hated her. She was beating me with her fists on the top of my head and she told me to shut the fuck up repeatedly. I finally quit fighting my mother and cried. When she saw how hard I was crying she stopped abruptly like she had just realized that she had lost control of the situation. My head was killing me from the pain of it being beat on repeatedly. I felt dizzy but that didn't stop me from telling my mother that I would no longer be staying at her house. I grabbed my coat and ran toward the front door. My mother tried to grab me but she couldn't because I weaved myself around her fast. She then yelled at Dale to grab me. Instead of trying to touch me, he ran to the front door and blocked it so that I would have to go through him to leave out of the house. When I saw that Dale wasn't planning to move, I felt defeated. I stopped and stood in the living room with tears falling from my eyes. I had no idea what my plan of action would be I just knew that I had to get out of there. I knew that I could call Misa, but I also knew that as much as Misa loved me she was not able to take care of me. I only had five dollars to my name so I felt stuck. My mother did something that I never saw coming. She ran up to me and grabbed me and gave me a hug. I cried in her arms like a small child as I yelled at her for letting Dale put his hands on me. I cried so hard that my body shook. Dale stayed by the door as though he thought I was still not to be trusted and I might try to run past him. Even though my mother had hugged me tightly, I was still bitter and I didn't plan to stay at my mother's home any longer than the following week. My mother said nothing at all, simply stood there and hugged me. She calmly took my coat off of me and after about five minutes of silence, told me to go into the bathroom and wash my face and lay down. She told me that we needed to calm down and talk tomorrow. I turned around and gave Dale the most foul look I could muster up. I truly believed I hated him.

When I went into the bathroom as my mother suggested, I became angry all over again when I looked in the mirror. I had the imprint of the belt on the side of my face. After about five minutes of me staring at my face in the bathroom mirror, my mother came and stood in the doorway watching me. For some reason, I assumed she was there to apologize for her role in our fight. My mother was actually there to tell me that I was wrong for fighting her like that. I carried guilt because she told me, "You are evil. I am too good to you for you to treat me like this. It's always you, Heaven, shoulda named your ass Hell."

I went to go stay with my father and his family the day after the altercation with my mother. I was completely over being in her house. My mother didn't appear to be upset. It was almost like it was a relief. I didn't learn until years later that my mother resented me for leaving her house. I felt bad knowing that my mother was angry with me for leaving. I just didn't know how to function in her house. I hated that jittery feeling I had when she was around me. The uneasy feeling that I got when my mother was around never left me. My brother, Leonard, cried when I packed my bags the night before I left. I told him I would be back to visit, but that I had to leave because I wasn't happy living in the same house as our mother. My sister, Angel, called the day I left to let me know how stupid I was. She felt like since I was going to stay in what was considered a rough neighborhood that I had to be stupid. Not to mention that I was going to live with a crack head. The truth was that I knew what type of environment I was going into and that didn't bother me. I was looking forward to something different because where we lived was so boring and quiet.

Chapter 7

I'll be moving on...

Whenever I went to visit my dad I would sit on the porch until the wee hours of the morning and people watch. It was anything but quiet. My father and his wife, Sonya's house sat on a very busy street. There was always something or somebody to keep my attention. I loved to watch the people walking the block. Most of all, I thought it was cool that much older guys flirted with me when I walked to the corner store by myself. My dad wasn't home very often, but when he was, we sat and talked for what seemed like hours if he wasn't in a bad mood. He seemed to get a kick out of the answers that I gave him when he asked me a question. It was like he knew that I was young, trying to sound more grown than I really was. I was trying to impress him because it was clear that he was listening to every word I spoke and I couldn't have him thinking I was stupid.

My father always made it clear to me that no matter what, he loved me. He stressed the fact that my mother was "different" and that he should never have dealt with her in the first place. He made it clear that he felt she had always been crazy. He would say, "Sharon…sweet and crazy as hell," and laugh to himself. My father and I sat and talked on the first night of my stay. Most of the time, I appreciated the advice he gave me. We were in our usual spots on the porch enjoying the cool breeze. He asked me what led up to the fight I had with my mother. I told him the truth. I chose to leave out the part about me having sex for the first time. I was trying to program myself to believe it didn't happen. After he listened to my version of the story, he sat in his chair on the porch and looked directly at me. He cleared his throat and crossed his legs as he hit the palm of his hand with his green box of More cigarettes. I didn't say anything, just sat across from him on the porch taking in the night air and watching cars drive by. He cleared his throat as he did often and said calmly, "In life there will always be a situation where your buttons are pushed. It takes a strong mind to decide that you won't allow yourself to be taken out of character. It's your job to always have self-control. I don't give a fuck if it's your mother or a fucking dog. We both know that something is wrong with your mother. Clearly she has a mental problem, always has. But you give her all the power once you show her that you can't control yourself and you act out with her. Sweetheart, that's a form of mind control. You allowed your mother to control your next move. Nobody should have that kind of power over you, but you." He paused to make sure it was sinking in. Then continued, "Now don't get me wrong, that's your mother. No matter how crazy she is. You need to always respect her, but when it comes to her acting a fool out of anger and the lack of self-control, what does that make you for reacting the same way?"

I tried to defend my actions. "I understand what you're saying, but you're forgetting that she hit me in my face with a belt!"

He calmly replied, "Being hit with the belt is neither here nor there. It doesn't really matter, because ultimately, if you would have been where you were supposed to be, none of this would have happened. Would being hit with the belt have been easier to digest if she had hit you on your ass instead of your face? Or is your main concern that you were hit with the belt period?"

I thought for a second because honestly I hadn't asked myself why I was so upset. It wasn't like I hadn't been hit with the belt on numerous times. I replied, "I think it's the fact that she hit me in the face. It was her way of showing how little respect she has for me. The look on her face was so mean that it terrified me."

My dad was still looking at me as he said, "There is nothing wrong with being angry, it's an emotion and you have identified it. Just try not to hold on to it. Understand that your mother handled it how she saw fit. She lost control of the situation before you did. We both know that she didn't have to hit you with the belt *anywhere*, but she did. That doesn't make it okay, but it happened. In the future, always be honest and stay true to your word. Otherwise, you will be viewed as untrustworthy."

I understood my father's advice, though sometimes I wondered if *he* followed his advice. His words gave me something to think about, and I didn't want to admit it at the time, but what he said made sense.

By the time I was fifteen years old, my mother had almost successfully brainwashed me and made me think my dad was just a stupid drug addict that didn't give a fuck about me. It's too bad almost doesn't count. I chose to store all the special things he told me in my heart. He was still my father, drug addict or not. Before I moved in with him I didn't get to see him very often, but when I did, we had really good conversations. My father always talked to me like I was a human being and that meant a lot to me. It felt so good to be in the presence of someone who had my best interest at heart. He didn't talk to me like I was a naïve sixteen year old girl. He talked to me like he knew that I comprehended what he told me. One of the many things I loved the most about my father when I was a young child was that he held me accountable for my actions. He wanted a valid explanation when he asked me a question. That was different for me because out of nervousness, I would always answer my mother with "I don't know" and look down at the ground. My mother never corrected me for not looking her in the eyes when I talked to her, it was like she took that to mean that she was more powerful. My father despised the fact that I had become shy in his absence. He would demand that I look him in the eyes when I talked to him or anyone else. He blamed himself for my low self-esteem, and told me that "a shy child is an ashamed child and you have nothing to be ashamed of because you're smarter and prettier than any girl I've ever seen before". My father always told me that he wanted me to stay with him, and he was going to get me into church because he knew a pastor that was a good man. My father claimed this pastor genuinely cared about the black youth. My father believed that he would be able to help sort through any issues that I was dealing with through prayer, and the good pastor.

My mother nicknamed my father that "lying, no-good son of a bitch" behind his back. I didn't see him that way, yet I understood that he wasn't perfect. While those things may have been true, I felt like my mother was speaking from a place of hurt. My family always told me that my father was a ladies' man, and that he cheated on my mother constantly. My father was definitely one of a kind and knew that he looked more innocent than what he was. His innocent looks seemed to work well with the ladies at some point in his life. My father learned to use his innocent boyish looks to his advantage and get over on people when he needed to. Daddy was a very handsome, charismatic man in his youth. He had a deep chocolate complexion with high cheekbones; his features made it clear that he was of Haitian decent. He had short soft, curly jet black hair. It was sad to see that over the years of continued substance abuse his looks were slowly deteriorating. He was always a smart and witty man. Even when my father was strung out on crack, he was still the most intelligent, articulate man I had known at that point in my life. He was known for being what they called a "pretty boy" back in the day, which simply meant that he liked to look nice at all times. My daddy, Leonard Sr., was always running the streets.

During the time that I stayed in the house with my father, his wife, and my three year old brother, Christopher Kyle, my dad was almost always on the go. I spent the most time playing with my brother and getting to know Sonya better than I already did. My father's wife was a petite woman who was just as feisty as my mother when provoked. She was almost always really laid back and sweet until my father pushed her buttons. Then it was like a beast came out of her body. One of the many times that my father was gone, Sonya and I sat and talked about things that probably would have pissed both my parents off, yet neither of them were willing to do it. When she asked me about sex, I thought nothing of telling her that I was a virgin. I had to get used to saying that I was a virgin. After sex with Joey, I came up with a "don't count" list. The list was exactly what it implied; people that I may have fucked, but for one reason or another, I became ashamed so they didn't count. As long as I didn't have any kids, I was cool because nobody could prove anything. Sonya was glad that I chose to remain abstinent. She told me a woman's body changed after sex. I didn't quite understand, but she said you smell different and you have to take extra special care of your vagina when you're sexually active. She mentioned STDs and that scared me. I wished I really hadn't had sex after I was done talking to her.

At some point, the relationship between Sonya and I changed, but the conversations we shared at that point in time were priceless. Sonya talked to me about sex before marriage also. Though I didn't follow her words, I never forgot what she said about having sex too soon. She believed that the sooner you started having sex, the more partners you accumulate. By the time you meet a man that you love and you decide that it's time to share your body, you've had sex so many times that it doesn't mean as much. She said, "Look at it like this, let's say there's a girl that's sixteen now. She has sex because she feels, at the time it's the right thing to do. Reality says that she won't marry him because she's a girl that has yet to grow into a woman. The commitment of marriage is the furthest thing in her mind. She gets her groove on and moves on to the next guy after about six months to a year, then to the next guy six months to a year after that and so on. That seems okay, right? But what if she doesn't meet that special guy until age twenty five? Can you imagine how many men she would have been with by that time? She has to decide that she doesn't owe a man her body in exchange for love. She should love herself enough to know that a man's love shouldn't ever validate you. *You* should validate you. This is something to think about. I'm not talking about you, though, you said you're a virgin. I know you're a smart girl. You want more out of your life than to lay down with any man just because it suits your needs for the time being."

When Sonya finally shut her mouth she looked at me like she was looking through me. Even if she had a clue that I had already lost my virginity, I wasn't planning on confessing. I felt like I understood and agreed with what Sonya told me, if I gave every man the best gift I had, what gift would I give a man to show that he was truly special to me? At some point, the most special gift I have would hold no value. Who wants a gift that everyone has had? I was listening to everything Sonya said, but I was having trouble respecting that it came from her. I was judging by the situation she was in. She said, "So try to wait until marriage to have sex. If you're good enough to lay down with then you're good enough to marry. If you do have sex before marriage, make sure you protect yourself. Men change after sex, Heaven, the thrill is gone and they become bored. Give him something to chase. I don't want to get too deep on you but never forget the power of what's between your legs, baby girl. If you ever meet a boy that pressures you, he is not the one."

Sonya and I could talk candidly this way before my father came home. The moment that my father walked into the house, Sonya's body language would change as fast as the subject. I felt sorry for Sonya and my brother because of the shit they dealt with where my father was concerned. Christopher Kyle was always right in the midst of their bullshit. When my father wasn't home the house seemed to be calm, and quiet. There were times when the house was peaceful when he was home, but when he became angry all hell would break loose.

The incident that happened my first week living with my father had me questioning where I really wanted to be. I was sitting on the porch watching the neighbor's teenage son. He was sitting on his parents' porch trying to act like he wasn't watching me from the corner of his eye. I was two seconds from asking him why he was sitting there by himself when I heard my father yell at Sonya.

"You stupid bitch! I'ma kill yo stupid ass!"

Sonya was in tears running from the kitchen, through the living room and up the stairs to get away from my father. My father was running just as fast as Sonya was running and finally caught her by her foot when she reached the top of the stairs. Sonya turned around as she fell and was screaming for help. "Heaven, call the police!"

I stood frozen for a moment at the bottom of the stairs. My father was dragging Sonya across the floor as she yelled, "Heaven, call your mother to come pick you up! You don't need to be here for this!" My father was oblivious to the fact that his kids were in the house as he behaved this way. I didn't call my mother to come pick me up because as selfish as it was, it wasn't me being chased down so I didn't feel like I was in danger. I ran up the stairs and stepped over my father and Sonya in the hallway to get to my brother. Sonya continued to scream as my father pulled her up forcefully, pushed her into their room by her neck and slammed the door shut. All I heard was what sounded like wrestling.

The next thing I heard was my father demanding that Sonya give him the money. He told her, "I'm going to ask you one more fucking time where the fuck that money is. I know you got some money, you lying bitch."

I stood in Christopher Kyle's bedroom looking around for him. I gently closed the door so that I wouldn't alarm him. I said his name softly, but I still didn't see him. I walked toward the closet where I heard slight movement. In the closet, I found my baby brother sitting quietly with his hands in his lap, looking down at the ground. He had tears in his eyes. I bent down and held my arms out to him. I had to blink back tears from my own eyes. It hurt my heart to see my brother hurting this way. He looked terrified, and he had every reason to be.

The yelling continued as I sat on my brother's bed rocking him and kissing his forehead. He was gripping the back of my shirt very tightly as though he was afraid I was planning to let him go. I turned the TV on in an attempt to drown the noise out. I could hear Sonya pleading as she got her ass beat. She was trying to make my father understand that the money she had was spent on the light bill. They didn't have much money since neither of them worked. My father's mother and Sonya's mother chose to pay the bills in the house during their difficult financial times. They had high hopes that my father would pull it together and leave the drugs alone. My father yelled at Sonya relentlessly, it was like he thought he was going to beat the money out of her. I had never experienced anything like that night in my life.

One of the most bizarre things about my father and Sonya was that they would fight one night and wake up the next day like nothing happened. I would lay in the room that I slept in while I was there and listen for trouble. Typically, the next day, there wouldn't be any trouble since my father would get up and leave early in the morning. He wouldn't come home for a few days and I was fine with that. When my father returned home from wherever he stayed overnight, Sonya asked no questions. I couldn't imagine living in constant fear and not being able to voice my opinion. As much as I loved my father I found that I was happier when he wasn't there because I knew he was where he wanted to be at that time in his life. If he was there I would be happy to see him rolling a joint. I felt like it was something to keep him calm for the time being until he was able to get his next piece. To me it seemed like smoking cigarettes only pissed him off when he was craving harder drugs, yet he smoked like a chimney when cigarettes were all he had to smoke.

I didn't know which household would be better for me. I couldn't find peace living with my mother, or my father. There wasn't really much for me to do there besides sit on the porch and watch cars or people. I remember thinking that I no longer wanted to live in the house with my father. Though he was kind to me, I hated the way he treated his wife. It also bothered me that he had no interaction with his son whatsoever. It was like my brother didn't exist to him. The fact that I realized that my father didn't deal with Christopher Kyle made me feel like my brother was the only thing that stopped me from leaving. I felt like he relied on me when his mother wasn't available.

Sonya was always there in the physical sense since she didn't work. I believed in the emotional sense she had checked out. She would stay in the bed all day sometimes. When I would knock at the door to see how she was, she would answer me while trying to act like she wasn't crying. She would come out of her room with puffy eyes and messy hair only to use the bathroom.

Chapter 8

Friends may come and friends may go…

While Sonya stayed in her room most of the time, and my father in and out, that left Christopher Kyle and I together. I remained in my favorite spot on the porch most days. It was on the porch that I met somebody that would impact my life in a major way. Before we actually talked, we would sit and watch each other for what seemed like hours without saying a word. He was on the porch at his father's house, and I was on the porch at my father's house. When he would look at me, I looked away and looked straight ahead. He finally came off of his porch and walked over to our yard. I didn't know what to say as I saw him walking up to me. He didn't look nervous in the least bit. He walked like he had a million dollars in each pocket. He was wearing a white t-shirt, a pair of flannel pajama pants that were so baggy I would bet they were his father's, and a pair of black corduroy house shoes. Christopher Kyle was sitting in my lap when he walked up to the porch. I checked my neighbor out as he approached, and he was just okay as far as looks go. I thought he was cute from a distance, now that he was closer I wasn't so sure. His eyes were too slanted and too far apart, his nose was long and skinny, his mouth was wide yet his lips were too thin. He stood at the bottom of the porch and leaned on the railing.

"What's up?" he said to me as he reached out to give my brother a handshake.

I said, "Nothing much. Just sitting here, watching you watching me." I smiled at him. I was still sitting in the chair holding my brother. Even though I was wearing a pair of boxers that I liked to sleep in and a t-shirt, I wasn't the least bit ashamed. I figured that since it was almost nighttime, I was safe from having to look decent. Besides that, he was ugly to me, so I didn't care if he liked what he saw or not. I had my hair wrapped in a scarf so that it would be nice looking for my first day at school the next day.

He smiled back and said, "I knew Leonard had other kids, but I don't think I've seen you over here before. What's your name?"

I told him, "Nope, you haven't seen me over here before. They haven't lived here long, and I didn't come around much because I lived further south but I live here now. My name is Heaven."

He smiled again and said, "That's what's up, Heaven. You mean to tell me your real name is Heaven?"

"Yep, Heaven is my real name. Why would I make that up?" I was smiling at him because it really was funny to me that people asked me if Heaven was my real name so often. I asked my mother what made her name her daughters Heaven and Angel; she said she wanted us to have unique names. In a perfect world she would have said that the reason she gave us our names was because that's what she felt we were.

My new friend complimented my name since it was different, and told me his name was Dontez. He wanted to know what grade I was in since he hadn't seen me leave for school since I had been staying with my dad. I told him I was in the eleventh grade, and that I was starting Bridgemont tomorrow. I had stayed with my father for a couple of weeks before I started school. I guess I was really trying to decide whether or not I really was going to stay with my dad, or go back to my mother. Dontez told me that he went to Bridgemont too, but he was in the twelfth grade.

After our conversation, I was concerned about how things would go at this new school. He told me that Bridgemont was a very rough school, and it would be difficult for me to make friends since I was pretty. That was the first time a boy had told me I was pretty, and given the way I looked at the moment, I just knew he had to be crazy. I was hoping Dontez was wrong about the way things would go at my new school. It was bad enough that I was going to be the new girl, and to find out that I might have to be prepared to defend myself simply because I was what he considered pretty didn't make any sense to me. Christopher Kyle started to whine and tell me he was sleepy, so I told Dontez I had to go into the house. He told me he would see me tomorrow at school. Before I walked into the house, he told me not to look so worried about the new school because he had my back.

Once I was in the house, I put my brother to bed in his room. Then I went into my own room and closed the door. It wasn't like I had tons of clothes to choose from, but I did have a few since my mother had come over to my dad's house bright and early that day and took me shopping at The Jones Store. I wanted to lay an outfit out to wear the next day because I was excited. My mother had made it clear to me that she didn't have to buy me new clothes to wear since I already had clothes that I wore to my other school. She also added that I was in my dad's care and that it really should have been him that provided clothes for me. She explained that when I stayed at her house she didn't ask for a dime, and he didn't offer one either. My mother must have been in a good mood because while we shopped, she told me that she wanted me to have a good start and feel confident. I wanted to know what made her come over and spend any money on me at all after the last exchange we had. The only thing I said after she explained her reasons for taking me shopping was a simple "Thank you, Mother." I made a mental note to apologize to her for being disrespectful when I stayed at her house when I felt the time was right. I didn't apologize the day she took me shopping because I didn't want to spoil the mood by bringing up something so negative. Where my mother was concerned, I had to watch any and everything I said because she turned everything into something negative.

After I laid my outfit out, I turned on the small radio that my dad had given me when I told him I needed music to help me relax. He told me that he had used that same radio to relax in the living room when Sonya got on his nerves. I laid the portable radio on my pillow right next to my head and hummed along with the song that played. I was lying in the dark wishing I had my pager. I knew the only people that would page me were my best friends. I hadn't talked to Tandra or Zandra since I had moved in with my dad. I missed the twins, and I missed my cousin Misa also. Most of all, I missed Leonard. He was coming to visit the following weekend and I was excited. I did make the time to call him, but it wasn't the same as seeing each other. I had so many thoughts going through my head that night. I wanted to make new friends, and I was hoping that I would fit in. Normally, I was the outcast, so not fitting in really wouldn't shock me. For some reason, I wanted things to be different at this school. I was still hoping for the best because I didn't want Dontez to be my only friend. He seemed nice enough but I wanted to hang out with other girls my age despite his warning that I would have a tough time dealing with the girls at Bridgemont.

The next morning I was up before my alarm clock went off. I was hyped about my first day at a new school. When Sonya heard my alarm clock go off, she peeked into my room with a warm smile. "Good morning, sunshine. Can I make you something to eat?"

I responded, "No thanks. I'm gonna wait until I get to school, but thank you." I knew I was lying, but I didn't want to hurt her feelings. I got along with Sonya well and I liked her, but her food tasted terrible. So far, I had been cooking my own meals, or getting chips from the store across the street from our house in an effort to avoid her food. As I ironed my clothes, I asked Sonya where my dad was. She told me that he hadn't come home last night and that he was probably tired from working, so he stayed over his mother's house. I couldn't believe she told me such a pathetic lie, but I just nodded. Maybe she was trying to protect me, but she had to know that I knew he didn't have a job.

I went into the bathroom and washed my face and brushed my teeth. One of the things I missed about my mother's house was the shower. The old house that my dad and Sonya lived in didn't have one, so I took baths at night then freshened up in the morning. I went back into my room and put my clothes on. I wore a black and white skirt that was short with flowers on it. My shirt was black with long sleeves and it showed my stomach. I wore thigh highs, with a pair of Dr. Marten's baby doll shoes. I also wore my gold herringbone. It wasn't real, but I didn't think anyone could tell the difference so I wasn't worried at all. I took my scarf off and unwrapped my hair in front of the bathroom mirror as Sonya stood in the doorway watching me smiling. I was excited and I felt good knowing that I had an outfit for every day of the week. Possibly next week also since it was a new school and they hadn't seen my old clothes.

Right before I got ready to walk out of the front door of the house, Dontez walked in with my father. I didn't understand why Dontez was standing in the living room looking so uncomfortable. Dontez spoke to me while not looking directly at me then looked at my father. I wasn't sure why he was there, I hadn't asked him to walk me to the bus stop and I wasn't sure if I wanted to start walking with him every day. I didn't say anything at the time because I was too focused on my dad. He was wearing the same clothes he had on when I'd seen him the other day. He had this cocky look on his face as he spoke to me. He looked defensive as he told me that Dontez was going to walk with me to the bus stop every day. After he gave me my orders, he took a long pull off his cigarette and exhaled. My father didn't seem to give a fuck that his wife had asked him repeatedly not to smoke in the house. I was afraid to ask why Dontez had to walk with me, so I just nodded and told him it was okay. Sonya just stood on the stairs and watched in silence. She had learned years ago not to intervene when he spoke to his children or anyone else for that matter. I had personally seen her get slapped for doing so. Dontez spoke up and said we better leave before we missed the bus. I grabbed my backpack and followed Dontez out the door.

Before I left, I walked up and gave my father a hug and a kiss on the cheek. He told me to have a good day and that he would see me later. I had the image of my father in my brain the entire time Dontez and I made the long hike to the bus stop. My dad's eyes weren't red, and he wasn't staggering or slurring. He just looked sort of out of it, like he wasn't himself. I felt sad, but I had to shake it off and focus on school. I hated seeing my dad so skinny and unhealthy looking. We had never addressed his drug problem with each other, so it was easy for me to live in denial when I stayed with my mother and believe that it wasn't as bad as it really was. Living in the house with him shed light on his habit and I hated that reality. He had offered no apology for attacking his wife behind money to feed his habit. He didn't bother to offer where he spent the night when he wasn't home with his family either. I knew not to ask him, but I couldn't help but worry. I made a mental note not to ever date a man that was into drugs. I also wondered as I followed behind Dontez to the bus stop if by me smoking weed, I would end up like my father. The thought of me becoming an addict scared the shit out of me.

Dontez and I waited at the bus stop in silence. I figured Dontez was silent because he sensed that I was silent due to being in deep thought. It seemed like I had a make-believe idea of who my father was. The level of disappointment I felt was enough to bring tears to my eyes. Dontez asked if I was okay, and I nodded to say that I was. He just stood there staring at me. Finally, after the silence, I asked Dontez why he walked with me to the bus stop. Dontez smiled and calmly said, "Let your father be a father. He wanted to feel like he was protecting you. He trusts me, and I ain't about to let shit happen to daddy's princess."

I was taking in what he said, but I wanted to laugh at him as he stood in front of me looking extremely serious about what he had just said. I found it to be funny that he was wearing a Stafford t-shirt with a pair of baggy jeans with heavy starch on them and a pair of Nike Air Max on his feet. I was genuinely concerned that he may get made fun of for wearing such a simple outfit. Though Dontez seemed to be a cool person, I knew he wouldn't be winning any best dressed contests anytime soon.

The bus took what seemed like forever and that pissed me off. I couldn't believe it wasn't a big deal that the bus was almost an hour late. We were in the month of September so it wasn't cold. It was more irritating to stand and wait for so long than anything, not to mention that I was so nervous that my stomach was hurting. Dontez calmly said that the bus being late was one of the differences in going to school in the inner city versus the suburban schools. He reiterated to me that things were going to be different at this school. I wasn't sure how he knew what went on in suburban schools, but for some reason, I believed him. All I knew was that at my school it had been hard for me to fit in, so I learned how to blend in by attempting to act like everyone else. There were very few problems at my old school. I was hoping this school wouldn't be too much different. If I didn't bother them then maybe they wouldn't bother me. The only people I talked to in school on a regular basis were the twins.

I left Woodson High during my freshman year, and I was happy to be gone. I didn't have any classes with my two best friends, the twins. I didn't bother trying to make new friends. Though both of the twins were my friends, I was closer to Tandra at the time. I met Tandra before I met Zandra We had a class together in the eighth grade. Their personalities couldn't be more different. While Tandra was more outgoing and approachable, her sister, Zandra, was more standoffish and introverted. Over time, Zandra and I became closer, but not as close as Tandra and I were by the end of eighth grade.

The only time I was able to hang out with Tandra and Zandra was at lunch, and sometimes after school. We had the same lunch shift and we would sit at our own table catching up on whatever was going on in our lives at the moment. Tandra was always being loud, or making an inappropriate joke of some sort. Zandra hated when she behaved that way, but I found it funny. Tandra was notorious for running and jumping on a boy's back just because she wanted to. Sometimes I would be afraid for her because not every boy thought it was funny. She would jump on their back causing them to lose balance while she was practically choking them. The funniest part of it all was that she would wrap her legs around their waist tightly. No matter how many times she got embarrassed she kept doing it. Tandra was confident to say the least.

We were walking down the hall headed to the buses after school when all of a sudden, Tandra said, "Watch this, he's about to get mad!" Before Zandra and I could say anything she took off running. She ran up behind KD and snatched his baseball cap off of his head. I stopped dead in my tracks and panicked in my head for her. KD was walking with his brother, and his best friend. They all turned around and looked at her.

KD said, "Damn, do I know you?" I could tell by his tone that he wasn't upset. Zandra and I stood frozen with eyes as big as saucers.

Tandra said, "Nope, and the only way you gettin' this hat back is if you give me your number." She was smiling like she had all the confidence in the world.

He gave her a sexy grin, and looked her up and down like he was contemplating giving her his number. Then his brother spoke up. "Girl, get yo ass on somewhere. Ain't nobody fuckin wit you like that." All of the guys started laughing.

Tandra laughed too and said, "Boy, here, don't nobody want yo hat or your number. I was playing." She handed him the hat so fast that it almost fell to the ground. She walked back over to me and Zandra and lied about what was said. I guess I would have too if I was blown off that way. From that day forward, she hated KD's brother, but she seemed to have fallen harder for KD.

The reason I didn't have many friends was because I simply wasn't a social person. Tandra didn't have many other friends because to a lot of the girls she was annoying. Zandra normally went with the flow. I think that's why she never irritated me, she never caused trouble. I knew that I wouldn't miss going to Woodson for the most part, but there were a few things that I would miss. Things like watching the boys at my school and being with my friend's every day would be the main things. None of the boys at my school had ever approached me, except for KeAndre Davis, and he had to be the most annoying boy that God ever made.

KeAndre had been bothering me, as well as the twins, since the eighth grade. He didn't bother us because we were special. He bothered us because he got a kick out of bothering almost everyone. KeAndre couldn't get me to entertain him if I was paid to do so. He was always loud talking in the hallway and picking fights that he always lost. I never understood why he behaved the way he did, yet his brother, KD, was totally different. KeAndre was in the same grade that I was in while his brother was a grade ahead of us. While KeAndre was loud and hyper, KD was always calm and laid back from what I saw when I watched him. When KeAndre would be in my face begging for my number, his brother KD would watch without saying anything to stop him from being so pushy. It was almost like he was amused by his brother and his antics.

I noticed instantly that KeAndre and KD favored a lot. KD was better looking, though. KeAndre was tall and skinny like Dontez, while KD was tall and muscular. KD wasn't skinny, but he wasn't fat either, more like solid. I thought KD was perfect as far as looks. His complexion was the color of smooth caramel and he had chestnut brown colored eyes with long eyelashes. I loved watching him laugh because his teeth were perfectly straight and white and his smile could light up a room. Normally, I went for the thuggish bad boy type, so I wasn't sure what it was about KD – aside from the fact that he was handsome and it seemed like all the girls wanted him. Not to mention the fact that he was cool with everyone. When I watched him, I never saw him being rude or talking to anyone like he thought he was better. I did see him flirt a lot, but I didn't fault him for that. He was too sexy not to flirt or be flirted with.

KeAndre was the complete opposite of his older brother when it came to personality. At least that's what it seemed like to me. I knew it was likely that I would never have a chance with KD, but it was nice to sneak and catch glances of him in the cafeteria when he would sit at the table with all the other popular senior boys. They didn't eat lunch, they just sat around making jokes and looking cool. The twins and I would watch KeAndre and laugh at him because he didn't have many friends in our grade. He was always hanging around his brother and his brother's friends trying to look as cool as they were. The only time KeAndre was respectful was when he hung with his brother. It was like he knew his role was to sit there and shut up or he wouldn't be allowed to hang out with them. Tandra was always begging me to give KeAndre a shot so that maybe she would have a shot with KD. Giving KeAndre a shot wasn't even an option. If I helped her get with KD then how would I get with him? I liked everything about KD from a distance. I even liked the nickname, KD. I could hear myself saying his nickname as he was making love to me in my mind. His first name was Kendall, but nobody ever called him Kendall. He went by KD since his last name was Davis and his best friend's name was Kendall also. I learned all these things by watching and listening to people talk to him and about him. There was no way I was giving KeAndre a chance when I knew how I felt about his brother. A part of me was disappointed that Tandra still liked KD after KeAndre told her to back up. I knew I wasn't the best looking, but I also knew that I wasn't about to settle for such an obnoxious person as KeAndre. If Tandra wanted KD she would have to set that up herself. I wasn't sure when I should have told her that I wanted him too. I didn't plan on letting him come in between our friendship, and if she was able to get him before me, I wouldn't be happy for her, but I wouldn't harbor any negative feelings either. The truth was, if I didn't have a chance with KD, Tandra most certainly didn't either.

The twins weren't the worst looking girls in the world, but they weren't what I would consider pretty at the time either. They were light-skinned to the point where they almost looked white. They had long dirt-brown colored hair that stopped at their waist. They thought their hair was their best feature since it was so long, maybe this was true, but I personally felt like they could have taken better care of it. It was thin, scraggly hair with split ends. The twins had skin that was always dry looking also. They had marks on their faces from all the times they picked at the pimples. It wouldn't be fair to say they were butt ugly, but they definitely had work to do on their appearance. What they lacked in looks they made up for with the way they dressed. They rarely wore the same outfit twice and they had shoes to match pretty much any outfit they wore. Regardless of the way they looked, they were my best friends and no matter what we went through, I would always have love for them. It was me and the twins that stuck together inside of school. Overall, my experience at Woodson High wasn't bad, but without friends like them, it would have been much worse.

Chapter 9

I stood at the bus stop waiting to tackle my first day at my new school. I went down memory lane in my head as I waited for the bus. I decided to ask Dontez what he knew about my father. I normally wasn't ashamed of my father, but I didn't want Dontez going to school telling everyone my family business. He looked at me seriously and told me that he knew enough about my father to know that he had a drug problem. Dontez informed me that my father was very close to his father who was a preacher. I must have looked confused because he paused for a second as though he was trying to let what he said sink in. I didn't understand why my father would be so close to the preacher, what could they have in common? I understood that the preacher could pray with my father, but how close could they be unless they smoked crack together? Dontez still stood looking directly at me as the light bulb went off in my head. I told him that couldn't be true. I mean, he was a man of God after all. Dontez told me at that time, titles in life mean nothing, and nothing is ever what it seems. I pondered his words as he continued to look at me without batting an eye.

All of a sudden, Dontez didn't seem like the corny little boy that I had taken him for. As I stood there judging him, I realized that I had previously misjudged him. I wondered why I had come to the conclusion that he was corny in the first place. It was like I was looking at him for the first time. I listened to him tell me that my father spent a lot of his time hanging out with his father, Pastor Harvey, inside of their house. He could have knocked me over with a feather when he told me that it was normal for both of our fathers to sit in the living room of his father's house and smoke from a crack pipe as though it was the most normal thing ever. My heart was beating fast because I was imagining them actually sitting in the living room smoking crack as though it was as common as sitting down eating dinner with the family. I had never personally met his father, but I had seen him coming and going. He was a tall skinny man like Dontez, and he always waved. His father always carried a Bible in his hand when I would see him. Dontez told me that his dad owned a small church that was walking distance from our block. He said it sickened him that his father was constantly lying to his fifty members saying that their church had been robbed or that not enough people tithed and that was the reason they didn't have a bigger church. I asked him what his mother said because I was curious about her. She never spoke when she was coming and going, she never even looked in my direction. Dontez informed me that the woman I was seeing wasn't his mother. That was his father's girlfriend, and his mother had left them when he was only five. His mother had never come back to visit or call him at all.

After listening to his story, my life with my mother didn't seem so bad after all. I tried not to look so disturbed by the things he told me but I was. This was the church my father had been bragging to me about and urging me to visit? This was the wonderful pastor with a great vision for the inner city youth? This was the same pastor that my father held a rally with to clean drugs off the streets? I recall being so proud when I saw him on the news. I called and told him that I saw him holding a banner that read "HELP US KEEP OUR STREETS CLEAN" with another man. That man was Dontez's father, Pastor Harvey. I was learning fast that seeing my father ever so often, versus living with him, was two totally different things. While I still loved him, I was starting to see him for who he really was and that made me sad.

The bus came, and Dontez let me walk in front of him onto the bus. When we got on the bus it went from being loud to quiet in a matter of seconds. All eyes were on me, this made me very uncomfortable. The first thing I noticed was the looks on their faces as I looked for an empty seat. When I made eye contact I would give a polite smile because I thought it was the right thing to do. I don't recall anyone smiling back at me. Almost every seat had two or three people already in it. I wasn't expecting the bus to be so packed. I walked slowly toward the back of the bus first, then back toward the front until I saw a girl sitting alone. Without asking, I sat down next to her. I saw her roll her eyes at me but I ignored her. Dontez went to the back and sat with some boys that I assumed were his friends. Our bus driver pulled off before we were even seated. I practically fell because I lost my balance. I couldn't help but think that if he would have been on time he wouldn't have to rush, or drive so aggressively.

The girl and I sat in silence while checking each other out at the same time. I noticed that she kept the same smirk on her face the remainder of the ride. This girl made it clear that she didn't want me in her seat. I wondered why she came to school dressed like she was a boy. I could see that she was a nice looking dark skinned girl despite the fact that she had on a plaid green and blue Nautica shirt with dark blue jeans. This was the type of outfit the boys at my old school usually wore. I wasn't used to seeing girls dressed like this. She had on a pair of Eastland boots that looked to be brand new. I noticed that she wore long acrylic nails that were painted neon pink. She had a cheap looking gold ring on each finger, including her thumb. Her herringbone was almost as big and shiny as the gold tooth in the front of her mouth.

Instead of looking directly at her, I kept sneaking glances when she turned her head. I hated her hairstyle and I didn't understand why it had to look so big. Her jet black hair was stiff like it was a statue. The hair in the back of her head came to the middle of her back, while the top was cut shorter. I could tell that it was a fresh style because there wasn't a hair out of place. While I tried to act like I wasn't watching her, she didn't seem to care that I knew she was watching me. She seemed to be amused by my outfit, I could tell because of the look on her face. She would look at my Mary Jane shoes and my thigh highs then turn around and look out the window laughing to herself. I wasn't sure that she had room to laugh, but I wasn't going to say anything to her. I just sat on the edge of the seat of the bus in silence holding my big fake leather backpack on my lap, since she didn't bother to move her oversized bootleg Coach bag over so that I could have room to sit comfortably.

As I sat on the bus in silence, I watched the route that the bus took because I hadn't really been around the neighborhood, aside from going to the corner store. I was amazed at how run-down the houses were, it was almost depressing to see. There was a nice car, with tinted windows and rims sitting in almost every driveway. Even at sixteen years old that struck me as odd. How were they able to afford such nice looking cars, yet their homes looked like a good wind would blow it to pieces? I didn't see one well taken care of house and it didn't make sense to me. I was also puzzled by the fact that almost every student that got on the bus wore name brand clothing. How did their parents have the money to buy such expensive clothes, but their homes looked shabby? It was becoming clear that this school was more about a fashion show than learning. I was so nervous that I was almost shaking. I wanted to get off the bus and run back to my father's house and change clothes ASAP. Every girl that got on the bus had a version of the outfit that the girl I was sitting next to wore.

I watched every person that got on the bus and I was able to tell who was considered cool by the way they dressed instantly. It struck me as odd that the girls seemed to wear the types of clothes at this school that the boys typically wore at my school. From what I noticed, most of the boys were wearing expensive tennis shoes, jeans that had so much starch they could probably walk themselves, and either Nautica or Tommy Hilfiger jackets. My skirt and cut off shirt were going to get me laughed at. Who could I call to pick me up before anyone saw me? Why was I the only person on the bus carrying a backpack? The girls carried their purses, and the boys carried nothing but a pencil in their hand at the most. I was feeling more and more out of place.

The bus came to a stop, and a group of kids got on the bus being very loud. The group consisted of three girls and two boys. The bus driver didn't say a word about the level of noise that they brought with them. They were laughing, and using foul language as they looked for a seat. I kept wondering if this was an everyday thing. There was nowhere for them to sit, so they sat in seats that were only holding two people. As they took their seats, they talked about the fact that there was about to be a fight at the bus stop that morning but the bus came too soon. I was sitting in my seat listening to the kids talk about how a girl was about to get her ass beat as a petite girl angrily walked toward me. She wore the same short style as the girl I shared my seat with except that her hair was shaved in the back. The girl stood right in front of me like she expected me to get up. I didn't move. I just sat and stared at her as I waited for her next move.

She rolled her eyes at me and said, "Uh uh, Danni, why she sittin' wit you? Do we even know...her?" She was talking to Danni but she never took her eyes off of me. Her question was more rhetorical than anything, because she knew that they didn't know me.

Honestly, I wasn't sure what to do, so I sat in the seat quietly and looked straight ahead. Danni looked at her and laughed and told her to sit down in the seat with us. The bus was moving, yet she still stood and watched me. Finally, the bus driver yelled at her to sit her "big head self" down. She plopped down on the seat with us after Danni moved her bag out of the way making room for me to scoot over. Danni sat by the window, I sat in the middle, and Danni's friend sat on the end complaining that she didn't have enough room on the seat. They leaned forward looking at each other as they talked as though I wasn't there. I wasn't sure how long I was going to last at this school if I had to deal with this every day.

Once we got to the school, I was shocked when everyone ran to get off the bus at the same time. There was no organization whatsoever. It was extremely chaotic, so I planned on sitting in the seat and waiting. I saw Dontez get off the bus with his friends, but I wasn't about to wrestle with the other kids to catch up with him. Danni's friend turned around and said, "OH MY GOD! IF YOU DON'T HURRY UP!" She was talking to me. She wanted me to move out of the way so that Danni could walk with her. I knew that enough was enough. I learned early in my life that you can only be so nice until people think they can take advantage of you. I also learned that when it comes to respect, it's something that you have to demand in the beginning of any relationship. I had tried to be as cordial as possible, but she couldn't talk to me that way.

I said to her, "Please don't talk to me like that. You don't even know me like that." My voice didn't come across as assertive as I would have liked, but at least I stood up for myself. When she yelled at me to hurry up I was sitting down, but I stood up to show her that I was defending myself. The few people that were left on the bus stopped and stared.

Danni reached around me and gently tugged her friend's arm and said, "Jania, just get off the bus, ok? Damn, it's not that serious!" Danni rolled her eyes at Jania.

Jania looked from my head to my shoes and laughed. She casually said, while looking right at me, "Yep, you are so right. Ain't nobody worried about this Blossom wanna be. With that wack ass outfit on!" I couldn't believe she said that to me. She said it loud enough for everyone to hear. She walked off the bus after she said it. I walked off the bus followed by Danni who was trying to hold her laugh in.

I was embarrassed, but I couldn't think of a comeback, so I just said, "You know what? You are so childish." I knew she didn't hear me because they were already off the bus. I was holding back tears trying to look like I wasn't bothered as I walked down the steps of the bus.

Dontez was waiting patiently for me in front of the school. He put his arm around me as we walked into the school and said, "I saw Jania talkin' to you like she had a problem. Don't worry about these sack chasin' ass broads. You look cute, they're just ghetto."

I smiled and told him, "Thanks. They were very rude and it's not even that serious. I'm gonna try to ignore them." I really appreciated Dontez being there for me the way he was. The only thing was, I was hoping that he hadn't developed a crush on me. I hadn't ever had a boy be that nice to me unless they wanted to fuck, and I most certainly wasn't planning on fucking Dontez. I was starting to view him as a big brother type.

After Dontez showed me where my locker and my first few classes were, he gave me a hug and told me he had to get to class. I nervously walked into my crowded math class. Once again, all eyes were on me. I went and sat down in an empty desk in an attempt to blend in. The teacher spotted me instantly and told me to move because that's not where she wanted me to sit. As I walked toward the front of the class she told me to come up to her desk. I heard laughter in the class about my attire. I heard one girl say, "Look at her shoes, y'all!" I ignored her and walked to the teacher's desk.

The teacher introduced herself as Mrs. Jenkins, the first thing I thought was, "I'm going to call her Jheri Curl Jenkins" because she had a long Jheri curl that reminded me of the pastor in the movie *Coming to America*. Jheri Curl Jenkins asked me what my name was. I told her my name, and she wasn't impressed in the least bit.

She said, "Ooh, chile, the names these parents come up with these days is just a shame. A cryin' shame. Go on and sit down, Heaven."

I gave her the meanest look I could come up with before I went to sit down at the empty desk that she told me not to sit in. It was only the first hour and I was already over this day. First the bus ran late, then those mean girls on the bus pissed me off, then more people laughed at my outfit, now the teacher was humiliating me. I tried to stay strong because I knew I had asked for this. Nobody told me to leave my mother's house and the school that I thought I hated.

By the middle of the day, I was numb to the looks I got in the hallway during the passing period. I was forced to sit by myself at lunch since I couldn't find Dontez. After lunch I had gym, and I sat by myself there too. The rest of my day at school went okay aside from gym class. Nobody tried to befriend me at all, even after the smiles I gave them when I entered the locker room. I didn't bring gym clothes to change into because I thought I had to order them like we did at my other school. I noticed the clothes the other girls were changing into, so I went into the gym teacher's office to ask him what my options were regarding gym clothes. The gym teacher quickly informed me that we were to bring our own clothes to wear during gym from home. He gave me a pair of short shorts to wear with a dingy t-shirt to borrow that was small enough to fit an eight year old.

When he handed me the clothes, I took them. After one look I said, "I can't wear these. They're too small and they stink."

The gym teacher gave me a sarcastic look and said, "I don't know how dey did thangs at yo otha school, but at DIS school when you don't dress out dats a F…fa da whooooole day! You oughta feel lucky cuz I didn't have to give you clothes ta wear, and I 'spect them to be in mah office when you done wearin 'em." He seemed to take pride in telling me the rules. I was more than pissed.

I said, "Well, I'll just take the F for the day. I can easily make that up, but I'm not wearing these clothes. Nobody told me that I needed to bring my own. IT'S MY FIRST DAY!" By that time we were both offended.

He made it clear that he didn't care about where I came from and how I was used to things going. He said, "So you can git ya proper tail in there and get changed like the otha girls or go head and take that F…cuz I don't do no makeup work." After he finished telling me how things were going to be, he turned his back to me and mumbled under his breath, "Come in here thankin' she a white girl or something,'" as he grabbed his whistle and put it around his old, wrinkled neck. I walked out of his office and slammed the door behind me.

I walked back into the locker room to find that the girls were all in the gym already. I sat on the side where I noticed nobody else had left their things sitting. Once I put the clothes on and looked in the mirror, I cried. This was too much for me, and I was planning to tell my dad that I wasn't coming back the next day. I was sitting on the bench in the locker room trying to decide whether or not to call my mother and beg her to let me come home. Why did she let me go through with this anyway? She had to know that I was making a big mistake. I was starting to wonder if Angel was right when she said I was stupid for making such a drastic move.

By the time I heard a bag drop onto the bench next to me it was too late to hide my tears. My head was buried in my lap when she came and stood in front of me. I looked up to find Danni staring at me with her hands on her hips. She didn't look like she felt sorry for me and I was happy about that. I didn't want anyone's sympathy. Danni turned her back to me as she opened her locker and grabbed a scarf to wrap her hair up, and gym clothes to change into. I said, "Why is everyone so fucking RUDE at this school?" My voice was shaking because I was still crying as I asked her.

She turned around and I thought I caught a glimpse of emotion in her eyes. She said, "Girl, you need to calm your dramatic ass down. It's not that bad. You're the one walking around looking like you think you're better than everyone. People started talking when they first saw you this morning. They say you're stuck-up, and that you have an attitude. I really don't know and I really don't care. You do talk like a white girl, though."

I sat there in disbelief because I knew I didn't think I was better than anyone, and I knew for damn sure that I didn't talk like a white girl. They were mistaking speaking proper for talking like a white girl. What the hell was I supposed to do? I couldn't change the way I talked to make them more comfortable, yet I wanted to be approachable. Would changing the way I talked and dressed make people like me more? Maybe it wasn't such a bad idea after all.

"Well, I don't have an attitude. I don't have time to worry about what people think about me. It's all good, though. Don't hate the player, hate the game." I told her that as I tried to pull the tiny shirt down to where it at least covered my stomach.

She busted out laughing after my speech and said, "Girl, stop. You don't have to do that with me, ok? All of a sudden you think you need to talk like you Brandy or somebody? Ol' I-wanna-be-down ass nigga. Just do you. It's simple." Danni smiled at me, it was the first genuine smile I had been given all day. Actually it was the *only* smile I had been given all day. It was like at that moment she decided that maybe I wasn't so bad after all.

We walked into the gym together that day and every day after that. Danni told me she was late to gym that day because she had been outside smoking a cigarette. The first thing I did was judge her. I believed it was a nasty habit and I had only seen adults smoke at that point. I had never met a girl my age that smoked cigarettes. Danni acted older than she was, there were times that I would tell her a story and she would stop me to tell me that she simply didn't care. Danni always said she had bigger things to worry about. She told me that her real name was Danielle, but she hated it, so everyone had called her Danni since she was in elementary school.

Once we were in the gym, I noticed that the other girls spoke to Danni to acknowledge her, but that was about it. I couldn't help but wonder why she was so standoffish with me. It wasn't like people were knocking her door down to be her friend. We were supposed to sit in five rows of six girls in alphabetical order by our last name. My last name was Stephenson, Danni's was Williams. Technically, we weren't supposed to sit by each other, but for some reason, the gym teacher didn't say anything to us. We would sit and laugh almost the entire gym period. Though her breath smelled like strong cigarettes, I got a kick out of Danni. Once she let her guard down she was a funny, down to earth person. We got along really well, and I appreciated her place in my life. For some reason, I couldn't shake the feeling that I was better than her. I knew she had suggested that I thought I was better than everybody when we had our first conversation, but I didn't think I was better than *everybody*, just her.

One morning I got on the bus and sat in my normal seat next to Danni. Jania still sat with us but she wasn't as annoying. I knew she still didn't like me, but she tolerated me because of Danni. I was bothered by Danni's outfit so I questioned her about it. I felt like I had room to question her. I was wearing my black bodysuit with a black and red plaid skirt with my black thigh highs. I decided after my first week at Bridgemont that I didn't care what they thought of my clothes. I had no choice but to develop that attitude since my mother refused to buy me more clothes, and my dad promised he would when he came across some extra money. I knew when my dad said "came across" instead of "when I get my paycheck" I better go ahead and find some level of confidence and ride it out. I asked Danni, "Why do you dress like that? You always have your jacket on with a t-shirt. It's like it's more important for your gold chain to show than a cute outfit to show." I laughed after I said it because I really thought it was funny. Danni laughed with me. To be honest, her laughter made me feel like she understood why I mentioned her outfit.

Then she said, "Yeah, I do like my chain to show. I mean, it's real and a lot of people don't have real chains to show. They just wear fake ones and try to laugh at other people when they don't have room to laugh at all."

When Danni mentioned fake gold chains my heart dropped. How did she know? Maybe she wasn't talking about me.

As if she was reading my mind she said, "Yeah, I'm talking about you. Don't be trying to look confused now, bitch". Danni was still laughing, so I joined in and laughed too. That was the first time she had called me a bitch. I didn't like it but I didn't say anything to her about it. It didn't seem to come from a mean place.

I just said, "Ok, so can you really tell my chain isn't real?"

"I CAN'T TAKE THE PRESSURE! Girl, please STOP! Hell YEAH, I can tell it's not real. That bitch gon' turn yo whole fuckin' neck green in NO time. Get a grip!" Danni was laughing loud and making a scene as she talked.

Jania laughed extra loud, she said to Danni, "Stevie Wonder can see that fake ass chain!" One of my biggest pet peeves had always been a person that adds their two cents when it wasn't asked for or needed. I was getting really sick of Jania and I would be glad when she left us alone. After Jania made her comment, Danni looked at me and laughed. I had my face frowned at Jania.

"Why don't you shut the fuck *up*? I'm so sick of your mouth, I *swear*." The bus was moving but that didn't matter to me. It was fine for Danni to have fun at my expense. Not Jania. She stood up while holding the seat so that she could control her balance. I stood up after she did.

She said, "Trust me, you don't want none of this. I'm not the one."

My heart was pumping, not out of fear. It was more like adrenaline. I was calling her bluff; getting the small amount of respect that I received from the kids at school wasn't easy. I wasn't about to lose it by backing down from her.

Danni started laughing and told us to chill. She sat between us so that we wouldn't attack each other. I turned around to see Dontez watching the whole exchange. I'm sure he didn't know exactly what was going on, but he knew that Jania was a loud person so he didn't look shocked. He looked like he was on alert. Once I calmed down, I had to ask myself if I was taking the fact that my chain was fake out on Jania. I really was more embarrassed than offended, but there was something hilarious about what Danni said about me. I made a mental note to make sure that before I said anything about anyone I was prepared to get made fun of as well. Despite the lesson I learned, I still didn't like Jania, and I still felt like I was better than Danni.

Regardless of how I truly felt about Danni, in school she was a lifesaver. When I didn't want to participate because I always hated gym Danni made up an excuse and walked me to the nurse's office. Danni always did sweet things like that for me. There was another time that I didn't have lunch money because my dad asked me if he could borrow five dollars until later that evening and never returned the money to me. When I asked him about the five dollars he looked at me and laughed and said, "Girl, quit playin' so much. I have enough problems as it is, don't lie and tell me you loaned me some money that you ain't got to loan in the first place." I was too ashamed to admit that I was broke, and Danni knew that, so she put the money on the table in the cafeteria when nobody was looking and got up and walked away. I grabbed the two dollars she gave me and ran up behind her to acknowledge her favor.

I said, "Girl, thank you. I don't know what I would do without a friend like you."

Danni stopped walking, and turned around and looked at me. "I don't have many friends because I don't trust many. If you don't plan on being real with me then leave me alone now. I've been crossed before because I'm too kind hearted."

I was uncomfortable by her straight forwardness and I assured her that I wasn't there to take her kindness for granted.

Chapter 10

I got five on it....

It was so weird how things were happening so fast. Though my first day was shitty, to say the least, the rest of the week actually wasn't bad at all. I went from being made fun of for the way I dressed, to being praised for it. A few girls had even come up to me and asked me where I shopped at and if I would go with them to get the same types of clothes.

By the middle of the week in math class, Jheri Curl Jenkins had to stop teaching because she felt that me and two other girls were disrupting her class. She very rudely put us in our place and made it clear that her class was not one to act a fool in. This was something new to me because I had always been quiet in class. I had never been reprimanded for being disrespectful in class. I didn't know what was different and why I was all of a sudden talking loud and feeling so free to speak up. After I gave it a bit more thought, I wondered if Danni's personality was rubbing off on me. She was something like a free spirit who said and did what she wanted to. After watching her, I wondered why I hadn't been that way all along. Danni would come over to my dad's house and hang out with me and Dontez after school sometimes. We would normally sit on the porch and talk, or walk the neighborhood out of boredom. Danni was always asking me to "hook it up" with her and Dontez. I didn't care about them dating at all, I just couldn't figure out if Dontez was even into girls. I had never seen him with a girl, and he never even mentioned a girl. He seemed to be more focused on getting money. Danni would flirt with him, but he would never take the bait. He would just laugh it off and tell her she was crazy. Danni insisted that I liked Dontez because I hadn't hooked them up. This couldn't be further from the truth. I thought Dontez was a great person, and I genuinely loved him like a brother. I couldn't imagine anything else with him. I just didn't like hooking people up when they could do it themselves.

A couple of months after I moved in with my dad, and was settled into my routine, my brother, Leonard, came to visit for the weekend. He was supposed to come sooner, but my mother didn't want him to. After begging for weeks, she finally gave in. He was kind enough to sneak and bring my pager with him. I was in complete shock, but I was happy that he did bring it. I hoped he understood that he would get his ass kicked for looking out for me. I don't think he could care less, he was genuinely happy to see the smile on my face when he opened his backpack and handed it to me.

After he opened his backpack to hand me my pager, he took out a small bag of weed and held it out to me like it was gold. I stood in Christopher Kyle's room checking the numbers in my pager. Leonard wasn't saying anything; he just stood in front of me holding the weed waiting for me to look up.

When I looked up and saw what was in his bag I was in utter disbelief. Where did he get it? When did he start smoking? Was he slowly headed down the same path as our father? I didn't want to panic, so I calmly said, "When did you start smoking weed?" as I snatched it out of his hand. I smelled it because it seemed like that was the first thing people did when they had a bag of weed. Christopher Kyle was standing next to me not saying a word. I was hoping he didn't know what was going on.

Leonard smiled coolly as he snatched the bag out of my hand and said, "Come on, Heaven, I'm not a baby no more. I get it from my nigga around the corner from mom's house. You know Boomer, don't you? He went to school wit you before he said fuck it."

I sighed and told him that I knew exactly who Boomer was and he wasn't about shit. I didn't know why or when he came into contact with my little brother, but I didn't like it. All I said was, "Oh" and made a mental note to find out more about my brother's relationship with Boomer. Boomer was into stealing cars and robbing people, and I didn't want my brother getting mixed up with people like that.

Even though it had only been months since I moved, my brother had changed. It was more than physical changes. He seemed different in the way that he carried himself. I had always known that he had a potty mouth, but the way he talked now was downright mannish. The little baby faced boy that I left no longer existed. I asked him how everything was at the house. Leonard told me that Dale still didn't work. He said, "I'm so sick of that bitch ass nigga, sis. This nigga asked me if I knew where to get some smoke from, knowin' fuckin' well that I got the green. But peep game, though, dude gon' tell me not to tell mama. So I did what any real nigga would do. I sold the nigga a sack and didn't say shit to mama about it. The way I see it, if I buy my own shoes and shit I can help mama out. Even if it comes from that bitch ass nigga. I mean, it ain't like that nigga is doing shit. That fat ass nigga still aint' got a job. She's too strong to deal with that nigga's bullshit. I mean, what else could I do, Heaven?"

I was amazed at his backward logic. He thought that since Dale didn't have a job it was only right to sell him weed. He asked me what else he could do, that was a hard one for me. I didn't have the same relationship with my mother that he did, so I wasn't as protective as he was. It was hard for me to feel sympathy for her when she's the one that had him staying with her. I wondered what would happen if he did tell her. That could go either way. She could possibly turn on her precious son for Dale, or she could flip out and kick Dale to the curb. I didn't really care too much about how she chose to handle it. I just didn't want to be around when she found out what Leonard was doing. I knew my mother would find a way to blame me. My real concern was the fact that my little brother had weed to sell to Dale. I wondered if he was selling it on the regular or if he simply sold him a sack from his own stash. My other concern was the fact that Dale didn't have money to help around the house, yet he had money to buy weed. Maybe my mother gave him money to spend. I was sure that the dime bag that my brother sold him wouldn't help with bills anyway, but it still didn't sit well with me that he was buying and smoking weed.

Leonard casually sat on the bed putting his weed in a Garcia Vega cigar. I stood in front of him in case Sonya walked past. Christopher

Kyle was being quiet, and I knew it was because he sensed that he needed to be quiet at the time. He was always intuitive in that way. Finally, I said, "You need to put that shit up while you're in here. He's a kid, and he's watching you. What type of shit are you on?"

Leonard looked up at me; he casually laughed and finished rolling his blunt. After he put his blunt behind his ear, he picked Christopher Kyle up and tickled him. I stood in front of them while our baby brother laughed hysterically. I wasn't amused at all.

Leonard said, "Girl, chill. This lil nigga is cool. Trust me, he's good. The nigga's daddy is a crack head. So you tellin' me what I do is somehow gon' fuck him up? Come on, Heaven."

I replied, "Leonard, are you that fucked up? So you're saying that since his father does that shit when he's around that it's ok for you to?" I didn't wait for him to reply. "Look, don't do that shit in front of him again. If his father is that fucked up why don't you try to be someone he can look up to? So all the men in his life are drug users and abusers?"

Leonard must have thought I was doing stand up because as I talked to him he laughed hysterically. He told me that he felt like he was in an after school special.

I took Christopher Kyle out of his arms, and carried him down the stairs. I grabbed Christopher Kyle a jacket and went to sit on the porch out of habit since there was nothing else to do. It was the month of November so it was getting colder outside, I knew I wouldn't sit too long.

Leonard came downstairs after me and walked by me saying he was going for a walk. I knew a walk meant that he was going to smoke his blunt. I wanted to smoke with him, but since I gave the speech about drugs, I didn't want to seem like a hypocrite. I chilled on the porch for a few more minutes until I decided that I was bored. I was hoping Dontez was home so I could shoot the shit with him. I was sure he wouldn't be around since he had been busy lately. I wasn't sure what was up with him. Dontez was more distant recently than he had been since we became friends. When I saw him last he was getting out of the passenger seat of a lime green Monte Carlo SS with gold Dayton rims.

Chapter 11

I know you fed up...

I couldn't see the driver because the windows were tinted, but I heard the music from down the street before they pulled into the front of Dontez's house. The song that was blasting from the speakers was called "Mr. Steep Pockets", the rappers were from our city. I knew the song because Dontez played it repeatedly. The first time I heard it I was impressed because of the beat. The lyrics blew my mind as well. I hadn't heard a lot of local rap music at that time, and Dontez found that to be hilarious. I got a kick out of Dontez when he listened to it because he would do motions with his fingers and bob his head hard to the beat like he was in another world.

When Dontez saw me he nodded and tried to go into his house without saying anything to me. I walked off the porch, oblivious to the fact that his friend was still sitting in front of the house. He was watching us. I asked Dontez who the person in the car was. It was clear that he didn't want to answer me. He nonchalantly said, "That's my nigga from way back." He left it at that, but I kept pushing for information.

"Where have you been? You haven't even been riding the bus."

"Damn, you nosey, girl. I been around. Chillin' and shit." We were standing on his porch talking. He was taller than me so I was looking up at him.

"Are you cool? I feel like something's wrong."

He replied with a smile. "Aww, Heaven got feelings too. Look at you. Nah, it's all good. On some real shit, it's better than good. I know how to take of myself, I'm a man."

I laughed at him and asked, "How are you taking care of yourself? When are you gonna be back on the bus?"

He looked at me in the same way that he looked at me when he was trying to decide whether or not I could handle his truth. "I can't even call it for real. I mean, I'm startin' not to even see the point of school, man. I'm feelin' like sayin' fuck that shit, Heaven. For real. Ain't like I'm goin' to college. This shit ain't set up for niggas to succeed. This is a white man's world, baby girl."

"So what are you saying?" I looked him in his eyes and waited for his answer.

He didn't bother answering my question about how he was taking care of himself. He matched my stare and said, "Man, fuck school. I'm tryna find a way to make it out."

After Dontez told me this information I was silent, because I really didn't know what to say.

He said, "I'm about to smash in a minute, so I need to go grab something."

We hugged, and went our separate ways. I was sure that Dontez would change his mind about being done with school. I knew he was too smart to say something so dumb. I wasn't sure where my life was going either, but there was something scary about dropping out of school. I felt like I had to go because it gave me something to do, and something to look forward to. I couldn't wait to walk across the stage like my sister Angel did. That sense of accomplishment was enough to keep me going. I understood what Dontez was saying about the fact that the world wasn't set up for blacks to win. I had heard my mother tell horror stories about the white people that she had to deal with at her job. There was also the fact that we were the first black family to move into a house on our block. We were treated like shit before the ink even dried to seal the deal on our new home.

My mother was so excited, it was something she never expected to do since she came from practically nothing. For her and her family it was about survival, not investing. She had just signed the papers that made the house officially hers that day. I don't think I had ever seen her as happy as she was in my life. My mother was referring to us as a family that day. She came and picked me and Leonard up early from school, and Angel was in the back seat of my mother's Buick when she arrived. I knew it was a good day because Dale had bathed. I was sure of this because the inside of the car didn't stink. He even smiled when we got in the car. My mother was rambling on about blessings, and how God was an on time God. I couldn't help but wonder if this was the same God she said could kiss her ass because He hadn't done shit for her anyway. My sister was even being nice. She was telling Leonard how handsome he was and that he was going to be a heartbreaker because of his dimples as we rode listening to my mother's Anita Baker cassette.

As we approached our street, my mother and Dale gave each other wide toothed grins. Dale leaned over and kissed my mother on her cheek and said, "You see, Sharon, dreams do come true. Shit, I knew we'd get us a house soon. We deserve this as much as the next person."

Angel looked out the window. Leonard and I looked at each other. We were communicating with our eyes. We knew not to say anything so we laughed silently. We never heard them talk like normal people and it was weird.

My mother replied to Dale, "That's true, babe. This is our house, only my name is on the deed, but that don't mean shit." My mother was removing the car lighter and putting her cigarette into it when all of a sudden she said, "Oh my God." Dale sat up in his seat. My siblings and I sat up as well. My mother pulled into the driveway of our new ranch style home. What we saw would change me forever. I didn't always agree with my mother, but nobody deserved to have their home vandalized.

Dale said, "I see right now I'ma have to kick somebody's ass." We all got out of the car and stood in shock. When we went to look at the house the day before all we saw was a house with a fresh white paint job. This day we saw the same paint job from the day before, but stick figured klansmen, 'KKK', and 'NIGGER GO HOME' was drawn in black spray paint on our new house. My mother was too shaken up for tears, so she stood in silence and smoked her cigarette.

Dale stood next to my mother with a single tear drop in his eye that wouldn't fall. I thought it was there on reserve in case he needed to put on a dramatic show. This was one of the first times I felt sorry for my mother. I watched her go from a negative place prior to even thinking about her house, to getting approved for her house and being positive every day leading up to her approval.

The next day the realtors came out and apologized for something like that happening. They were kind enough to paint the house free of charge. I knew I didn't have a say so in the matter, but I was pissed beyond measure and didn't want to move into the house. I didn't care how nice the house was. I decided that I hated white people at that time. I had a sour taste in my mouth about starting a new school that was full of them. My mother called the police and reported the incident.

After the police came and got the information they needed, they left. A local news crew came to our house shortly after the police left. As the news crew set up their equipment, Angel stood next to my mother and told her she was sorry this had to happen to her. Leonard grabbed a weed from the neighbor's yard and gave it to mother as a flower. I didn't know what to do to console my mother, so I awkwardly walked off and looked in each and every window of the house. When I walked back to the front of the house there was a camera pointed in my direction. I gave a wave, and walked toward the car so that I couldn't be seen.

I watched the interview that Dale gave and had to fight laughter. Leonard and Angel were standing by the car with me. Leonard was ten at the time, and I was twelve. We found it to be hilarious to listen to Dale talk.

Angel was pissed at us for laughing, she told Leonard, "You're smarter than that. Don't be stupid like Heaven and laugh at something serious."

I didn't say anything to her in my defense. I just went and sat in the car and continued to watch, but from the window of the car. My mother stood by Dale's side with more dignity and pride than I'd ever seen in her before.

Dale said into the microphone, "This here, this don't make no sense. We all human beins' and ain't nobody gon' run us off this here property!" The lone tear drop fell from his eye, and the interview was over.

We rode home in silence while Dale and my mother held hands.

Chapter 12

Not tryna put a rush on you, I had to let you know...

Just as I suspected, Dontez wasn't home contrary to what I had hoped. Christopher Kyle said he wanted a snack and I was getting antsy. I was getting this feeling that I needed something to get into. I had been nice and respectful since I moved in. With my dad constantly gone, and Sonya locked in her room, I had become Christopher Kyle's caregiver. Most days that was fine since it was only after school and on the weekends. Other days I felt trapped and overwhelmed. A walk was what I felt would do both myself and my brother justice. I wasn't planning on going too far, just across the street to the store. I went to the bottom of the stairs and yelled up to Sonya that I was taking Christopher Kyle with me to the store. As the days went on, Sonya stayed in her room more often. I knew I was a welcomed relief for her since I was more aware than ever before that she was mentally incapable of caring for her son. At first I wasn't sure if she was taking advantage of me or not. However, as time went on, I realized that there was no way she could have been faking her behavior. I don't think I had met anyone in my life that cried as often as Sonya. I blamed my father for Sonya's current condition.

After I told her we were leaving, she opened the door to her room, stuck her head out and said, "Ok, you guys be careful. Need some money?" I told her that we did need money. She came down the stairs wearing her robe and handed me two wrinkled dollars.

When Christopher Kyle saw his mother he became excited and ran toward her and yelled, "MOMMY'S WOKE!"

Sonya smiled, kneeled down to Christopher Kyle's level and gave him a warm hug. He was hugging her tightly with a smile on his face. I knew that my brother loved me, but I also understood that there was nothing like affection from your mother, or the lack thereof. I didn't want to be rude and stare, but as Sonya hugged her son I couldn't help but to notice her appearance. She looked awful to say the least. Her wig was sitting on her head crooked and it actually looked more like a lion's mane than hair. When she noticed me looking at her hair she ran her fingers through it, which only made it worse. I gave her a genuine smile and asked her if she wanted anything. After telling me no thanks, she released her son, blew him a kiss then turned around and went into her room and shut the door.

As I walked to the store I wondered if my father had a type. Either he attracted crazy women, or he drove them crazy. The look in Sonya's eyes was weird to say the least. It was like she was trying to keep it together but not having much luck. I wondered how long she planned on putting up with my dad's shit. I liked Sonya, and I appreciated her lectures, but on the other hand, I found myself thinking that she needed to shut up. She seemed to have a lot of answers about men, yet she was clueless when it pertained to her leaving her abusive husband. What was keeping her there? Why not pack up and run away? What made her think she should be any voice of reason regarding my life? I didn't plan on telling her my personal thoughts. Sonya was already an emotional wreck.

Christopher Kyle and I ran across the busy street and toward the store. The store had a small parking lot but it wasn't uncommon to see cars parked right in front. I noticed the same lime green Monte Carlo SS that Dontez was riding in the last time I saw him. It was parked in front of the store. I wondered if Dontez was in the store with this mysterious person that he had been hanging with recently.

As I approached the store, I gave the car a quick glance and walked into the store holding Christopher Kyle's hand. I loved that car, it looked masculine. The body of the car was shiny like he had just left the car wash. When we got into the store I looked for Dontez but I didn't see him. Christopher Kyle jerked away from me and ran toward the candy section. I called his name, but he didn't bother listening. My frustration was setting in. I loved him a lot, but I wasn't blessed with patience. The first thing that came to my mind was that I was going to beat his ass when I got to him.

As I walked toward my brother I heard a male talking. "What's up, bro? Let me get a pack of Back Woods." We became aware of each other's presence immediately. He heard me approaching and turned around.

I had to catch my breath. I had been going to my new school for a while now, I had seen Dontez and most of his friends and none of them compared to what was in front of me. He made KD's looks seem mediocre. I was looking at the sexiest chocolate male I had ever laid eyes on.

Christopher Kyle ran back to me with two bags of chips, and a candy bar before I made it to the candy section to grab him. My brother was tugging my arm in an attempt to get my attention. He said, "Heaven, this is what I want! HEAVEN!"

I was back to reality for a minute, but in my mind I couldn't get over this handsome man. He had jet black cornrows that sat on the middle of his back. I could tell his hairline was cut with a razor. His mustache and beard were trimmed perfectly. His eyes were his best feature. They were shaped perfectly for his face, and he had long eyelashes. I tried to guess how tall he was. He wasn't as tall as KD, maybe a little shorter than Dontez. I would say about six feet. As long as he was taller than me I was cool. There was no way I could afford to buy all the snacks Christopher Kyle picked up. Sonya only gave us two dollars and I didn't have any money at all. We stood in line behind the guy that I could only assume was Dontez's friend since I saw his car at Dontez's house first.

I was holding Christopher Kyle's hand in silence. I had yet to break the news about him not getting his all of his snacks. Once Mr. Chocolate paid for his Back Woods, he slipped the package into his baggy gray sweat pants pocket and turned and gave me a slow up and down glance then turned to leave. He was wearing a fresh pair of Jordan tennis shoes and a Stafford tee-shirt that looked to be brand new. I was sure he was a drug dealer. I peeped his wad of money and the expensive watch on his wrist. He was wearing a simple gold rope that had the letter "A" hanging from it. I wondered if it was his or his girlfriend's chain. I was used to males being louder with their jewelry versus a simple gold chain. I was even shocked that his diamond stud earrings in each ear were so small.

After he walked out of the store, I grabbed the candy bar and one bag of chips. I told Christopher Kyle to put the other stuff back as I sat the things we were getting on the counter. He flipped out. He had never behaved that way with me before, he was normally mild mannered. The store employee stood behind the glass wall looking like he felt sorry for me. I got pissed and said to Christopher Kyle, "Since you wanna act like a brat, you won't get shit." I was pissed and I wasn't about to start dealing with this behavior. When I became rude, my brother reacted. He threw himself into the floor, and embarrassed me even more. I grabbed his arm and walked out of the store. I noticed Mr. Chocolate from inside the store was sitting in the car that I figured was his. He was finishing rolling his blunt, I could tell because he was licking it to seal it when we locked eyes again. I tried to act like I wasn't paying any attention to him. I really was focusing on getting my brother back home, but I knew that I was exaggerating the situation now. I was busying myself by telling my brother unnecessary things as I looked down at him so that I wouldn't have to look up at that sexy chocolate man. "So if you act up like this the next time you won't get anything, you hear me?"

That's when he hopped out of his car and slammed the heavy door. "Excuse me, can I talk to you for a minute?"

I was about to cross the street. He was leaning on his car. If he hadn't tried to get my attention I would have been disappointed. I turned around and looked at him but I didn't move toward him. I was hoping to give off the vibe that I didn't care about anything he had to say.

He calmly said, "You might as well come here, you'll be my girl pretty soon anyway." He smiled at me showing two gold teeth with diamonds in them in the side of his mouth.

I smiled back at him, for whatever reason I didn't feel nervous as I walked toward him. I could have kicked myself for coming out looking the way I looked, even if it was just the store. My black leggings and Gap sweatshirt surely let him know that I was young and broke. My hair was in a ponytail and I wasn't wearing earrings. He didn't have on anything too fancy, but somehow I knew that if he wanted to get spiffy he could. I walked over to him and he put his hand out to shake mine while he looked directly in my eyes. He said, "Your hands are soft. I like that." He looked down at my brother who had tears in his eyes. Then back up to me and said, "Damn, what you do to lil man?"

I told him, "He was in the store throwing a fit because he couldn't get all the stuff he wanted." I refused to go into too much detail about the reason he couldn't get all of his junk food. He reached in his pocket and pulled out his money. He peeled off a twenty dollar bill and handed it to Christopher Kyle.

After he gave him the money, he told him, "Tell your sister to take you back in there and let you get whatever you want. Then maybe she'll let me take her out to get anything she wants." Although I was impressed with him handing out money like it was nothing, I chose not to address it so that I wouldn't seem ghetto.

I laughed and said, "Are you flirting with me?"

"His reply was, "Whatever you wanna call it, baby."

With a straight face, I asked him, "How do you know he's not my son? You've been asking questions about me?" By then I was flattering myself, I knew he would have had to ask Dontez about me. I just wanted to hear him say it.

"Yeah, I gotta know if my future wife got kids already or not. I don't wanna have to fuck your baby daddy up when he finds out he lost you." He smiled at me again and I told him he was full of shit.

I didn't give him the number to my dad's house because I wasn't sure if I could talk to guys, and more importantly, I wasn't sure if the phone would be on since it was always getting cut off. The thought of giving him my pager number popped into my head, but I wasn't sure if I would be able to keep my pager after Leonard left, so that may not have been a good idea. I took his pager number, and home phone number. I wasn't sure if I was going to call him, I would talk to Dontez about him first. Then I would decide. As I walked off, he said, "When you ask Dontez about me tell him I said, thank you."

"Who said I was gonna ask Dontez anything?"

He didn't reply, he literally walked off and got in his car. He started his car and revved the engine.

I walked over to his car and said, "I don't even know your name."

"It's Aaron, don't forget to call me."

This time I walked off. I turned around to see him watching me in his rear view mirror. I noticed he didn't ask for my name. When we got into my yard Aaron sped off.

I picked Christopher Kyle up and was about to carry him into the house when he said, "Heaven, look at my DOLLAR!" I had forgotten about the twenty dollar bill that Aaron had given him because I was so focused on all the possibilities of dating Aaron. At that moment, I wondered why he gave my brother twenty dollars so easily. Apparently he had money to spend. I was impressed. I knew I had to take the money from my brother, if my dad found out that his son had twenty dollars there was no telling how things could have gone.

Chapter 13

My first name must be he ain't shit...

Before we walked into the house, I told Christopher Kyle, "Give me your money, I'm gonna hang on to it for you. I don't want you to lose it."

He said, "If you keep it like Daddy did, I'll be sad." I promised him I wouldn't keep his money, and I meant it. He handed the money to me and we walked into the house.

Leonard looked bored, and high. He was sitting at the kitchen table shuffling cards. When I came in he looked up and signaled for me to come to the table.

I sat across from him and he leaned in to say, "Sis, these mufuckas are crazy as fuck." His eyes were bloodshot red, and glassy and he was looking like he was about to explode with laughter. I wondered if he was able to smoke weed at home and walk around casually like it wasn't a big deal. I didn't laugh because I was sure that he was talking about the madness that took place on a normal day.

"What happened now?" I asked him.

He said, "Daddy came in and told Sonya to open all the fuckin' doors in the house, and turn on all the lights. She looked at me like I was supposed to say something. I just sat right here and looked at her. Maaaan.....tell me why Daddy yelled like he was King Kong in this mufucka! He told her to do that shit now before he fucked her up. This nigga meant *every* fuckin' door and window in the *house*. I think he forgot I was here or something because he never even looked in my direction. Sonya did what he said, then went upstairs and slammed the door to their room. Daddy just sat on the couch being quiet. He wasn't moving or saying a word. I asked him if he was good. He just sat there with his back to me. Then he jumped up and walked outside. I got up and turned some of the lights off. Neither of them have jobs, and this nigga wanna leave lights on and shit."

I just sat there and listened. I really wasn't in the mood for my dad's shit that day. It would have been nice to have a normal day just once while I stayed in the house. I was about to respond to Leonard when my dad walked in. He was very loud when he greeted us. He stood in the middle of the dining room staring at us with huge pupils.

He said, "CHILDREN! DADDY'S HOME." Leonard and I just sat and stared because neither of us knew what we should say next. My dad spoke again. "Where's that bitch Sonya?" he said with a smirk. He was amusing himself. Leonard didn't say anything, Christopher Kyle didn't say anything either, he simply gripped my hand and I gripped his back. My dad's behavior was erratic and it was really starting to bother me, I was sure that he would drive Christopher Kyle crazy soon. I rolled my eyes at my dad out of irritation. I made sure he saw me. He ignored me and went upstairs, then came right back down and said, "I wonder what kind of mood she's in. She's washing her funky ass today. That's refreshing." He did an evil laugh. My dad was talking to himself as he searched feverishly for something in the living room. He was using his cigarette lighter to see under the couch that he lifted with his hand. He was searching high and low. He would get frustrated when the flame of his lighter went out and curse every minute or so. Leonard, Christopher Kyle, and I sat and watched in silence. Leonard was kicking me under the table until I gave him a shitty look. It wasn't like I didn't see what was going on.

Finally, I asked, "Daddy, what are you looking for?" Maybe I could help him find whatever it was. My dad was obviously in another world. He didn't bother to respond. As I got up to move closer to my dad, Sonya walked down the stairs.

She casually said in the harshest tone that I had ever heard her use, "He's not looking for shit. He's high, just like a FUCKING crack head. Look at you. JUST LOOK AT YOU."

I turned and looked at Leonard with bugged eyes, I wasn't expecting Sonya to behave this way. My dad was ignoring Sonya, it was like he really didn't hear her. She was going to make sure he heard her. I decided to move into the living and watch the argument from the stairs. Sonya went and stood behind my dad as he was bent down steadily looking from the couch to the coffee table. She said, "You ain't shit. Your fucking kids see you, and you don't even give a fuck. You are a pathetic excuse for a man. I see why that Sharon didn't want Leonard, Jr. over here! And I can't, for the life of me figure out why she would release her sixteen year old daughter to your sorry ass!"

My father cocked his head to the side like he had just realized that Sonya was insulting him. When she was telling him about himself, she had her hand on her hip with her head moving from side to side. When my dad slowly turned around and got up, she started to lose her confidence. My dad grabbed her by her shirt and said, "Bitch, don't you ever talk to me like that in front of my KIDS." He shoved her so hard that she flew into the staircase. She landed right by my foot. I got up to help her, she looked disoriented. Christopher Kyle started crying hysterically. My dad turned toward the dining room and yelled, "STOP CRYING LIKE A LITTLE BITCH ALL THE FUCKIN' TIME!"

He turned back around and went to grab Sonya who was screaming, "Don't you talk to my son that way!"

I didn't know how far this was going to go, so I ran and grabbed Christopher Kyle and I told Leonard to come on. I ran next door to Dontez's house. By this time I was in tears. I didn't know what my plan was as far as staying with my dad, but I knew I wasn't going back to my mother's house. There was no way I was leaving Christopher Kyle. The way that I talked to him earlier popped into my head. I felt awful about it.

I calmly knocked on Dontez's front door. I tried to wipe my tears, but they kept coming. Leonard stood behind me, I could tell he was nervous but he was trying to act like he wasn't. I could hear Sonya screaming next door as Dontez opened the door for us to come in. He looked concerned instantly and said, "What happened?"

"It's a long story, just call the police over to the house before my dad kills Sonya."

Dontez refused. He said, "Heaven, I'm not about to call them boys. What the fuck do you think they gon' do? Ain't no Officer Friendly over here, baby girl. We'll be lucky if they even show up." He spoke to Leonard. He hadn't ever met him so he was wasting time on making bullshit small talk.

I interrupted him and said, "Dontez, what's gonna happen then? You think it's okay for him to beat her ass all night?"

"No, I'm not saying that, but I'm sayin' I'm not callin' the pigs. I'll go break that shit up myself before I do that." He was grabbing his coat as he talked. "Just chill here for a minute with lil dude. Leonard, come on, bro," he said to my brother. "This is your daddy. Maybe you can calm his ass down some."

Leonard said, "I don't know him any better than you do, but I'll go." Leonard was being honest in his statement. He wasn't ever close to his father.

I asked Dontez who was home because I wasn't trying to have his daddy get pissed because I was there and he didn't know it.

He said, "They're upstairs in their room sleep. Just chill, we'll be back in a minute."

I did just that, I sat on the couch that my dad and Pastor Harvey sat on when they smoked crack. I turned the TV on and kept the volume down low. Christopher Kyle was on my lap, he was resting his head on my chest dozing off.

After about ten minutes, Dontez and Leonard came back from my dad's house. Christopher Kyle was asleep. I laid him on the couch and covered him with his jacket. Leonard came and sat next to me. I tried to feel him out to see how he was doing. Dontez told me to come with him. I followed him into his small room. I hadn't ever been in his house, let alone his room. I sat on his twin bed. As he talked to me I looked around. There wasn't much furniture in the room. There was a small TV sitting on his dresser and a bed. I noticed that the only decoration he had on his wall was a picture that said "Money Over Bitches" with a dollar that was drawn right under the saying. He said, "Are you listening to me?"

"No, I wasn't, what did you say?"

He smiled and said, "I was telling you it's cool over at your pops crib. Ol' girl is in their room, your dad was cool. He wasn't trippin' about me coming over there. He told me that if I hadn't he could have really fucked her up."

"Thank you, Dontez. I was scared to death over there. I doubt they'll ever stop that shit, and it doesn't look like he's planning on getting clean anytime soon."

Dontez was standing in front of me with his hands in his pockets and said, "So what you plan on doing? You know I got you regardless, Heaven, right?"

"Yeah, I know that, but I'm not gonna make my problems, your problem."

Dontez came and sat next to me on his bed. He said, "Look at me."

I did as he asked me to. I had started crying again, so I tried to look away.

Dontez gently grabbed my face so that I couldn't look away and said, "I told you I got your back. Your problems are my problem, that's why I'm here. I'll always be here. You're the sister I never had. Feel me?"

I forced a smile and told him that I did. We sat in silence for a minute until Aaron popped into my head. I asked, "So how do you know Aaron?" Dontez looked surprised by my question. Before he could answer me I said, "I went to the store earlier and met him. I recognized the car he drives because you were riding with him before. He gave me his pager number and his house number. Should I call him?"

Dontez looked like he was trying to choose his words carefully. He looked at the floor as he thought then he looked up at me and said, "Like I told you before, that's my nigga from way back. He's a cool dude."

"Ok, so should I call him? Does he sell dope?"

Dontez looked at me, laughed and said, "Girl, I can't tell you if you should call the nigga. You should know that. I don't know how he get's money, you gotta ask that man."

"Oh my God, Dontez! Should I call him or not? When you say you know him from way back what the hell does that mean? Why are you being so vague?" I was getting impatient because I really wanted to hear Dontez say this dude was great and that I should call him.

Dontez laughed and said, "I know him from around the hood. He's cool, he looks out for me. He's something like family to me for real. I'm not being vague. I just don't ask how he gets money. That's not my business. Feel me? He just slides through to swoop me sometimes because my pops is a bitch. I thought I was gonna have to beat pops ass the other day. I been stayin' at Aaron's house until I get my place."

Dontez had my full attention at that point. What he said was a mouthful. I asked him before if everything was cool, and he didn't tell me any of this. He was always trying to protect me, and I didn't do anything for him. I felt bad; the least I could do was listen to him. I knew he wasn't the type to vent about things. He would try to fix things himself. I figured he didn't have much respect for his father, but I didn't know it had gotten that bad. The other thing he mentioned was that he had been staying over at Aaron's house. Aaron had his own house. I wondered how old he was so I asked Dontez, "How old is he?"

Dontez said, "He's nineteen, Heaven. I'm not answering no more questions about him, aight?"

I nodded and told Dontez that I was sleepy anyway.

He said, "Look, I'ma tell you the same thing I would tell you if it was anybody else. Don't get played by no nigga. You are so fuckin' pretty, and it's cool because you don't realize how pretty you are yet, but you will soon."

I laughed and told Dontez, "Aww, thank you, big brother!"

He chuckled and said, "Come on, let's go."

I hesitated and said, "Dontez, I have one more question. Why do you think he gave my brother twenty dollars like that?"

Dontez just laughed and said, "I guess he has it to give."

We got up and walked into the living room where Leonard sat quietly watching TV and Christopher Kyle snored. I can't imagine how tired that poor baby was. I had missed lots of rest in the short time that I had stayed in the house with my dad, so I assumed he lacked proper rest also.

As Dontez walked us next door to our house, I couldn't help but wonder how things went for Christopher Kyle when I wasn't there. The front door was unlocked, so we walked right in. Dontez walked in behind me then walked in front of me. We didn't see anyone and the house was quiet. Dontez didn't say anything, he pointed up the stairs to signal that he thought that's where they were. I turned and gave Dontez a hug, this time I gave him a kiss on the cheek as well because I truly appreciated him and I couldn't imagine my life without him. I said, "I love you, Dontez. I just want you to know that."

He smiled and said, "Thank you, baby girl. I love you too. Go get some rest. I'll check on you tomorrow." Dontez got ready to leave out the door, then he turned around. He looked at me for a second and said, "Everything is gone be cool, stop lookin' so sad, baby girl." He left with me standing in the living room wondering what the hell I should expect next.

The house was too quiet. Leonard was sleeping with Christopher Kyle on the floor. I grabbed some blankets from the hall closet and covered them up. I went upstairs to change into my night clothes and go to bed. As usual, I could hear Sonya in the room crying. I wasn't sure how much more I could take. Why wouldn't she just leave? What was the point of speaking out, and yelling like she was crazy then turn around and go upstairs and leave it at that?

I decided to sleep downstairs on the floor with my brothers. This way if they started fighting it wouldn't be as disruptive to me while I slept. I walked past the bathroom and smelled a weird odor. It smelled like burnt plastic mixed with piss. The smell was nauseating to say the least, I felt like toxic fumes were floating around the hallway. I knew my dad was in the bathroom, because Sonya was in their room. I just sighed and went downstairs to lay with my brothers on the floor.

I was up for what seemed like hours crying. When I was finally able to get to sleep, I was abruptly woken up by my dad. He wanted to talk to me. He was wide awake. He said, "Heaven, wake up. It's time for us to have a father daughter talk."

I sat up and looked at him knowing that it was going to be a bullshit talk. At that point, I had lost most of the respect I previously had for him.

He said, "Listen, I'm not sure how much longer your stepmother and I will be together. She's just getting to be a bit much to deal with. I mean, did you see how she talked to me earlier?" He was sitting next to me on the floor smoking a cigarette. He was talking like he was innocent. My dad was pissed off all over again, like the mention of Sonya talking to him some sort of way set him off.

I said, "Daddy, you were saying horrible things to her. How would you feel if someone talked to me like that?"

He looked at me like he was taken aback. He said, "I was only kidding her, she always was too uptight. I just don't know how much more I can take. She's… she's stressing me a lot. I've been smoking more weed than ever since you've been staying with us. Haven't you noticed how I've been acting?"

I sat in the living room in disbelief. He was only kidding? He was so stressed that his weed habit had gotten out of hand? I was shocked that he chose to stay in denial about his drug addiction to heavy drugs, not just marijuana. How could I not notice the way he had been acting? I was speechless.

He continued, "Nobody would ever talk to *you* that way. You're *my* daughter."

I sat silently listening to my father as he calmly explained his point of view. I couldn't believe that he thought just because I was his daughter, I was above being disrespected.

"I'm just gonna sleep down here for tonight, I don't want to be in the same room with her. I can't stand that bitch." He said this as he reached for the lamp to turn it off.

I said, "Daddy, you gotta do better by Sonya."

He didn't reply, then ten minutes later, he was snoring. Eventually, I dozed off as well. I don't know how long we'd been sleeping but it couldn't have been very long. We were awakened by Sonya standing in front of us holding a butcher's knife, and a pot of boiling water.

She alerted us of her presence by saying, "WAKE UP, MUTHAFUCKA. I'MA KILL YO ASS, YOU BLACK SON OF A BITCH."

We all sat up and looked at her like she was crazy. We were in a state of shock. We all got up slowly and stood still. I wasn't sure what her next move was. Sonya threw the entire pot of boiling water on us. My right ear was ringing from the boiling water. After the ringing stopped, there was a sting inside of my ear. I couldn't believe she went to such extremes to make my father pay. I felt like she could have at least grabbed her son. She was responsible for protecting him, and she had failed miserably at that point. I had this belief that when the father fucks up, the mother has to step up. What happens to the kids when both parents are fucked up? I guess I could ask that question about myself. Leonard ran and stood behind the couch, he was screaming at the top of his lungs. I grabbed Christopher Kyle and went and stood next to Leonard behind the couch.

My father said, "Sonya…Sonya, you better put that fuckin' knife down, bitch!" His tone was warning her but she didn't listen to him. I'm not sure why I wasn't afraid of what could have happened. Looking back, I'm sure it was because I felt like I was the oldest and I needed to protect my siblings. Leonard could have pissed himself, he was that scared. He never stopped screaming his terrified high pitched scream. I was still holding Christopher Kyle and trying to cover his face so that he couldn't see any of what was going on. I didn't know what else to do. Sonya chose not to take my father's warning.

Sonya said, "Heaven, call your mother! You don't need to see this! Leonard Jr., go upstairs!"

I didn't move, nor did I reply. I decided that I hated Sonya at that time. I hated my father also.

Leonard looked in my face and screamed, "Heaven, call MAMA!"

I still didn't move because if this woman was really as crazy as she was acting, she could easily put that knife in my back when I went to grab the phone. Sonya decided that she was done asking me to call our mother to get us out of the house before she killed my dad.

My dad looked like he was amused by her dramatic show. He stared at Sonya with evil eyes as he stood directly in front of her. She tried to come at him with the knife but he grabbed her wrists in an attempt to make it fall from her hands. My dad wrestled her to the floor as he called her stupid bitches. He was shaking her wrists demanding that she drop the knife, but she refused to.

My brothers were still screaming and crying, so I took them upstairs into Christopher Kyle's room.

I wasn't sure what was to happen next, but I was ready to whoop Sonya's ass myself for behaving this way. The sad part was that I couldn't blame her for finally flipping out. A person could only take so much abuse. I went to the top of the stairs and I could see them still in the living room wrestling. When Sonya dropped the knife she paused and looked at my dad. She was silently asking for mercy. Without her weapon she lost her confidence, so she jumped up and ran out the door in her nightgown and no shoes. My dad chased her out the door while he yelled that he was going to kill her repeatedly. Leonard walked up behind me sitting on the staircase. I didn't have any idea what my plan was, but I knew things were going to get worse from here on out.

Leonard sat next to me and said, "I called mama. Heaven, I gotta go. I love lil bro too, but these mufuckas are crazy. She's on the way."

I looked at him and said, "Why the fuck would you call *her*? What do you think *she's* gonna do?" He started tearing up, and I said, "I don't care if she comes or not. I'm not going with her. I can't stand her, and I'm not leaving Christopher Kyle."

Leonard didn't say anything; he just got up and packed his clothes.

Chapter 14

That's what you are sunshine and rain...

Fifteen minutes after my dad chased Sonya down the street, they came back to the house. The police were with them. When Leonard said he was calling our mother he didn't mention that he was calling the police at the same time. Leonard ran down the stairs when he heard movement and talking downstairs but I didn't. I stayed in my spot at the top of the stairs. By this time, Christopher Kyle was sitting next to me waiting for my next move. Before Leonard came and told me that our mother was there, I already knew. I heard her outside demanding to know what was going on. The front door was open, so it was easy to hear my mother's loud raspy voice.

She said, "What is going on? I send my son to his daddy's for the weekend and I get a call telling me to pick him up. I'm disappointed as a mother. This is senseless, and it has to stop."

The white officer assured my mother that he was there to put an end to the madness. He appreciated my mother's concern. He told her, "Ma'am, I couldn't agree more, your…is he your…were you guys married?"

My mother lied and said they were married at one time.

The officer jotted down notes on his pad and continued, "Your ex-husband is being given the opportunity to put his shoes on and he's coming with us."

I finally went downstairs and peeked outside because my curiosity had gotten the best of me. Sonya was talking to an officer. She was visibly shaken. When she noticed me standing there watching her, she gave me a shitty look.

My dad went into the house to get shoes, and came back out.

The officer that was talking to my mother turned to my father and said, "Now, Leonard, we're asking that you come with us without any trouble."

I couldn't read my father's expression, and he didn't say a word to the officer, or to anyone else for that matter. He simply put both hands out to say that he was going willingly.

The officer read him his rights as he handcuffed him and escorted him to the car.

My mother made sure Leonard was okay then told him to get his things while she waited for him in the car. Leonard begged me to come with him and my mother. I knew there was no way that I could go with my mother at that point. I was hurt. My mother hadn't asked about me at all.

I was too ashamed to tell Leonard how much this hurt me, so I told him, "Call me later. I'll be fine here."

He hugged me and left.

I told Christopher Kyle to come with me into his room. I was going to lay with him until he fell asleep then go to my room and go to sleep.

Sonya came in after the police left. She walked into her son's room and picked him up like he was an infant. She forced his head into her neck as she looked at me like she hated the mere sight of me.

Christopher Kyle hugged his mother and gladly lay on her shoulder.

Sonya said, "I hope you got somewhere to go because you're not staying here anymore. When your dad gets out of jail he won't be coming here either. I'll give you until the morning, then I'm calling child protective services on your sneaky ass. You really think you're slick don't you? Well, all you are is a pretty face, and that ain't gonna get you very far, sweetheart."

I was shocked at the way she was talking to me. I hadn't been anything but respectful to her, and I thought we had a better bond than what she showed me that night. I said, "I see why my daddy beat your sorry ass. You pathetic, bitch." I figured that if I called my mother a bitch when she was out of line, Sonya surely wasn't exempt. After the shitty things she'd just said to me she still managed to look shocked when I responded to her insults. I knew she hadn't expected me to talk to her that way. I had purposely come off innocent to her, especially when I talked about my mother. I was aware that my mother was wrong for the things she said and did. What I never mentioned to Sonya during our talks was my reactions when I would get to my "You got me fucked up" point. I didn't feel like I needed Sonya either way, so I wasn't going to entertain her behavior. I walked past her and purposely bumped into her.

She turned around to see what my next move was. I wasn't going to disrespect her anymore, but I knew she wasn't sure what was going to happen next.

I went into the room I slept in and packed my things. I had no idea where I was going, but I knew I couldn't stay there for the night like Sonya said I could because we would probably kill each other. I was feeling sad because I had twenty dollars in my pocket. It was the twenty dollars that Aaron gave Christopher Kyle to buy anything he wanted in the store. I never imagined that it would come in handy. I would find a way to give the twenty dollars back to my brother one day.

Sonya followed me into the room while I packed my bags like there was something to steal. She said, "You're just like your sorry ass father, and I want to be done with all of you. Forget I ever existed."

I casually put as many clothes that I could fit into my bag without responding to her. I was extremely close to responding to Sonya but I honestly thought that it wouldn't make a difference what I said. My father had told her so many things that I didn't think anything I said could compete. Also, I didn't know when I would see my brother again, and I didn't want his last memory of me to be whooping his mother's ass.

I walked out of the house without saying bye to my brother. It hurt a lot, but I couldn't focus on that. I had to go into survival mode. I went next door to Dontez's house and knocked on the door. I wasn't concerned about the fact that it was almost four a.m. I wanted to talk to Dontez right at that moment. I banged repeatedly and got no answer. Feeling defeated, I walked across the street to the store to use the pay phone. I thought about calling Misa, but I figured she didn't have the gas money to come from the suburbs to get me. I knew that the twins had started stealing their father's car to joy ride at night, but I couldn't call the house at that time. They may have been out joyriding at that moment. I didn't want to get them into trouble. I had one other person to call, and that was Danni. I was nervous, but I didn't feel like I had a choice.

Chapter 15

I done dug myself a hole now I'm trying...

anni's mother answered on the first ring. I hadn't ever met her mother so I didn't know what to expect. I said, "Hello, may I please speak to Danni?"

Her mother said, "Can I ask who's calling? Danielle is in the bed."

I sighed while trying to fight the tears. "My name is Heaven." I paused then said, "I'll call her back later. I'm sorry for calling at this time." I was sniffling and wiping my tears as I talked.

She said, "Heaven? Her new friend from school?" I told her yes, and she asked me why I was crying. I gave her the brief story of what happened as I checked my surroundings. I saw a woman standing a few feet away from me talking to herself. She was getting louder and louder, so I had to talk louder to drown her out. Her mother said, "And what did you expect Danielle to do, sweetheart?"

I was honest with her mother. "I don't know. I just don't know what to do. I can't call anyone else." She asked me where I was, and I told her, "I'm at the Corner Stop on fiftieth and Woodland."

She got quiet for a second then said, "Okay, I'm coming to get you."

"Thank you so much," I said, relieved.

She said, "You're welcome. I'm only ten minutes away. Bundle up while you wait, it's chilly out." We hung up and I waited for her. The thought of being cold didn't cross my mind. I was too busy thinking about what my next move would be. I needed to stay with Danni for the night, but I knew I couldn't stay with her and her family forever. I refused to go to my mother's house. I was willing to be homeless before I went to stay with her.

It was almost exactly ten minutes after I hung up with Danni's mother that she pulled in front of the store. She said, "Heaven?"

I waved then went and got into the passenger side of her old beat-up minivan. I had to open the door and shut it twice to get it to close all the way. It had rust stains on the body and ran loud. I wasn't in the position to make fun, so I just rode in silence. I wondered why she didn't bring Danni with her.

As if she was reading my thoughts, she said, "I didn't wake Danielle up. We had a busy day with her helping me out at my job and that poor child was exhausted. We had a bake sale and they're always packed." Her mother's voice was smooth and calm. I felt comfortable with her instantly. She asked me if I went to church and my answer was no. I wasn't planning on starting either.

Danni's mother was a heavier version of her. She had beautiful dark skin with a short haircut. She said, "Oh, I forgot to introduce myself to you. I'm Diane. It's nice to meet you, although it's under a sad circumstance." I liked the way she talked. For some reason, I expected Danni to have a loud talking mother with nails just as long as her daughter's. She was the total opposite. She was calm but she spoke very clear and precise. Her nails weren't painted at all, and the only ring she wore was her wedding ring.

When we got to their house I wasn't shocked that it wasn't as big as my mother's house. It was a very small house, but it wasn't old and raggedy looking like I expected. The yard was nice and neat also. Her mother had green astro turf on the stairs that led up to the house. We walked in and she told me to make myself comfortable. The inside of the house was neat and clean, it felt what a home should feel like. She showed me where the bathroom was and then led me upstairs to Danni's room, which was the only room upstairs. She was in the hallway talking low, telling me that Danni wakes up early for Sunday school so try not to make too much noise getting settled.

I told her that was okay, but in my mind I was panicking. I truly didn't want to go to church because I truly believed that overall, church people were full of shit. I would go and fake it for the time being if I needed to. I wasn't going to be ungrateful for Danni's mother taking me in like she did.

After Diane left out and went down the stairs, I quietly took off my shoes and placed them against the wall. I was looking in my bag for something to wear to lie down in when Danni turned over. She opened her eyes briefly then closed them, then opened them again and jumped up. She said, "Oh my God, Heaven, what the hell are you doing here? You scared the shit out of me!"

I went and sat on her bed as she sat up. I told her, "Sorry, Danni. Long story short, I called you because my dad went to jail and Sonya kicked me out. I didn't know what to do and Dontez didn't answer, so your mom answered the phone when I called you. Your mother answered and offered to come get me. Here I am."

She laughed, shook her head and said, "That woman is so kind hearted, I swear." Danni moved over so that I could lie down. She told me to sleep at the foot of her full sized bed because she didn't want to sleep close to a female. Thank God for that, I wasn't sure if she was really into pussy or not. I was judging her by the way she dressed and the fact that she smoked cigarettes. I lay there for a few minutes then asked her if I had to go to church with the family.

She laughed and said, "No, you don't have to go to church, crazy girl. Hell, this will be a good excuse for me not to go. We will say that you're stressed and we need to sit home or something."

I replied, "Cool."

The next day, Danni and I sat around her mother's house not doing much but catching up. I gave her the full story of what happened with my dad and Sonya, and she was shocked. She asked me how I was feeling without Christopher Kyle right by my side. I told her how much it hurt me, and the fact that Sonya could treat me that way was wrong. Regardless of what happened between her and my father, I took care of her son when she needed me to. Danni laughed when I told her that I called Sonya a bitch. She said, "You didn't have to call that woman a bitch, girl!" I agreed with her, I didn't have to. But I did. We were sitting outside on the porch while Danni smoked her cigarette. I was shocked by the fact that her mother knew about her habit and she wasn't all over her about it. She told me that her mother wasn't a real judgmental person. Danni told me that her mother was thankful to have her since life was so short. She knew her mother's mindset had to do with her father dying a couple of years ago suddenly from a stroke.

I asked, "Why does she wear a wedding ring if your father died?"

Danni took a pull from her Newport and said, "She doesn't want to date anyone. She really believes there's not a man that can love her or take care of her like my dad did. So, it's just us two." I nodded while Danni put her cigarette out. She got up and said, "Come on, let's get out in traffic. It's Sunday in the city." She was looking like a Sunday in the city was a big deal. It was kind of cool out so I couldn't imagine what we would get into. I followed her into the house and up to her room. Diane had left for church earlier that morning and had yet to return. Danni told me as we climbed the stairs to her room, "Oh, and my mother said you can stay as long as you need to. She seems to think you might be a good person."

I laughed and said, "I'll tell her thanks when she gets home, and I *am* a good person, bitch." It was the first time I called Danni a bitch but she thought nothing of it. She laughed with me.

After our laugh, Danni told me casually that Jania normally came over on Sundays and they hung out. I asked her what they did because I didn't want to intrude. I told her I would gladly chill at Danni's house by myself. I wanted to call and tell Dontez what was going on anyway.

Danni said, "At some point, you and Jania are gonna have to get cool. What's the problem *anyway*?"

I looked at Danni like she was crazy and said, "What do you *mean* what's the problem anyway? Her big nose ass doesn't like me. She was hella foul out the gate." I rolled my eyes at Danni; it was second nature for me to become defensive when I was questioned.

Danni told me she forgot because it was so long ago. She said, "Really I don't care." She paused and looked at me like she was waiting for me to respond, but I didn't because I really didn't care either. Danni changed the subject. "The park might be packed and if the park ain't jumpin', Prospect might be. If both of those are dead, it's all good. We can slide through Club Milan and pimp the parkin' lot." She was talking like this was typical, but I didn't know what the hell she was talking about. I was wondering why I didn't know what she was talking about. We spent many days chilling on the porch at my dad's after school, so it was weird that I hadn't been invited to actually go hang out. I must have looked confused. She had her head cocked to the side and said, "You really are one of those out south girls!" She laughed and said, "Just get cute. You'll see some of everybody today."

I asked, "Ok, so what will you tell your mother? And how are we getting around?"

Danni was gathering things to get into the shower. She sighed and said, "Girl, will you relax? Jania has her license and she borrows her mother's car. I do this every Sunday. I don't really tell my mother too much other than I'm going to chill with Jania. My mother knows I'm not stupid. I'm not gonna get into no bullshit."

I nodded but I didn't know if I believed her. It didn't make sense that she didn't have to have every single second accounted for.

Danni went downstairs to the bathroom and took a shower. I went downstairs to look around some more. I noticed how warm and cozy the house felt. I was walking barefoot on the soft and thick burgundy carpet. I saw pictures of Danni when she was younger. I saw family pictures with her late father as well. Her mother had a painting of Jesus on the cross on one wall. Another wall was a shrine of Danni. There was a picture of her on a pony in preschool, and one in front of a fake fireplace. There was even a picture of Danni with a fake library behind her. I laughed in my head because those were pictures that let you know you grew up in the eighties. As I looked at the other pictures I began to wonder where my baby pictures were. I wondered why there were no pictures of any of my mother's children sitting in her living room, aside from Leonard.

I was getting ready to sit down on the couch when I saw a car pull into the driveway through the window in the living room. It was Jania driving a white Geo Prism. She checked herself in the mirror, then got out and slammed the door to the car. She walked into the house like she was a member of the family. I didn't want to admit that she looked cute because she had such a bad attitude. She was wearing a pair of dark blue Levi's that fit her thick body like a glove and a long sleeved turquoise shirt that accentuated her breasts. Her white K Swiss classic tennis shoes went perfectly with the outfit. When she walked in we both just looked at each other. I said, "What's up, Jania?" As I sat on the couch I was thinking that I was starting to get a kick out of her attitude with me. I couldn't believe she was this shitty to me because of her friendship with Danni. Why couldn't we all be friends?

She said, "Hey. Where's Danni?" Her tone was rude and she couldn't care less. I told her Danni was in the shower. Jania didn't say anything to me in response. She simply went upstairs to Danni's room. Once Danni got out the shower and was dressed, she told me to come upstairs.

Once I got upstairs, Danni said, "Ok, girl, what are you wearing? I don't want you to embarrass me, or yourself." She was looking through her closet like she had the best clothes. I told her that I refused to leave looking like a nigga. If she didn't have anything feminine I just wouldn't wear it. I was nervous about what to expect anyway. Jania stood in Danni's room looking at me like I had nerve. Danni said, "Girl, please." She looked in her closet and tossed me a black sweater that was sheer around my waist and hung off of one of my shoulders. She said, "I guess your jeans are cool. Are they real Guess jeans or are they fake like your chain?" She had a smirk on her face, then her and Jania exploded with laughter. I had to laugh too, but I refused to wear my chain anymore.

I said, "For the record, my jeans are real." I showered, and when I came out they were waiting for me. I didn't care, I wasn't rushing for anyone. I took my time when I curled my hair, and put mascara and lip gloss on. Then I was ready to go.

Chapter 16

I hit the parking lot and watched convertibles...

Riding with Jania was actually fun, she drove fast and played her music loud. I didn't appreciate riding in the back seat but I knew there was no way I going to be able to sit in the front seat since Jania really didn't want me there in the first place. I sat quietly in the back seat watching Jania and Danni rap to a song word for word.

Danni got quiet and started rolling a blunt while bobbing her head. Once the blunt was rolled, she held it up and looked at it like she was proud of herself, then she ran it through her lighter to dry it. Then she lit it. Danni was hitting the blunt when Jania asked her, "Where did you get that? I hope it's not bunk. That shit will give me a headache." I couldn't believe how much this girl complained, her whiny, high-pitched voice was annoying. Danni told her she got it from the same dude she always got it from on her block. We all smoked and chilled, listening to the music. We all sang, *"Be about yo paper"* as we approached the park. I stopped singing to the music because my surroundings shocked the hell out of me.

We rode past Swope Park and couldn't find a place to park. Jania said, "Maaaan...it's not even packed for real."

I disagreed with her in my head, if that wasn't packed then I must have been crazy. There were cars and trucks everywhere. I hadn't seen so many nice cars and rims in my life. I heard loud music, I saw pretty boys, I saw thugs, I saw pretty girls, and of course, the uglies were out.

Seeing the park from this aspect was something different and I loved it. I was ready to get out and chill for a bit, but Danni said, "We might as well leave, it's not hot out so it's not gonna be packed."

Jania must have agreed because she said, "Fuck it, you right, ain't shit crackin' here." She maneuvered around the lot and pulled out.

Danni said, "Well, go see what's up on Prospect." Prospect was a regular street on Sundays during the day, by Sunday night it was a hangout spot. Danni told me that in the summertime it would get so packed that the police would have to direct traffic. Both Danni and Jania laughed about all the fights they had seen on Prospect. I listened and laughed too, but in all honesty, I hoped that wouldn't happen tonight. I knew fighting led to shooting, and I wasn't trying to dodge bullets anytime soon. "Yep, we gotta find something to get into," Danni said.

In about five minutes we ended up on Prospect. It was more packed than Swope Park. I was sitting up in the back seat because there were so many people there. I thought Danni was exaggerating about seeing any and everybody. Jania started the song over right before we were within earshot of people. She had the music blasting so loud that I couldn't understand the words, all I heard was static. We parked in the lot of an auto shop.

Danni turned around and said, "You nervous? I know this is different for you, my little suburban friend." She was being funny again. She continued, "Niggas are everywhere! Let's get out and look cute." I couldn't lie, Danni was looking cute and it was nice to see her feeling confident. I think she was trying to show me that she didn't always have to dress like a tomboy. She wore a pair of blue Tommy Hilfiger jeans with a Tommy Hilfiger shirt that was tight fitting and had the name "Tommy Hilfiger" on the front.

I looked at her and said, "One thing about you is that you love your gold rings. Do you sleep in them?"

She laughed and said, "Bitch, shut up!" Jania got out of the car without laughing at anything we said. I found myself thinking that I wasn't going to kiss her ass but I knew to be cool because she was driving. I couldn't get left in a foreign place. Danni and I got out and leaned on the hood of the car. Danni and Jania looked so natural and comfortable. It was clear that this wasn't their first time being on Prospect to hang out. Danni and Jania yelled when they saw people they knew, they would also leave and go smoke with guys that offered them weed then come back to lean on the car. I passed on smoking with people I didn't know, but I was enjoying myself. We all had jackets on in the car but since we were trying to be cute, we left them in the car.

Jania had the idea to walk. She said, "Come on, y'all, let's go find some niggas." Jania was hyping herself up, and she was talking louder than she needed to. If she heard a song she liked she would stop and dance to it like she was a stripper. When we would walk past males she walked different and made different facial expressions.

I was watching and learning because it had never dawned on me to actually try to look sexy, maybe it could work for me too. Danni knew when to turn on her sexiness too. I wasn't going to go as far as dancing in front of cars, but I did want to master looking sexy without looking like I was trying to look sexy. I was shocked that I got the hang of making myself believe I was sexy very quickly. The fact that I still had a little buzz from the weed helped me. I felt like I had a chilled out vibe going and I liked that. The males were very aggressive, I hadn't expected them to come at a female they were interested in that way. Somehow, we all understood that if we weren't interested in a guy we still needed to be respectful because nobody wanted to be called a bitch or anything other than her name.

The closer we got to the crowd, the louder the music became. I realized the music was coming from the green SS that Dontez's friend, Aaron, drove. I didn't see Aaron, or Dontez, but I figured Aaron had to be somewhere close since his car was there. I wondered where they were, I was ashamed that I was more interested in seeing Aaron than Dontez. I hadn't called Aaron, but I was curious to see if he was still interested in me despite that. There was a gang of guys standing in front of the car wash talking loud and watching people.

Chapter 17

When I saw him, my heart dropped. He was just as handsome as I remembered. I didn't tell Danni or Jania that I knew of him, or that I had spotted him. I wasn't sure about how I was planning to handle seeing him and I didn't want them to get me any unwanted attention before I was ready. Should I speak to him? Or make eye contact and hope he noticed me? I didn't have to worry for too long because he spotted me. Jania had Danni's attention, they were pointing at a guy they knew.

When Aaron spotted me he took a long glance at me like he may have been trying to decide whether or not he knew me. I'm sure I looked different because the last time I hadn't done anything to myself. This time I had myself together. When he decided it must have been me he got his friend's attention by nudging him in the chest, he nodded his head in my direction. His friend was leaning against the brick wall with Aaron. They both watched me like they couldn't care less that it may have been uncomfortable having them boldly stare at me.

Danni saw them looking in our direction and quietly said, "Look over there. Bitch, I think your yellow ass is gonna pull somebody before me again."

Jania did a coy laugh like she didn't believe it to be true that she could have their attention. We all looked in their direction.

As we approached where they were standing, I quickly decided that I would walk past them because I was feeling shy all of a sudden. Aaron didn't move at first, he just stood and watched me. I was almost past him when he gently grabbed me and wrapped his arms around my waist from behind me and whispered in my ear, "Damn, baby, you didn't call me. This time I'm not lettin' your pretty ass out of my sight." I was turned on by his confidence, and I couldn't believe how good he smelled. He was being aggressive without making me feel like he was being disrespectful.

Jania and Danni stood there looking shocked.

I turned around and laughed and said, "Is that right?" I was using the looks that I had seen Jania and Danni use when we first arrived.

Aaron replied, "Fuckin' right. I told you, you'll be my girl soon." He was looking at me like he knew he had the gift of gab. I think we both knew he wasn't being serious. He was playfully flirting, and I thought it was cute.

"Aaron, I don't even know you," I said as I looked him up and down to let him know that I was checking him out.

He took a step back so that I could take all of him in. He gave me a cool smile and said, "Well, get to know me. You gotta call me, see what I'm about." I wasn't sure how to take him. It was clear that he was in flirt mode, but I decided at that moment that he was my type. I told him I would call him. He said, "That's what's up."

I asked him," Don't you wanna know your future girl's name?"

He replied with a chuckle, "Come on now, Heaven. You already knew I was gon' ask Dontez what your name was. I had to be able to tell my mother my new woman's name." He gave me that sexy smile again.

I loved all the flirting he was doing, but I wanted to know what Dontez had told him about me besides my name. "What else did Dontez tell you about me?"

"He didn't tell me nothing else. All I wanted was your name. Anything else I need to know, you can tell me." He was looking me in my eyes again. It was the first time that I sensed he was being dead serious.

Danni and Jania stood behind me talking to Aaron's friends. Aaron was standing in front of me, not taking his eyes off of me for a second. I didn't sense the least bit of nervousness from him. I said,

"Cool. So are you ready to talk for real, or do you wanna keep flirting?"

He put his hand on his chest like he was hurt by what I asked, and said, "Who's flirtin'? See, you hurt my feelings already. Now you gotta make it up to me." He was smiling at me again. I felt like I had to look away from him because his look was so intense. I felt like he was staring at me trying to decide his plans for me. He continued, "Heaven, pretty name for a pretty woman."

I laughed and said, "You are a mess. You never stop, do you? You are so full of shit."

We both laughed.

I said, "When do you want me to call you?"

"Shit, you can call me anytime, pretty woman," he replied, still smiling.

I smiled and told him, "Thank you. You're kinda cute yourself." Something was happening to me. I was starting to think I was pretty based on what people were saying to me and about me. My confidence was sky high.

He said, "Kinda cute, huh? I bet you are sneaky as hell. You're too pretty not to be."

Dontez walked up as I was talking to Aaron and put his arm around my shoulder. I hadn't ever known Dontez to be the worst dressed person in the world, but he wasn't ever the best. I wouldn't have expected Dontez to show up wearing what looked to be brand new clothes and fresh new kicks. I didn't recall ever seeing him wearing baseball caps either. His new look was cool, but he still wasn't what I would consider nice looking. I hugged him and said, "What's up, bro?" He was looking like he had something he wanted to say to me but not at the moment. I figured he either wanted to ask what I was doing hanging out at a place like this, or about what had happened over my dad's house.

He said, "Not shit, you good?"

I told him, "Yep, I'm good. What about you? I went by the house and nobody answered."

He casually said, "Yeah, I'm not fuckin' with them. I told you where I'll be for a minute."

Aaron broke into our conversation and said, "So you can feel free to come see 'bro' anytime." He added emphasis when he said "bro" like it was a joke, but I did plan on using the fact that Dontez would be there to my benefit. The three of us stood talking for a few more minutes until Danni and Jania interrupted us to see what was going on. Danni spoke to Dontez, and Jania didn't speak to anybody. I wondered if she was mad because nobody was entertaining her so she was pouting.

Aaron asked me, "So, what you about to get into, you headed in for the night?" I told him we were heading to Danni's house where I stayed to get ready for school the next day. He paused like he was trying to figure out how old I was. I didn't volunteer my age because I knew he was older and I didn't think I could get away with lying about my age. I just watched him try to figure it out. He decided not to ask me my age, instead he said, "Follow us to my house." Danni perked up like it was a great idea. I was ready to go to his house as well. I wasn't driving, neither was Danni, so we had no say so about going to Aaron's house. Jania was the driver and she looked pissed.

She rolled her eyes and said, "I gotta get home, so if y'all riding with me we need to go."

It was official, I didn't like Jania. Danni looked disappointed because she had a crush on Dontez, and this could be her chance. Aaron was talking to Dontez while we figured out what we were going to do.

Finally, I said, "Aaron, can't you take us back to Danni's house later, so Jania can go home?" I knew what I said pissed her off because of the foul look on her face. I didn't give a fuck. It wasn't like she was *my* friend. I wanted to go with Aaron. I was confused about the look on Dontez's face. Clearly, he didn't like the idea of all of us going to Aaron's house to hang out.

Aaron either didn't notice or didn't care. He said, "Yep, let's ride."

I turned to Jania and said, "Girl, you should come with us, we won't stay long."

She gave me an evil look because she knew I wasn't being genuine, then she walked away without saying bye to me or anyone else. I followed Aaron and Dontez towards Aaron's car. Danni walked Jania to her mother's car then came back to Aaron's car. Aaron was in the driver's seat, and Danni sat behind Aaron.

Dontez opened the door to the passenger seat and stood beside the car looking at me. He didn't say anything, but he was pissed about something. I didn't know why he was looking at me like he was mad at me when I didn't do anything to make him upset.

I said with an attitude, "If you wanna sit in the front go ahead. Damn, it's not that serious." I tried to say it quietly so he wouldn't look like a bitch in front of people.

Aaron spoke up and said, "This nigga ain't trippin' off the front seat, baby, go ahead and get in. Only dimes ride shotgun with me."

Dontez gave a fake laugh and said, "Girl, just get in, I don't know what you talkin' about." He got in the back, and didn't say anything else for the remainder of the ride unless it was very brief. When Danni tried making conversation he gave short answers to make it clear that he wasn't in the mood. I thought about Dontez's attitude and I figured that he was mad because he hadn't been able to dodge Danni. I was going to ask him about his issue with giving Danni a chance. Danni wasn't ugly and she was the most down to earth person I had come across in my life. I couldn't see what the problem was.

Aaron weaved through the traffic like he was used to driving in such chaos. He was bobbing his head to his music, not saying anything. When he saw someone he knew, he yelled out the window, or stopped in the middle of the street to speak. I wasn't sure if I should have been offended when he stopped to say what's up to a really pretty girl or not. When Aaron spotted her, he stopped and leaned out the window. "What up, fam?"

She walked over to the car to speak to Aaron. Dontez leaned in to speak to the girl also, then leaned back into his seat. I looked in the back seat at Danni. She looked at me like she was just as confused as I was. The girl looked like she belonged on Prospect. So did the group of girls standing behind her, they looked like they had just left an audition for a rap video. I was used to seeing a group of girls with at least one unattractive girl, if not two. I counted six girls standing on the curb watching their friend talk to Aaron. They were all gorgeous, but they were dressed like whores. I wondered if they were cold in their open toe shoes, sleeveless shirts, and tiny skirts.

The girl leaned into the car and gave Aaron a hug and a kiss on the cheek then said what's up to Dontez. I decided to look out of the passenger window because I felt disrespected. Danni sat up and whispered in my ear, "Do you think you and her look alike?"

I turned around and gave the girl a quick glance and said to Danni, "Nope, don't see it." I dismissed Danni when I actually did see it. I thought she looked better than me, so I wasn't going to admit to any resemblance. The girl asked what they were about to get into.

Aaron said, "Nothing for real, about to turn some corners. Let me get at you later, though."

She smiled and said, "Ok, playboy," and walked away.

I thought he was going to be uncomfortable since he stopped and talked to a girl in my face. He wasn't, and he offered no explanation as to who she was and why she called him playboy. I gave it some thought, and I wasn't concerned about getting information. Dontez would tell me when we were alone.

"Do you live far from here?" I asked Aaron as I watched him reach for his ashtray and grabbed a blunt out of it.

"No. If I did, I wouldn't be ridin' four deep." He put the blunt in his mouth and reached in his pocket for a lighter. After he grabbed his lighter, he lit the blunt. He took a long pull from the blunt first, then let the smoke slowly slip from his mouth then sucked the smoke back into his mouth. He released the smoke from the blunt then hit it again. I sat in the passenger seat mesmerized by him simply being him.

I said, "What's wrong with riding four deep?"

Dontez cut in, sighed and said, "You don't know why it's not cool to ride four deep? Come on, Heaven. Are you really a valley girl like *that*?" Dontez laughed after his attempt to insult me.

Aaron looked at me as if he was asking how I planned to handle the rude comment that Dontez made. I felt like we all knew that Dontez was trying to embarrass me and I didn't appreciate it. I was shocked because that was out of Dontez's character.

I turned around and said to Dontez in a nasty tone, "It was a *question*, and I wasn't *talking* to you." I knew he wasn't expecting me to be so defensive since I hadn't shown him that side of me, but I wasn't about to deal with anymore of his behavior.

Dontez attempted to answer my question. "Okay, put it like this...like, you see how we smokin' and shit? Okay, so if..."

Before he could finish, Aaron cut him off. "Ridin' four deep, especially leaving the park or anywhere that young black people chill like Prospect is like asking to be pulled over." As time went on I learned that on Sunday nights Prospect Ave was the busiest street in the city. There was nothing unusual about seeing fights, hearing gunshots, seeing drug deals, guys with their dogs, and anything else you could think of. Aaron continued his explanation, "Plus, we got weed on us. Not enough to sell, but enough to go to jail. Since I don't live far from here, I'm not trippin. "

I nodded and said, "I figured that, just wanted to be sure."

Aaron looked at me and said, "It's all good. If you didn't know, you didn't know."

The aroma of the weed was so powerful that Danni said to Aaron, "Damn, nigga, what are you smoking? That smells lovely." Whatever type of weed he smoked smelled better than the weed we had been smoking, but Danni didn't have to act so excited about it. She was loud when she asked him about his weed, and she scooted to the edge of the seat so that he knew she wanted him to pass it to her next.

Aaron passed the blunt to Danni and said, "No stems, no seeds."

Out of nowhere Dontez looked at Danni and said, "Damn, you hood for real, ain't you?"

Danni looked at Dontez as she released smoke and said, "And proud of it. You are too, right?"

He said, "Nah…I'm *from* the hood, you *are* hood."

Danni laughed and said, "Yeah, ok. You forgot I've been to your house, right?" Dontez just looked at Danni while she continued, "Don't get it twisted. You're hood, you just don't understand that being from the hood doesn't have to be a bad thing." They didn't seem to be offended by their exchange of words.

Aaron shook his head while laughing. "Tez, you are a fool, bro."

Dontez didn't reply to Aaron, he was looking at Danni smoke. He said, "Gimme a charge." His tone was demanding and rude.

Danni said, "NO! Will you leave me alone?"

Dontez didn't leave her alone, he said, "Gimme a fuckin' charge."

I looked at Dontez and said, "What's up with you? What the hell is a charge anyway?" I was getting impatient with him and I wondered why he even came if he was going to behave this way.

Dontez said to no one in particular as he looked at the roof of the car while he spoke, "All she gotta do is stop tryin' to be so difficult and put the lit part of the blunt in her mouth and blow into my mouth."

I said, "And that's it?" I was being sarcastic and Dontez picked up on it, I knew because of the way he looked at me. I didn't know up until that night that Dontez had this side to his personality since he came off so cool when we met. I was starting to wonder if anyone was who they claimed to be. I hadn't ever seen Dontez smoke, and he hadn't ever seen me smoke.

Danni passed the blunt to Dontez and said, "Either you hit it like this or not at all."

He hit it a couple of times with no further complaints.

Aaron drove in silence for about a minute then asked me as if Dontez wasn't in the car, "Why did he call you a valley girl?" He was pulling into the driveway of his house.

"I guess it's because I went to a school with a lot of white people before I went to live with my dad so the way I talk is different," I replied. I was purposely vague when I talked about myself. I hadn't even told Danni much about myself and I was with her daily. Aaron asked me what school I went to before I moved in with my dad, and I told him.

He said, "That's what's up, baby. It's better than the school he's going to." Aaron took the keys out of the ignition and turned to look at Dontez and said, "I'm fuckin' wit you, bro." Aaron was laughing as he talked to Dontez.

Danni and I tried to turn our heads while laughing out loud at Aaron's joke. Dontez laughed while leaning forward to pass the blunt back to Aaron.

Aaron took a pull then laughed at his own joke, while holding the blunt and shaking his head. He looked at me and said, "You don't smoke?"

I turned around and looked at Dontez.

He said, "Girl, ain't nobody worried about you. Do what you do." It was odd that he told me to do what I wanted to do yet he didn't pass the blunt to me.

I took the blunt from Aaron, and didn't bother to respond to Dontez. I hit it once then gave it back to him. I knew Aaron had to live fairly close to Dontez and my dad's house, but didn't know he was within walking distance. I wondered how I missed seeing Aaron come and go since he had to pass our house to get to the store on the corner. I began to feel sad almost immediately, but I tried to keep my game face in front of everyone. It was hard acting like I wasn't bothered by the fact that Christopher Kyle could be home with his mother, and I was this close but I couldn't see him.

Aaron got out the car and held the door for Danni as she got out. I opened the door, got out and reluctantly held the door for Dontez. I was irritated with Dontez for the night.

Dontez got out of the car with red, glassy eyes. He stretched, then yawned and blew his foul breath in my face. I had never known him to have such bad breath, the smell made me feel nauseated. I wondered why his eyes were so red. I didn't understand why he looked so out of it but nobody else did. He looked at me like there was a secret that only the two of us knew. I ignored him and walked toward Aaron who was still standing by the driver's side watching us with a smirk on his face, he seemed to be amused.

Danni said to Aaron as we all walked toward the front door, "They are weird." She had her nose turned up like she was irritated with both of us, but I was feeling like I was done with Dontez. I didn't feel like he was the big brother that I never had.

Chapter 18

I guess I want you too bad....

After we walked into Aaron's living room, I sat on his couch and watched him turn on the lights. There wasn't a single light on in the house when we walked in. Once Aaron turned the light on, I was able to look around. It was a nice house for a nineteen year old to have. Everything was up to date and it was clean. My curiosity for what he did for a living was really getting the best of me. After Aaron turned on the light in the living room he came and sat next to me and handed me the remote to his TV. I flipped through channels awkwardly, not caring about watching TV and not knowing who was going to make conversation. Danni was sitting in a black leather chair in the corner with her feet kicked up on the ottoman. She was being unusually quiet. She was in her own world studying her nails and biting them. I was starting to get worried because I didn't want her to get bored and start being a bitch like Jania did earlier. I knew she had hoped that Dontez would be interested before, but I was sure she wouldn't want him following his antics earlier. Dontez was in the other chair in the living room with his head leaned back, with his mouth wide open, snoring. At that point, I was more than sure that Danni wouldn't want him. How could he fall asleep in front of all of us so quickly and snore so loudly?

Aaron looked at me and gave me a light pinch on my side. "So, what's up? Tell me something good," he said, smiling.

I returned his smile. "You, being here with me."

He nodded and said, "Yep, that's good." Then he said, "Tell me how old you are, and don't lie."

I said, "Why would I lie about that?" I responded to Aaron like it was unfathomable that I would ever lie about my age. "I'm sixteen."

He shook his head and said, "Damn, baby…sixteen? You act older than sixteen. You *look* older than sixteen, too."

I didn't realize Danni was even paying attention. She spoke up and said, "Age ain't nothing but a number."

Aaron laughed. "You keep something to say, don't you?" Then he looked at me and said, "She's cool as fuck. Good people." I gave a fake smile because I didn't want to seem rude. The truth was that I didn't care to hear compliments about Danni. I asked Aaron how old he was because I wanted to be sure that Dontez's information was right. He said, "I'm nineteen." He paused and waited for my reaction. "Is that cool?"

I replied, "I guess it's cool."

He smiled. "That was close. I thought I lost you that quick. You just made my night."

Danni laughed out loud and said, "You are crazy, boy!" I was happy that Dontez fell asleep at first, but with Danni butting in like she was I almost wanted to throw a bucket of water on him to get him up to keep her company. Aaron wasn't bothered by Danni, so I tried to play cool.

I said, "So y'all telling me that Dontez's snoring is only annoying me?"

Danni said, "Hell yeah, that shit is annoying! I should wake his ass up."

Aaron laughed and said, "That's Dontez for you, he was like that when I first met them."

I asked, "How long have you known Dontez?"

Aaron looked toward the ceiling like doing so helped him to think better and said, "Since he was about eight. We all grew up around here."

I said, "Who, you and Dontez?" Aaron looked at me like he was wondering if I was serious.

Aaron said, "And his brother."

"I didn't know Dontez had a brother," I replied.

Aaron said, "Whaaat? You didn't know bro had a brother?" I knew he was being condescending.

I laughed and said, "You are rude. You know Dontez isn't my brother."

He shook his head, and said, "Never rude, just real. Come here, I wanna show you something." He got up and gave Danni the remote and asked if she was cool. Danni said she was fine since she was bored and about to wake Dontez up.

I walked toward the back of the house with Aaron, and up a flight of stairs. I couldn't imagine what he had to show me. The more I looked around, the more I felt like there was a female's touch there. There was a warm, cozy vibe over Aaron's house. Joey's apartment lacked that warmth, but it was what I would have expected from a bachelor pad at their age.

Before he opened the door to his room, we stood in the hall and he looked at me and said, "Don't panic, alright?"

I looked at him and said, "What's in your room that would make me panic? I'm starting to panic already."

He grinned. "It's nothing bad like that, chill." He turned the knob, and we walked into his room. I didn't see anything out of the ordinary. There was a queen sized bed, a black bedroom set, his closet and an aquarium. He walked over to his dresser and took his watch off then placed it on his dresser. Then he turned the light on in the aquarium in the corner of his room. He calmly said, "Come here. I just got him a few weeks ago." I wasn't smiling because I was terrified of things that crawled in cages.

"What is it? I'm serious."

He laughed at me and said, "I wouldn't let him hurt you, woman. It's just my iguana."

I refused. I said, "I'm not coming near that thing. It probably carries diseases on it. So, hell no."

Aaron said, "No, I keep his area clean."

I told him, "Aaron, I'm not coming to see that thing, ok? So just put him up before I leave."

He laughed and said, "Such a girl" as he put the iguana in its cage. I didn't understand why he would have a pet iguana anyway.

I said, "So, are you into reptiles or what?" I was standing in his bathroom watching him wash his hands.

He said, "I wasn't before I got the iguana. My six year old nephew runs game on my sister all the time. She promised to get him anything he wanted if he behaved in school for a week, instead of just beatin' his ass. After the week was over, he told her he knew what he wanted. It was the iguana. When he got the iguana he was cool, then a couple of days later he decided he was scared to sleep in his room with the iguana in there. My sister was ready to beat the shit out of him, so I told her I would take it for her. I'll probably get rid of him soon because I'm not here enough to take care of him." I nodded to him but in my head I was thanking God that he wasn't a reptile loving freak. He dried his hands off while he stood watching me in the doorway. After he hung his towel up, he said, "Can I get a voluntary hug? The first one you gave me was shitty."

"I've never given you a hug," I said.

He walked closer to me and said, "My fault. I guess I'll take one now then."

"You guess, huh?" I said as I grinned and looked up at him with my arms open. He wrapped his arms around my waist. I wrapped my arms around his neck. We hugged for less than a minute but it felt so good, I couldn't remember when I had one before that unless it was from Christopher Kyle. I wasn't concerned about the time because I was enjoying being in Aaron's company.

He said, "You smell good. I like that."

"Thank you." I walked over to his bed and sat down. I grabbed the remote because I planned on hanging out for a while.

"You ready?" he asked. "Y'all got school tomorrow and shit." I decided that I wanted to be honest with him.

I said, "I know I have school tomorrow but I'm cool here with you right now, is that ok? Or do you have other plans?"

He said, "That's what's up." He asked if I wanted to watch a movie, as he put in *I'm Bout It* without waiting for my response. He turned the light in the room off and sat down next to me. I forced myself to watch the movie and not him. "Are you cool? You can get comfortable." As he told me to get comfortable, he stood up and unbuttoned his plaid Nautica shirt and took it off. He had on a white t-shirt under the plaid shirt. He got up and hung his shirt in his closet then came and lay at the head of his bed.

I sat up and took my shoes off then relaxed at the foot of the bed. I was lying on my stomach with my face resting in the palms of my hands watching the movie. Before that night, I hadn't seen nor heard of *I'm Bout It* and I couldn't believe how good a movie it was. When I turned around to look back at Aaron, I felt a tingle that went from my stomach to my pussy. His attention was on the movie so I didn't think he was focused on me. He had his head resting on the headboard of his bed with his legs crossed. As usual, his braids were neat and fresh looking and he was as handsome as ever. He had his arms folded across his chest when I got up and went to lie in his arms. I wasn't ever an aggressive person, but I couldn't deny my attraction to Aaron. He was so confident and grown man like, it made me want to match him and be confident and grown woman like. His smooth chocolate skin, with his long eyelashes and thick lips were driving me crazy. His perfectly trimmed mustache and beard were so sexy to me, I really felt like I couldn't resist him. When I went to lay with Aaron, he didn't move at first. He just sat and looked at me. I looked him in his eyes and said, "Are you gonna uncross your arms?" He uncrossed his arms and pulled me close to his face and lightly brushed his lips over mine. He slowly kissed me a few more times on my lips. I didn't expect him to kiss me but when he did, I felt butterflies in my stomach. His scent was almost intoxicating and I felt like I couldn't get enough of it. I had only kissed one person before Aaron and that was Joey.

The first kiss Aaron gave me was without tongue, yet it felt more passionate than any kiss Joey could ever have given me. I had my arms around Aaron's neck again as I lay on top of his body. I could feel him getting hard and I experienced a different feeling. My vagina was throbbing because I was so aroused. He had his arms wrapped around my back at first, then he slowly rubbed my backside. I kept telling myself that I should stop him, but I couldn't. I had my eyes closed as I gave him soft kisses on his neck. He was kissing my neck as well. His slow kisses were making me want to moan, but I contained myself for the time being. He slid from under me and got on top of me. We could see each other from the light of the TV. We made eye contact for a second. Then he began to kiss me with his tongue. I followed his lead, and it just felt right. He stopped tongue kissing me, and sucked on my bottom lip for a second then stopped and got up. He looked at me like he knew I was going to ask him what was going on.

"There's plenty of time for that, baby," he said. "I shouldn't have let it go that far. You're young, so I wanna make sure you know what you want. You don't understand that, though."

I sat up and said, "Understand what?" I despised anyone telling me that I was too young to understand anything.

He said, "Baby, you're young. I can't deal with you fallin' in love and losin' it and shit. Feel me? I already know you're not a virgin by the way that you carry yourself. But I can tell that you don't have a lot of experience because you can't kiss. You probably can't fuck for real either."

I sat up and looked at him. "Oh my GOD, you are so RUDE, and you don't know if I'm a virgin or not."

He grinned and playfully slapped my thigh and said, "I think it's sexy that you can't kiss. That just tells me that you haven't fucked the whole hood. I can teach you some shit."

I said, "Aaron..." and rolled my eyes at him. I was smiling so he knew I wasn't mad.

He said, "I gotta make sure I want you to fall in love with me before I give you the business." This time he wasn't smiling. He got up and pulled a tray full of weed from under his bed then rolled a blunt as I sat next to him.

I said, "After you have sex with a girl, do you feel like the cha—"

He cut me off with a sigh and said, "Are you about to ask me if I leave 'em alone after I hit?" Yes, I was curious about Sonya's philosophy on waiting to have sex, and her idea that after the chase is over, ultimately, so is the relationship; depending on how young you are. So I said, "Well, I guess I was, but you cut me off."

He sighed and said, "Peep game, a nigga won't ever leave as long as he's getting pussy and the female he's getting the pussy from stays cool. It's really when a female starts actin' crazy and psycho *after* she gives up the pussy that a nigga wants to leave her alone. Females start thinkin' that sex means a relationship or marriage, and that's bullshit. So when a nigga show 'em what they should have already known, they start talkin' all greasy on some, 'that nigga used me' type shit when that's not what it is. Feel me?" He was looking at me like he really wanted me to understand what he was saying, but I didn't.

Well, maybe I did understand when it pertained to some other female, but not me.

"And what do you mean when you say as long as she's cool?" I asked. Aaron exhaled his smoke then passed the blunt to me. I smoked the blunt as I listened intently to his explanation.

He said, "See, you young, you don't feel where I'm coming from, but it's all good."

"Aaron, I'm asking you to explain what you mean when you say as long as she's cool. This really isn't about age."

He said, "Alright, like going from calling to see what's up and we kick it when we kick it. Then to calling the house back to back, and blowing up pagers and shit after we fuck. Makin' a nigga wanna go to a fat, ugly female or something. It's always cool starting out, but feelings change that shit. And for females sex brings feelings. Even though y'all try to front and say it don't."

I laughed hysterically at what he said, and asked, "So, you mean you would have sex with someone that is unattractive to you just for sex rather than someone that you *are* attracted to because she might cause too many problems? Get a grip, Aaron."

He wasn't laughing when he replied. "See, that's what I'm sayin', baby, you are young. Pussy has no face. If I'm not looking for a relationship, why would I give a fuck what she looks like? I'm not knocking her up or no shit like that. I can hit, and be done. A lot of ugly women already know their role. Just like pretty women know theirs."

"And you don't think an ugly female would do the same thing that a pretty female would do eventually? I mean, being ugly and pretty are opinions anyway. You can't say that just because a girl is ugly she can't catch feelings from sex."

He replied while shaking his head. "We *both* know what ugly is, baby. Your home girl downstairs is cool as hell but she's ugly, and you're pretty. So the shit that she settles for, you wouldn't have to. It's just like when niggas are broke and don't have the shit females like to see. They don't get to be choosy, they take the type of female they can get for what they got. You dig? So, to be honest, even if the ugly chick does catch feelings she doesn't even feel confident enough to speak up because she knows she ugly, so she takes what she can get."

I was stunned at what he said about my friend. I said, "Aaron, you just said my friend was ugly."

He said, "Am I lying?"

"Okay, I'm done with that because I don't feel what you're saying at all. So what types of things do females like to see?"

He laughed and said, "You can answer that. Are you a female?"

I said, "Of course I am, but I wanna know what you think a female wants to see."

He said, "Well, first y'all like seeing money." He looked at me like he was waiting for me to say something, but I didn't. He continued, "You like seeing money just like the next female. I put that twenty in your brother's hand then I watched your reaction. You handled it cool, but I knew eventually you would call me because you probably figured I wasn't broke. My father told me a long time ago that women like security. When they see money, they start thinking about being taken care of."

I sat in his bed and looked at him like he was crazy. "So how many twenties do you lose trying to show females that you're papered up? Who's the real dummy? And you really think that when a female sees money it automatically means that she's broke and looking for a trick?" It was his turn to laugh out loud.

He said, "You got it wrong, baby. I felt bad for your brother because I know what that's like. To want something so bad but you can't have it. So I gave that to him, but I'm no dummy. I know seeing me give him that money fucked with your head a little bit. Tell me you didn't ask Dontez about me and what kinda bread I'm workin' with. But to answer your question, it doesn't always mean that a chick is broke, but y'all like security. Why would a female with money fuck with a broke nigga? A smart female wants a dude with as much as she got, so they can make moves. I'm tellin' you, my parents gave me the game early."

I said, "Well, okay. I need to go so that I can get ready for school tomorrow." I got up and started putting my shoes on. I was done with listening to him for the night. Aaron was opinionated and he couldn't care less who liked it or not.

He stood up and said, "That's what's up. Can I see you after school?" He didn't bother to ask why I ended our conversation abruptly. He stood in front of me with his hands on my waist. He was looking at me as he bit his bottom lip. He said, "I fuck with you, though. For real. You still got growing up to do, but trust me, I'm the realest nigga you'll ever meet. I can teach you a lot." Aaron was looking into my eyes again. "You ready?" he asked.

"Yeah, I told you I was. I have school in the morning." He grinned and shook his head like he knew that I knew what he was talking about.

"I know *that*. I mean, are you ready for this, for us?"

I said, "I'm ready to go for now."

We were about to leave his room and he said, "Where's your jacket?" I told him it was in Jania's mother's car. He went and grabbed a hoodie sweatshirt from his closet that smelled just like him. I told him thanks and put it on. "It's all good," he replied. "I can't have my baby gettin' sick." I couldn't figure Aaron out because one minute he seemed genuine then the next he went back into bullshit mode.

Chapter 19

Cheers to you for giving me a chance....

We walked downstairs and into the living room. Dontez and Danni were sitting on the same couch, and sharing a blanket. Apparently, Dontez had changed his mind about not dating Danni. Dontez looked up at me first, then at Aaron. Dontez was accusing us with his eyes. I looked away and adjusted Aaron's hoodie on me because I felt guilty for some reason. Though Aaron and I hadn't had sex, we had still turned each other on and I didn't know if it was right to do that with Dontez in the house. At that moment, I realized that I still viewed him as my brother after all. Aaron noticed the look on Dontez's face also. He didn't look amused by the look on Dontez's face. He said, "You good, bro?" The question wasn't asked in a way that suggested that Aaron gave a fuck. It was more like a warning for Dontez to mind his business.

Dontez said, "Yeah, man. I'm straight. I'm just tired, bro."

Aaron absent-mindedly said, "That's what's up," and grabbed his jacket and his keys. Danni was surprisingly quiet. Aaron held the door open for me to walk out. He watched me with a mischievous grin until the moment that I got in the car then he followed me to the car. I knew we had stayed over Aaron's for a while because I could hear birds chirping. Danni came out of the house without Dontez. I got out of the car to let her in the back seat. I was trying to feel her out because she was different after I came downstairs.

Danni didn't live far from Aaron. I gave him directions and we were at her house in five minutes. As Aaron drove, I asked Danni if she would get in trouble for staying out so late. She calmly said, "Girl, no, we'll be fine. She won't hear us come in." There was a level of sadness in Danni that I hadn't seen before, but I could tell she was trying to be her normal easy going self. When we made it to her house, I got out of the car and let Danni out. Danni walked into the house without saying bye to Aaron. Aaron walked over to the passenger side and asked me when I would call him. I told him that I would call sometime later that day. He said, "Do you live here?"

I told him, "Yep, for now I do. I told you that earlier." I didn't explain any further.

"Why though? Where's your family, baby?" he asked.

"It's a long story," I replied with a sigh. He wasn't buying my answer.

"Well make it short." I told him that I didn't get along with my mother, and the short version of my dad and Sonya getting into their arguments. He said, "Damn, that's fucked up. Let me know if you need anything." I told him I would, and he said with a straight face," You know I hand out twenties like it's nothing." I laughed at him then he laughed with me. He pulled me into his arms for a hug then he gave me two soft kisses on my lips. Every time he touched me I felt a tingle through my body. He looked down at me and said, "Kiss me back. Or at least try to." The way that he looked at me gave me chills. I leaned into him more and followed his lead again. He said, "Yeah, I like you."

"I like you too," I replied, smiling. In my mind I was thinking that I loved him, but I didn't want to seem like the girls he talked about earlier, and we hadn't even had sex yet.

"Can I take you out tomorrow?" he asked. I told him I would find out. He wanted to know who I needed to find out from. I told him I wanted to make sure I didn't leave Danni out. He said, "Bring her too. I think Dontez is feelin' her now." Aaron reached in his pocket and took out money for me.

"Thanks, but I don't need it. I have lunch money for tomorrow. And please don't ever make it seem like money is the only reason I like you."

He walked around to his driver's side shaking his head. He looked at me and said, "What we got going can't be bought with money." I smiled and walked into Danni's house wearing the same smile. Danni left the front door open, so I came in the screen door as quietly as possible. I crept up the stairs and went into Danni's room. She was about to lay down when I walked in.

"Well how was your night?" She had a smile on her face that I took as genuine.

"I really like him. Don't you think he's cute? Just can't stop staring at him," I continued.

Danni laughed and said, "Yeah, he is sexy as hell. He's your speed. Aaron looks like he would be your type."

I smiled and said, "He is my type."

I was in deep thought thinking about Aaron when Danni said, "Did you fuck him?"

I looked at her and laughed. "No, I didn't, but I wanted to. We could have, but he stopped kissing me and told me there's plenty of time for that."

Danni said, "Oh my GOD, Heaven. You are so *fast*. You probably already had sex, haven't you?" I was busy taking my earrings off, but I stopped and turned around to look at her.

"No. I haven't," I replied.

Danni laughed. "Bitch, you're lying!" I tried to lie but I couldn't, not to Danni at least.

I said, "You haven't had sex, Danielle?"

Danni said, "Oh, shit, you're calling me by my real name, it must be serious...No, I haven't."

"Why not?" I inquired.

Danni replied, "Well, to be honest, I told my father that I would wait until I got married, and I really want to keep my word." I sat in the same spot watching her.

"Well he's dead now, so what difference does it make?"

Danni said, "Heaven, you need to have my mother give you a Reiki treatment. You are so negative!" She laughed after she said it.

"Whatever that is," I replied. "Anyway, I did it one time, and I didn't like it. I was so mad when I was done because it didn't feel good like people said it would."

Danni said, "Well, you shouldn't have done it anyway."

"Oh, well, I decided that I'm a virgin again anyway. I gotta learn how to kiss before I lose my virginity to Aaron. He said I can't kiss, but that's a good thing because he will teach me how to, but I felt so stupid when he said that. Who doesn't kno…"

Danni cut me off. "Do you think Dontez likes you, Heaven?" She was looking at me.

"No. I honestly think he hates me. Did you see how shitty he was toward me tonight? I was ready to smack him in the fucking face."

Danni sighed. "But that's kinda what I'm talking about. He was cool as hell with you until Aaron came around, then he started acting different. When he woke up and asked where you were, and I told him where you were, he tried to play it off – but he was pissed."

"Well, if he does he better get over it, because even before Aaron, he didn't have a chance. I know you like him but he's not my type at all. Why don't you ask him?"

Danni replied to me, "I guess it really doesn't matter, he's not into me anyway. He was so cool when it was just us two downstairs. He was mad at first, then he smoked and calmed down." I lay on my end of the bed and Danni was on her end.

I finally asked, "Is that why you were acting kinda different?"

"Yes! I don't know why I like him so much. It probably seems stupid to you because you can get anybody you want."

I laughed at Danni in my head because she had me mistaken. I wasn't the girl that got anybody I wanted. The truth was that I needed to figure out what was going to happen with me and Aaron. I knew that I liked him, and I knew that he said he liked me, but what did that mean? I had watched my cousin Misa go through guys and she had been hurt before. I wasn't trying to experience that at all. I didn't see what Aaron could have liked about me. I started thinking that I was pretty, but that still didn't mean that I would compliment Aaron in any way. He was put together better than I was. He mentioned his sister, and nephew, and even his parents when we were over his house. I couldn't help but wonder if they were a close family. If they were a close family, where would my fucked up family fit in with them? I wouldn't ever be able to take him around my family. I casually said with a chuckle, "Danni, I can't have anybody I want; I can only wish life was that simple."

Chapter 20

He can't love you like I can...

School was the last place that I wanted to be the next day, but I decided to go anyway. I thought about dropping out of school numerous times, but I chose to keep pushing forward. By going to school in one district, and then moving to the next, I learned that it really didn't matter what school you went to. In the inner city, you had mostly Black teachers that didn't give a fuck, and in the suburbs you had mostly White teachers that didn't give a fuck. Yet I understood that I had to get in where I fit in because that little piece of paper called a diploma would at least give me the confidence to believe I could do something positive. I hated the fact that both schools were extremely easy and the complete opposite of thought provoking.

When Danni and I woke up the next day, her mother was in the kitchen preparing food. Diane always had a peaceful look on her face. Danni walked up to her mother and gave her a kiss on the cheek. I thought it was special because her mother's eyes lit up when she walked into the room. We sat at the table talking as if it wasn't six in the morning. We never did those types of things when I was with my mother or my father either for that matter. When I stayed with my mother we all decided that we would be in bad moods from the moment we got out of bed each day. Our excuse was that it was too early in the morning. I hadn't realized how dysfunctional my home really was until I went to stay with Danni and her mother. Watching her mother cooking breakfast, and humming made me realize that I had no reason to think I was better than Danni. What gave me the right? I loved Danni and her mother, but I was envious. I wondered why I had to come from such a fucked up mess. I sat in another woman's kitchen with my best friend, and I was hurting on the inside. It seemed like they thought nothing of the normalcy in their home. The house was clean and I felt like there was a positive vibe in each room. Danni grabbed three plates as I sat and watched her. I didn't know what to do to help because I wasn't used to this type of unity between loved ones.

Diane was watching me and I didn't know it. She said, "Heaven, how are things going for you?"

"Things are going okay."

She nodded, "Well, we're glad to have you here, sweetheart. You can stay as long as you need to."

I nodded and told her thanks.

She was still looking at me. "Where's your mother?" she asked. Concern was written all over her face.

I shrugged. "I don't know. I guess she's at home."

Diane nodded. "Okay, when you're ready, I wanna talk more about what's going on. Is that okay?"

I told her it was okay as Danni listened silently while she set the table. Her mother made a vegetarian dish for breakfast. I wasn't a vegetarian, so I told them that I would rather not eat anything.

Danni laughed. "I know what you're thinking because I'm the same way. I'm not into the things that my mother eats since she became a vegetarian. This is a cheesy potato casserole, with sun dried tomatoes. Relax, it's not like there's a bunch of weird stuff in it."

I decided to go ahead and try the casserole that Diane made and it was delicious. They both laughed at me because I had three plates of it. We left for school, but we were exhausted because of the lack of sleep. I wasn't mad about being tired because of losing sleep. Being around Aaron was more than worth it to me. I could hardly focus from thoughts about Aaron and what we could turn into. I couldn't wait to see him again. I still planned on asking Dontez about the girl that we saw when we were hanging out. I had been in denial about Dontez dropping out of school up until that day. I heard Aaron's joke about my school being better than Dontez's and I knew he was saying that Dontez didn't go to school, but I was still hoping that something would make him come to school. I knew my reasons for wanting Dontez to be at school that day was selfish, but I had to ask about the girl that we saw on Sunday. I couldn't let it go. After I gave it some thought, I figured that she wasn't his girlfriend, but she had to be someone close because Dontez knew who she was too.

When the bell rang, I met up with Danni and Jania. I wasn't sure when Jania would warm up to me, but so far she hadn't. We all got off the bus at Danni's stop and went into her house. Danni and Jania sat in the living room staring at the TV; they were watching Jerry Springer and loving every minute of it. I tried to hold back, but I paged Dontez after becoming bored of watching the talk show. After I paged Dontez, I returned the cordless phone to Danni. She sat it next to her thigh like she was expecting a call. When it rang, she answered and said, "Did somebody page *who*? Who is *this*?" I was sure that Danni knew it was Dontez, but I still chose to entertain this game she played.

I said, "It's probably Dontez. I just paged him. I'll take it."

Danni put her finger up to her mouth to let me know she wanted me to be quiet. Jania sat on the couch laughing saying, "Danni, he's gonna clown you if you don't stop." Danni had a grin on her face like what she was doing was funny. I rolled my eyes because there was nothing funny about it. He didn't like her, and she knew that.

Then she said, "Oh, it's you. Hold on."

I took the phone. "What's up, brother?" I asked.

He said, "Why did you let that bitch answer the phone?" I hadn't ever heard him call anyone a bitch, and I wasn't sure who else he thought should have answered the phone. After all, it was Danni's home.

I tried to act like we were having a casual conversation since Danni and Jania were in the room watching me like hawks. I did an uncomfortable laugh and said, "I don't know, what are you doing?"

He replied, "Shit...makin' moves. Hustlin'."

"Oh, okay. Well I have a question for you."

He responded, "If it's about Aaron, you can ask him. I'm not in that shit, Heaven."

I got up and walked out of the room and into the kitchen. "Why are you so shitty now? Do you want me to stop calling you? You were foul the other night, and I'm still kinda pissed about that."

Dontez said, "The other night...did you fuck Aaron?"

I got loud with Dontez. "WHY?! And if I DID?"

"See, that's what I'm sayin'. Bitches always fall for that nigga's bullshit then get hurt and cry like little bitches." Dontez sounded annoyed.

I said, "Excuse me? Who the fuck do you think you're talking to? You better watch it before I hurt your feelings, okay?"

Dontez sighed and said, "I'm not talking about you, Heaven. I'm sayin' that I don't want you to be like the other ones, baby girl. He's just gonna hurt you. Trust me."

I sat down at the table, and pondered what Dontez said. "Well, he seems cool so far, and nobody said we were getting married. We will just kick it when we see each other and leave it at that. We're just cool."

Dontez laughed out loud. "So he has told you the line already? My brother and Aaron have gotten so much pussy from telling these bitches that shit."

I made a mental note to ask about his brother, but it wasn't important enough at that point for me to mention. "Is that right?" I replied. "Well, if they're able to get so much pussy from using that line it must work. Why don't you use it? Sounds like you need a line or two."

Dontez said, "Trust me, I gets pussy. Bitches love me. I'm a cold piece of work."

"Okay, if you say bitch one more time I'm hanging up," I warned.

"Did you fuck him?" Dontez asked me again.

"It's not your business. Why don't you ask Aaron? He's your boy, right?"

Dontez said, "Well, you're the one that's dumb. You met his bitch last night, he had just fucked her right before we got on to Prospect." He hung up without waiting for me to reply.

I hit the off button and went into the living room and sat it on Danni's lap then went upstairs to lie down. Ten minutes later, Danni came upstairs and gave me the phone. It was Dontez again.

"I'm sorry, baby girl. I fucked up. Can I slide through and talk to you face to face?"

I said, "Dontez, I wanna take a nap, let me call you later."

"I won't be long, come on, Heaven."

I agreed to let Dontez come over to Danni's house and talk to me. He was there in five minutes. I went outside despite the cold and sat in the raggedy car Dontez was driving. "Whose car is this?" He told me it was his car. I laughed and said, "Well, looks like quitting school really worked out for you."

He laughed too as he tried to fix the ceiling of his beat-up two door Cutlass. "I wanted to tell you I was sorry about the shit I said to you. It wasn't cool."

"So Aaron isn't still with that girl?"

Dontez said, "Don't get me wrong, he is, but I shouldn't have told you that shit just because I want you for myself."

I was shocked and uncomfortable. Danni was right when she said that Dontez had a crush on me. I couldn't mess with Dontez like he wanted me to. He simply wasn't my type. "Dontez…"

He cut me off. "I know…you fuck with Aaron. That's cool; I just wanted you to know what was up with me. I hate seein' that nigga run the same game all the fuckin' time, but he had me fucked up when he started playin' you. You don't have to tell him anything I said, just watch him. He got so many bit--I mean, women." Dontez shook his head like the thought of Aaron having a lot of women sickened him. He told me that he knew I fucked with Aaron, as if that would be the only thing holding me back from him.

I was starting to wonder if Dontez was mentally fucked up. I kept asking myself why Dontez would care if I told Aaron anything. If what he was saying was true, and he was looking out for me, what difference would it make if I said anything?

He was watching me as I looked straight ahead not saying a word. There was silence in the car, then he said, "Promise me you won't say anything to Aaron about what I told you."

"I don't know if I can promise that, Dontez, this is scandalous. I mean, don't you stay with him?"

He said, "I got my own shit now. I don't need him for shit, he's not my nigga for real anyway. I know he just looks out for me because my brother is in jail, but I don't need neither one of them niggas for real."

"Since when do you have your own place?" I asked. I didn't know if I should believe him. I said, "You don't even have a job."

"But I got money," Dontez replied.

Chapter 21

A penny for your thoughts, a nickel for your kiss...

"Why are you so quiet?"

We were sitting in Bennigans eating and I hadn't said much because I was really bothered by all the things Dontez told me earlier that day. Aaron was a damn good actor if what Dontez said was true. I found Aaron to be irresistible, and he seemed so genuine.

"I don't know," I replied. "I guess I don't have much to say." I was looking down at my food, and picking at it.

He looked at me and said, "I thought you told me you liked this place."

I looked at him and said, "I do."

"So what's wrong?" he asked, resting his arms on the table, leaning forward to look at me.

"I'm just tired. And I don't mean sleepy."

Aaron said, "What are you tired from?"

I was holding back tears. "I'm tired of feeling like I can't trust anyone. I don't know who's real or fake and I'm so sick of it." It wasn't that I was in love with Aaron, it was the fact that Dontez could be so cut throat. He was nice when I first met him but his true colors had come out. I didn't know how much longer I could be around him. One minute he was trying to belittle me in front of Aaron, the next he was in my ear telling me negative shit about Aaron. It was hard for me to believe that Aaron was so foul, he had given my brother twenty dollars just because he wanted to, he let Dontez stay with him when Dontez's father got on his nerves, and he had been nothing but cool to me. I didn't know who to think was genuine. Aaron came off kind hearted but that didn't necessarily mean that he was genuine, and the fact that I had known Dontez slightly longer than I knew Aaron didn't mean much to me because Dontez was cool when we first met but now I wasn't so sure. After the way he acted in the car with Aaron that night I found myself with my guard up with him. The fact that he would gossip to me about the things that Aaron could be doing bothered me a lot also. It was at that moment that I realized that I couldn't trust anyone. Everyone that I should have been able to trust had failed me.

Aaron said, "Baby, we all get tired of that. You just gotta open your eyes and pay attention to everything. You got good people around you, though, so you good."

"Who do you think is around me that's good?"

He looked at me like he thought I was crazy. "You need me to answer that?" he asked. "Well, I'd be tired too if I was that clueless. It's all good though, you still young."

"Aaron, you're so quick to tell me that I'm young before you actually listen to my question. I want to know in *your* opinion who you think is good."

He smiled at me and leaned across the table. "When you roll your eyes and get sassy, that shit turns me on." He sat back in his chair with a grin on his face.

I sat in my chair and looked at him, not cracking a smile at all. I said, "I'm serious."

"Me too," he replied.

"Aaron, answer my question," I said with an attitude.

He replied, "Shit, your homegirls are cool. Even the one that's quiet."

"Jania acts like she doesn't like me, and she never says anything to me," I told him.

"She just doesn't know you that well not to like you, but she's solid. She's just trying to make sure you are," Aaron informed me.

I said, "How do you know all this?"

"Because I know people. I watch people. That's how I know you're good people," Aaron continued, "I see your heart. I wouldn't ever do anything that I thought would hurt you because I just see…something in you. Do you believe that?" He was looking me in my eyes so intensely that I looked away. He said, "Look me in my face. I really wanna know."

I said, "I don't know. You can just show me."

Aaron shook his head. "I feel that. I can show you, I plan to. But you have to trust me. You just gotta know what it is with me and you when these hoe ass niggas and silly ass females get in your ear."

I stared at Aaron trying to figure him out. He was very convincing in his approach.

He said, "What do you want from me?"

I replied with a smile, "Oh, that's easy. I want you to always be honest with me."

Aaron was still looking at me. "That's all? I can do that. That's my word. Anytime you ask me a question I won't lie to you," he said with a shrug.

"Who else do you think is solid that I hang out with?"

Aaron said, "Are you trying to ask me if Dontez is cool?"

"Yes, sometimes he acts weird and I don't know which way to go with him."

He took a sip from his water and said, "I bet Dontez would be a lot cooler if you weren't so pretty. He wouldn't give a fuck about what you do if he didn't wanna hit. He likes you so much that he can't think straight. That's my nigga's lil brother, though, so I'll always show him love. Even if he does want a piece of my baby." He grinned at me and said, "Women and money can bring out the best or worst in a man."

"What makes you think he likes me?" I inquired.

"I'm a man, baby. I just know. It's the same way that you will know when a chick is diggin' me, at least you should know."

"Well, he's been shitty to me recently, but he was so cool when I first met him."

Aaron laughed. "He's tired of waiting on you to see that he has a lil crush. He probably feels like he's been nice enough. Now you my baby so he knows he doesn't have a chance. Niggas always start off nice when they want some pussy."

"Is that why you're nice?" I asked him.

He looked at me and said, "Who said I was nice? Who said I want some pussy from you? I know how to treat a female, but I never said I was nice. And I don't have to be somebody that I'm not to get some pussy, baby. I'll always be me."

"What if I told you that Dontez told me some stuff about you?"

Aaron replied with a serious face, "I would say that you gotta be smart enough to judge for yourself what's true or not. If what he said makes sense and you don't wanna fuck with me, that's cool. I can live with that. But don't ever tell me something that another nigga said about me because it doesn't matter, feel me? You gotta figure out who you with. People will always talk shit. If you believe every fuckin' thing you hear that's a problem." I asked Aaron if we could leave, and he said, "Let's ride, Princess."

After we left the restaurant, Aaron asked where I wanted to go. I looked at him and said, "I'm going wherever you go."

He nodded and said, "You don't have school tomorrow. Come chill with me for a minute."

I told him I would go and chill with him. He turned the music up and went from Bennigans by my mother's house in South KC, to his house in the city.

The next day was a staff development day and I was excited not to have school that day. I didn't have school the day after the staff development day either because of parent conferences. I called Danni from Aaron's house and told her my plans to spend the night with Aaron. She told me to use a condom. I laughed like the possibility of having sex was a crazy one. I was hoping that we were going to have sex, but I wasn't going to come on to him because he seemed like the type that would think I was a slut if I was too aggressive. I asked Danni to tell her mother if she asked that I stayed with my mother for the night to possibly work things out. Danni told me she would and we hung up.

Aaron's phone rang about two minutes after I hung up with Danni. He answered it on the third ring and I was sure it was a female on the phone because of the way he was talking. He wasn't calling her baby or other pet names, but it was the tone of voice that he used that was bothering me. Whoever he was talking to on the phone was being talked to the same way he talked to me. He was flirting. I was almost boiling listening to him talk, and I couldn't believe he could be so rude to me. He was catching up, and telling her that she was a stranger and how she doesn't fuck with him because she hadn't called him in a week. After the five minute call he said, "Let me get at you later. I'm chillin' with my company for a minute."

I was heated. His company? That's it? In the restaurant I was princess, baby, pretty, and whatever else. To his caller, I was "company". Before that call I had every intention on having sex with him. I decided that I would not have sex with him until I knew what was going on with the other girls.

Aaron hung up the phone and said to me, "So, is everything cool? Did you talk to Danni?"

I looked at him like he was stupid. I said, "Yes, I was just on the phone with her before your phone rang. Remember?"

He smiled at me. "My baby got a smart mouth. I like that shit. But you just gotta know when to use it. I'm not putting up with a shitty attitude all the time, kill that shit."

I said, "You sound like a woman beater or something. What do you mean 'you're not putting up with it'?" I was trying to show him that I was angry, and hoping that he asked me what was wrong. He didn't.

He looked at me and said, "A woman beater?! Girl, you're young for real. What type of gutter ass niggas have you been around? Just because I say that I'm not putting up with something doesn't mean I have to beat your ass. If you can get me to that point then I don't want shit to do with you at all. For real. When I say I won't put up with something all it means is that I won't fuck with you. If anything, I would say some shit to fuck your head up. I know how to talk bad to you if you make me mad enough. That'll last longer anyway." He was irritated by my statement, and once I said it, I felt stupid. He continued, "Why the hell would I make myself look like a bitch by hitting you? If I hit you I know I can fuck you up, but what the fuck would that mean?" His face was frowned like I said the most stupid thing he had ever heard. He looked turned off completely while I tried to clean my dumb comment up.

"I wasn't serious. You take everything I say too seriously. Relax."

"Yeah, ok." He sat back on his couch and turned the TV on. We sat in silence for a couple of minutes then he gave me a quick look. He went back to the TV, then right back to me and said, "I'm not gon lie, I know you're young but you gotta watch what you say to me. That's one of the reasons why younger chicks get fired by me."

I never felt the pressure from being around Joey that I always felt being around Aaron. Aaron made me feel like whatever I said was stupid. I looked at him and said, "Okay."

"You look sad now, chill out. It ain't shit, I fuck with you. You just got some growing up to do." He gave me reassurance that he forgave me for what I said, and for some reason I felt better. We lay on the couch for a while watching a movie, after a while I dozed off. When I woke up, I had a blanket on me and Aaron was gone. I sat up and looked around. He was nowhere to be found. I was sure he hadn't gone too far since he left me in his house alone. After a while I was scared because the house was too quiet and it was dark. When I got up to turn the lights on I heard a knock at the door. I sat there frozen because I didn't know what else to do. The knocking continued for a couple more minutes then stopped. I grabbed the phone and paged Aaron to find out when he would be back. Thirty minutes later he called back. When I answered the phone he said, "What's up? You cool?"

I said, "Yeah, I guess I'm cool. I woke up in your house and you were gone. Why didn't you tell me you were leaving? Somebody came to the door beating like the police."

He said, "Baby, I didn't wanna disturb you. I'll be there in a minute. Get ready for me."

I laughed. "What does that mean?"

"Be naked in my bed." We both sat there not saying a word. Then he said, "Hello?"

I cleared my throat and said, "I'm here."

He laughed and said, "I'm fuckin' wit you this time. I'll be there in a minute."

I didn't know if he was playing or not, but I was planning on taking him up on his offer. I wanted to show him that I was a woman and I wasn't as childish as he thought I was.

"Where are you at?"

"In traffic, I'll be there in a minute. You missing me?"

"I am." I told him.

"Alright, show me when I get there." He hung up. I went into panic mode because he told me that he was playing about me waiting on him naked, but he also told me to show him when he got back. What the fuck was I supposed to do? The first thing I did was check to see what kind of panties I was wearing. My panties were big and baggy, my mother never believed in buying attractive panties, so they were all I had. They were pink with a bow on the front. I thought about taking them off, but what would he think if I wasn't wearing panties? Maybe nothing would happen anyway, I was probably over-thinking the whole situation. I went upstairs to Aaron's room then came back down immediately and stood in the hallway. I had forgotten that he had that iguana in his room so there was no way I could stay in there by myself.

Chapter 22

And when your boys come around...

Aaron walked in ten minutes later smelling like strong weed and looking sexy. When he was high he never became goofy or stupid looking. When he smoked weed I thought it brought out another level of sexiness in him. He was wearing a pair of jeans with a white t-shirt, and as always, a fresh pair of tennis shoes. I never wanted to stare at him too hard, but it was hard not to. I thought it was so cool that he didn't overdress, or wear loud clothes to look nice. He had on his rope chain with no other jewelry besides his watch. I was lying on the couch under the blanket that he left me covered with. I turned the lights off in the house so that I wouldn't feel silly when he came and lifted the covers off of me and saw that I was naked.

He looked at me and said, "Damn, baby, why is it so dark in here?" He was turning the lights on as he asked me. I should have known he would turn the lights on. He walked over to me and said, "You sleep?" He had to know that I wasn't asleep. As he lifted the blanket off of me, I tried to grab the blanket before he could pull it off of me. I wasn't successful at grabbing the blanket. He managed to grab the blanket and held it in his hands for a second and stared at me. "Damn....you know you sexy, don't you? Stand up, let me get a good look at you."

I laughed and said, "No!"

He playfully pulled me up. "You might as well show Daddy all of you." When he got to my pussy he paused and gave it a long look. I was starting to feel myself because I knew he was turned on. Out of nowhere, he started laughing loudly and hysterically. I stood in front of him looking confused, he was laughing so hard he was bending over and holding his stomach.

I said, "Okay…what are you laughing at?"

He could barely speak as he said, "MAAAAN….YOU GOT A HAIRY ASS PUSSY! It's a seventies bush, baby. Shave that shit off. I can't even see it because of all that hair!"

I laughed too but I was embarrassed. I said, "Is it that funny? You don't have hair?"

He was still laughing, and said, "I'm a man, baby. I'll always have hair, but damn, you really got a bush!"

I tried to grab the blanket but he put it above his head so that I couldn't reach it. He was still snickering and said, "I'm fuckin' with you, come on. Come take a shower with me."

I told him okay, but I wanted him to go first so that he wouldn't make another one of his random jokes.

"No, I wanna watch you walk. You go ahead." He was grinning as he said it. I grabbed my clothes and he said, "I'll carry these for you." I walked in front of him up the stairs leading to his room. I sat on his bed while he started the shower water. He came out of the bathroom and said, "You ready?" I went and got into the shower; he got in after me and said, "Here, I want you to shave some of your hair. Cool?" I told him it was cool and took the razor blade without looking at him or his body. I shaved all the hair that was easy to see, and he said, "Turn around, and bend over."

"Huh?"

He grinned and said," I wanna make sure you got it all."

I did as he asked. I turned around and bent over and touched my ankles. My hair was getting wet but I didn't care, my goal was to show him that I wasn't childish. I was positioned right in front of his hard dick. He sighed while shaking his head and said, "Girl…shit…you are a mess. Damn…" He put his hand on the bottom of my back to let me know to stay in the position I was in. I felt his finger playing with my clitoris from the back. His middle finger was moving in a "come hither" motion as I moaned and dropped the razor that was in my hand. He slid his finger in and out of me slowly then went back to slowly stroking my clitoris. He stopped touching and fingering me so I stood up, I turned around and looked at him because I was so turned on. He tried to put his fingers in my mouth after he fingered me, and I moved my face. He said, "What you trippin' for? It's your pussy."

"That seems nasty, Aaron."

"No, it's not. It's yours, and nobody is here but me and you. Chill out, baby." He moved his fingers toward my face again. I licked his fingers while he watched me. I hadn't ever felt like he had just made me feel and I was willing to do anything to show him what that meant to me. I didn't know what to expect next. "Look at me," he said.

I told him, "I am looking at you." I traced the scorpion tattoo on his chest with my finger.

He started kissing me on my neck while I moaned. "Look at that." He was looking toward his hard dick. "That's all you." He kissed me in the mouth, this time I was able to follow his lead when we exchanged tongues. He grabbed my hand and put it on his dick. I hadn't ever stroked a man's penis but I decided to go with what turned me on. It seemed to work because he didn't stop me. Aaron pulled me closer to him and wrapped his arms around my waist while his dick was touching my pussy. He stopped and grabbed a towel and soap and washed my body, then washed his own body. He reached around me and turned the shower water off. We got out of the shower and went back into his room.

The room was dark, so I reached for his hand and followed him to his bed then lay next to him. He wasted no time climbing on top of me and kissing me. He used his index finger and his thumb to softly pinch my breasts. Then he licked my nipple slowly between sucking my breasts. My body was on fire. I lay under him with my legs wide open in hopes that we would go ahead and fuck right then and there. I felt his fingers teasing my pussy again, and I started squirming while I moaned. His index and middle finger slid into my vagina easily. He said, "Damn, baby, you are so fuckin' wet. Feel that shit, baby." He took my hand and guided it toward the wetness that he wanted me to feel. He kept his hand on my middle finger and moved it around with his hand. "You like that?" I told him I did and he rested my hand at my side. His face was so close to my pussy that I could feel him breathing. The closer that his face got to my pussy the more turned on I became. He moved and laid his head on my stomach while he slowly moved his fingers in and out of me. I felt his finger around my butt and tried to move. He kissed my stomach and said, "Just relax." I did as he asked while he slid his pinky finger sideways into my anus while at the same time sliding his index and middle fingers in and out of my vagina. I moaned louder and louder, I barely recognized my own voice. When I said his name I shocked myself, but I couldn't help it. All of a sudden, I felt pressure building up all over my body. I started moving my pelvic area involuntarily because my body felt so good. I gripped the sheets with both of my hands and opened my legs as wide as possible. My whole body was tingling. I felt like I had the urge to urinate but it felt a million times better. I let out one last moan, and said Aaron's name again as my vagina started pulsating. He didn't stop fingering me until I stopped moaning. I was breathing hard and my heart was beating fast. Aaron kissed my pussy and came and lay next to me. He said, "I had no idea that you could get wet like that. Damn."

I said, "I didn't either." I felt embarrassed and I wasn't sure why.

Aaron pulled me closer to him and said, "Had you ever came before tonight?"

"Never," I replied.

As if he had just decided that he had some sort of use for me, he said, "Yeah…I don't want nobody touching you but me."

I said, "I don't want anyone touching me but you."

"That's what's up," he replied.

I was ashamed to admit that I was sleepy so I lay next to Aaron and listened to him talk to me while trying to fight the sleepiness that kicked in. I didn't know if I was more in love with the way he made my body feel or the way that he talked to me. He was always direct without being rude, and I loved our conversation as well. Somehow I got the feeling that he wasn't the type to talk to any and everybody and I needed to know where we stood.

"Aaron, how do you feel about me?" I interrupted what he was saying, but I wanted to know because I needed to tell him how I felt.

He said, "How do I feel about you?" He paused and said, "Honestly, I'm trippin' because I haven't felt like this about anybody, especially this soon. I like you, a lot. You'll always be my sweetheart. I know that for sure. Even when you get pissed at me."

I said, "Why would I get pissed at you?"

He chuckled. "See, that's what I like about you, that innocence. It seems crazy to you that you could get mad at me because of what you see right now, right? It's because you're young. Sometimes your age is a problem, but other times it's cool."

I said, "For once you're wrong. I asked how I could get mad at you because you're like…I don't know…Like a breath of fresh air. I come from so much bullshit that it feels good to be around someone that knows how to make a joke with me, but not making a fool of me. I feel protected around you. I really think that you wouldn't let anything happen to me. And…I love that about you." I wasn't ready to tell him that I loved him because somehow I knew it was too soon for that, so I chose to find a way to mention love.

Aaron said, "That's what I picked up on. You need to be protected, I'll always protect you. Trust me."

"I do trust you."

He kissed me on the cheek, and said, "Is shit really that fucked up that you gotta stay with your girl?"

"Yes, it is that bad," I replied. "I will do whatever I have to not to go back to my mother, or father's house."

He said, "Yeah, right. It can't be *that* bad. You probably just spoiled."

I said, "I know that's what a lot of people think. Until they've seen this shit for themselves." We fell asleep facing each other, but when I turned around, he wrapped his arms around my waist.

I woke up because I heard loud music downstairs and Aaron was nowhere in sight. I jumped up in panic and turned on the light. I didn't want to put my dirty clothes back on so I looked in his dresser and grabbed a white t-shirt that covered right underneath my butt. I walked quietly down the stairs and walked down the hallway that led to his living room. As I approached the room, I could hear Aaron's voice talking over the music.

"Nigga, this bitch is pretty as fuck. I bet none of y'all can fuck with my shit." His friends laughed and talked shit back to him, and he continued. "Fuck wit me. She makes my other bitch look like nothing at all." They all laughed out loud and continued to brag about whose bitch looked better than the other.

I was on the verge of tears. I was shocked to hear Aaron talk about me that way. He came off so nice and respectful, why did he have to keep calling me out of my name? I peeked into the living room from the dining room and they all looked up. I tried not to look shocked by all of the guns and weed that sat on the coffee table. There were three guys in the living room, one I remembered seeing the night that I left with Aaron after hanging out on Prospect. The entire room was cloudy from weed smoke. As soon as they looked up they looked away. Aaron put the gun in his hand down and muted the stereo with the remote. He told me, "Go get some clothes on, baby. Then you can come back down."

I felt like his friends were sneaking and staring at me but I didn't care. I said, "Okay, but can you come here for a minute?"

He got up and followed me upstairs. "What's up?" he asked.

My eyes were filling up with tears. "Why are you calling me a bitch like that?"

His face frowned instantly then relaxed. "Huh? What are you talking about?"

I said, "I heard you say that your bitch is pretty, and I make your other bitch look like nothing."

Aaron laughed so hard that he had to lean against the wall.

I stood in front of him with a straight face. I was just about to tell him that I was done with him. I still hadn't mentioned anything to him about what Dontez told me, and I was dying to. I was offended because he was calling me out of my name like it wasn't a big deal. My logical mind was telling me that all signs said to say 'fuck him' but I chose not to.

He replied, "Are you serious right now?" Aaron was still laughing but not as hard. "So you think I would call you a bitch? And if I did, you think I would do it front of my niggas? I wouldn't do that shit. Chill out. I was talking about my gun, baby. Damn."

My face was full of shock and embarrassment.

He read my expression and said, "Yeah, my gun." He lifted his shirt to show me a 9mm pistol, then put his shirt down and continued, "You come in at the end of us talking and you automatically think the worst."

I said, "Well, I don't know what else I should have thought. I mean, I didn't know people called their gun their bitch."

"Oh ok, so because you're used to niggas calling their girl a bitch you thought I was calling you one. Those out south niggas got your mind all fucked up."

I said, "Whatever, Aaron."

He pulled me into his chest and grabbed my ass. He looked me in my eyes and said, "Don't ever come around my niggas wearing only a shirt. Lettin' them see my shit."

I said, "I didn't know anyone was here until I got closer and actually heard them talking and laughing. I couldn't help but peek and see who it was. Right?"

Aaron replied, "However you wanna put it, but the next time before you even come downstairs put some clothes on just in case." He kissed me on the cheek and went back downstairs.

Chapter 23

I guess I'm tryna be nonchalant about it...

I decided against going back downstairs, and paged Danni instead. When she called back I knew it was her, but I let the phone ring since I was in Aaron's house. He called me to the steps and gave me the cordless phone like he forgot that he had a phone next to his bed. It was the wee hours of the morning and Danni was wide awake. I asked her why she was up and she said she was talking to Dontez. "You mean right now? As in he's there?"

She laughed. "Yes, crazy girl. Here, right now. He told me to tell you that your daddy is looking for you."

I said, "Well he can keep looking because I'm not fuckin' with him or his bitch wife."

Danni said, "Mama really thinks you're trying to work it out with your mother, but she said she still wants to talk to you about everything that happened."

I sighed and asked, "What does she want to know? It's all bad, and I don't have anywhere to go. Can you ask Dontez if he'll take me to my mother's house to get more clothes?" I was shocked that Danni didn't seem to appreciate me asking if Dontez could do me a favor.

She said, "Where's Aaron? He can't do it?"

I said, "Well...I guess I can ask him. Are you and Dontez like messing around or something? You seem irritated. I didn't mean to offend you."

Danni said, "I don't even know yet."

I asked her if she wanted to come over and hang out since it was just me and Aaron's iguana upstairs.

She told Dontez she would be right back then she whispered into the phone. "I might, we're sitting here bored, trying to be super quiet because mama is sleep. We need something to do but anything is better than going to his place. Did you know he had a place? We ran by there today so he could show me and it was nasty. And did you know Dontez sells dope now? His house looks like a dope spot or something."

I said, "Nope. Didn't know any of the above. I know he was in that shitty car when he came to your house to talk to me. He had on a new outfit and new shoes, so you know he was probably feelin' himself. It's so stupid; his daddy smokes the shit that he's selling. No wonder he wanted to drop out of school. He thinks he's about to be a baller or something."

Danni said, "Okay, Heaven, you sound like you're offended for real. It's his life, not yours."

"Danni, Dontez is like a brother to me. Okay? So when he fucks up it does bother me. You're not trippin' because you still think he likes me, are you? And I KNOW you don't think I like him."

Danni ignored my question and was talking to Dontez in the background then she said, "Okay, we'll be there pretty soon." I asked Danni to bring me some clothes to wear because I wasn't comfortable wearing Aaron's shirt after he told me to come upstairs and change. I told her to bring them up to me once she got there. Before I invited Danni over, I thought about going to sleep, but I changed my mind when Danni said they were coming over. There was a part of me that was irritated because I genuinely cared about Danni and I didn't want Dontez to cause any animosity between us. But he really was somebody that I loved despite the fact that he got on my nerves sometimes.

Aaron came and laid a pair of sweatpants, a t-shirt and a pair of my panties on his bed that Danni brought from her house. He had a grin on his face. I wondered what he was laughing at until I grabbed my panties. Somehow he didn't see my panties from earlier, and if he did he didn't say anything. He said, "Can I take you to get some cool panties? Those damn things are a turn off."

"Will you shut up? I'm so sick of you saying shit about me."

He said, "I wasn't making fun of you this time. I was serious. Do you want me to buy you some panties or not? Stop acting like a brat." He was smiling at me like he got a kick out of seeing me irritated.

I said, "I thought Danni was bringing my clothes to me anyway."

He said, "No, its daddy."

I laughed as I sat on his bed putting the t-shirt on and said, "Daddy….is that right?"

He looked at me and said, "You heard me. Daddy. I can't wait to hear you say that shit in my ear, and scratch my back and shit."

I laughed out loud because I knew he was serious, the truth was that I couldn't wait either. He got ready to leave then turned around and looked at me. "What are you looking at?" I asked.

He said, "You. Is that cool?"

"Aaron, you have that look in your eyes. Go back downstairs. You have company."

"It's just Dontez, and your girl," he replied. "Everybody else left."

"Well that's even worse. I don't want to seem rude."

Aaron said, "That's what's up. I don't want to seem rude either."

I replied to him, "Cool, let's go."

He gave me that mischievous smile and said. "Lay back, real quick. So we don't seem rude." I laughed and tried to get up and go downstairs. Aaron came up to me while I sat on his bed and got down on his knees. He spread my legs apart and kissed my inner thighs, then slowly licked my clitoris. The lights were on in his room, so he saw my eyes get big and he watched me cover my mouth. He looked at me and laughed as he pushed my stomach for me to lie down. He got up and turned off the lights then came back to me.

His tongue was so soft and wet as he glided it slowly up and down my pussy while I moaned louder than I ever would have imagined. I grabbed his head and pushed it towards me so that his tongue could go in as far as possible. He stopped and pulled his pants down, and told me to come lay next to him. I lay on my back next to Aaron. As soon as I lay down, he climbed on top of me. He tongue kissed me aggressively while I wrapped my arms around his head and kissed him back. We stopped kissing and he repositioned himself so that his face was right in front of my pussy, and his penis was right in front of my face. I had never sucked dick, and I never planned to, so I let him continue to kiss my pussy as I lay back and enjoyed myself. I thought my body was going to explode as he licked from side to side, and up and down while rotating the tip of his tongue. I could feel the tip of his tongue giving soft licks then more firm licks. His dick was right in my face, yet I still hadn't touched it with my hand or my mouth. I kept trying to act like it wasn't there by turning my head. I felt him pushing his dick toward my face, so I decided to grab it and give it a massage. I was about to have another orgasm when he said, "Taste it, baby." The first thing I thought was what the fuck I would say if someone found out that I was sucking dick. It was the one thing that my friends and I had agreed to never do. I opened my mouth wide and took his penis into my mouth. I had no idea what I was doing, so I just licked. I couldn't get his entire penis into my mouth because it was so big. My mouth and my jaws were hurting from the few attempts that I did make at taking his penis into my mouth. I couldn't focus on him going down on me because I focused on going down on him. He wasn't moaning like I was when he did me. When he slowly pushed his penis deeper down my throat so that I could take more I gagged. I stopped and sat up abruptly as I coughed loud. My eyes were watery, and I wanted to cry. There was no way I was doing that again.

Aaron got up and turned the light on. "Are you cool?" he asked. I told him I was but I felt like I was talking like I had cotton balls in my mouth because my mouth felt so stretched out. He wiped his mouth and said, "Put some clothes on. We don't wanna be rude." He laughed like he was trying to make light of the situation but I was pissed. What the hell was he thinking? I wasn't ready for that. I didn't say anything to him. I just got up, grabbed my clothes and put them on. As we walked down the stairs, Aaron said, "We'll fuck around and watch a movie so that you'll know how to do that shit the right way." He slapped me on the ass.

We walked into the living room and sat down. I spoke to Dontez and Danni. Dontez spoke and Danni laughed and said, "Y'all nasty! What took so long?" I was uncomfortable and I didn't want to sit too close to Danni because even though it didn't stink, I had a fear that she would be able to smell penis on my breath.

Aaron acted like it was not a big deal at all. He casually said, "That's your homegirl. Always wanna talk." He poked me and laughed like he knew this was awkward for me. I laughed awkwardly while trying to act natural. When Aaron looked at me, he laughed loud and said, "Girl, you are fuckin' funny as hell. What is wrong with you?" Everyone was laughing at that point but Dontez, he just looked at me like he was making some sort of assumption. I wondered how long they planned to stay because I wasn't in the mood for company anymore. Aaron and I had yet to go all the way but my body still felt tired. Aaron and Dontez went into the kitchen and talked for a minute. Whatever it was that they were talking about looked serious. Danni and I could see the kitchen from where the living was situated.

Finally, Danni moved to the couch that I sat on and said, "Seriously, bitch, did you fuck him?"

I said, "NO! We haven't fucked, why are you asking me that? Do I have the 'I got some dick' face or something?" We both laughed.

She said, "You are silly for that one. Did he go down on you? You probably sucked his dick!" I went into panic mode. Keeping my face casual was difficult, and I hated that I was about to lie to my best friend.

I chuckled and said, "Why did you say that? No. We didn't do none of that." I knew I didn't sound as confident as I did when I told her we hadn't had sex.

She said, "Oh my GOD! Heaven, you are lying!" She busted out laughing.

I replied, "I'm not lying, Danni. Now will you be quiet before they hear you?"

Danni was still laughing, but she wasn't as loud with it. "So why are you sitting like that? You have your legs crossed tight or something."

I laughed at her and said, "You just don't stop, do you? Ok…" I looked in the kitchen to make sure Aaron and Dontez were still busy. I continued, "We didn't actually fuck, but he went down on me. You better not tell Dontez anything because it's not his business and I don't want him looking at me like I'm a ho."

Danni's eyes got big and whispered, "Oh my God! You sucked his dick too!"

I laughed. "No, I didn't. I just licked it and I didn't like it so I stopped."

Danni said, "Okay, you are lying!" She was still laughing when Aaron and Dontez came back into the living room. Danni and I tried to look natural when they walked into the living room and sat down.

Aaron stretched and said, "So what y'all about to get into?" We all knew that was his way of saying he was ready for them to leave. It was almost four in the morning, so I didn't mind them leaving either. There was a knock at the door just as Dontez and Danni got ready to leave. Aaron got up and asked who was at the door as he opened it. I couldn't hear the name, but Dontez looked at me like he thought I was stupid. Danni was standing next to me trying to make conversation but I was preoccupied with the knock at the door. Aaron opened the door and it was the girl that we saw when we hung out on Prospect. I wondered what the hell she was doing there, and at that time of the morning. She only spoke to Dontez and followed Aaron into his kitchen. I was pissed because she was dressed better than she was the last time I saw her and she was prettier than I remembered. Aaron was breaking weed down on the counter and bagging it up to hand her.

She smiled and handed him twenty dollars. As she walked off she said, "Thanks, daddy. The next time answer my call." Aaron didn't respond to her but I was glad the cordless phone was upstairs when she called, I was hoping that made her think he didn't like her. He grinned and shook his head as he watched her ass while she walked out the front door.

Dontez and Danni were about to walk out the door when I said, "Wait a minute, I'm going with y'all. I don't want to stay here after all." I didn't give them the chance to say yes or no because I walked out of the living room. My feelings were hurt, and I couldn't understand how he could flirt with her right in my face and not think anything of it. I didn't have a lot of things to grab, just one outfit so I wasn't upstairs long.

When I walked back into the living room with my clothes in my hand Aaron said, "What's up, baby? You cool? I thought you said you would chill with me tonight."

I tried not to show how pissed I really was but I wasn't successful. I told him, "No, I won't be staying here. I don't think you need me to stay here." I rolled my eyes at him.

Danni said, "Aaron, you really are wrong for that. How do you think that looks? Chicks coming over and flirting with you and shit, when you know how much Heaven likes you."

Aaron became defensive, he gave Danni an impatient look and said, "Tez, get your girl. Tell her to stay the fuck out of my business."

I was shocked that Aaron was being so rude to Danni. I said, "Aaron! Don't talk to my friend like that!"

Dontez sighed. "Are we leaving or what?" he asked.

Danni was getting ready to respond to Aaron but he cut her off and said to me, "Come holler at me real quick."

Dontez sighed again and said, "If you're coming you need to come on."

Danni was irritated, and I could tell because she was watching Aaron like a hawk with her arms folded across her chest.

Aaron told Dontez, "She'll be right back, bro."

I followed Aaron into the bathroom and he asked me what was wrong. I whispered so that there was no way that Dontez or Danni could hear anything I said. "Aaron, you're not good for me. You sell drugs for one thing. I have been wondering what you did to get money but I didn't want to ask you. Dontez already told me that you're a player so I should have known what to expect, but I never would have thought that you would have a girl over here like I'm not here. I saw the way you watched her when she walked past too, and she called you Daddy. What kind of shit is that?"

Aaron stood in front of me and said, "You think I sell drugs?"

"Aaron. I saw you sell drugs."

He replied, "I don't sell drugs. I sold her a sack from my shit because she's my homegirl. It's nothing like you're trying to make it, she said that daddy shit to fuck with you, and I see it worked. You let her see you sweat, and that's what she wanted. I knew that pissed you off, but you can't get mad at me for something she did. Saying you're leaving when you said you would stay with me is silly." He shook his head. "That's that young shit. That's why I really don't fuck with young chicks."

I told him, "You're trying to twist this."

Aaron replied, "I'm not trying to twist anything, baby, I'm being honest like I told you I always would. She's cool as a fan but I don't fuck with her like that. I like you, I'm just trying to see where you plan to let me and you go. It's all on you."

I replied, "Well, I need to go, they're waiting on me."

Aaron said, "Ok, well, I'll go and tell them you changed your mind. You chillin' with me? I won't try anything. I just wanna chill with you."

I told him I that I would. I knew I shouldn't have given in so easily but I chose to stay because I loved him. The need to play tough simply wasn't there.We walked back into the living room and Aaron said to Dontez, "Alright, bro, she's in for the night. We'll see what's up with y'all tomorrow."

Dontez said ok and I went to give him a hug. Danni looked like she was mad at me about staying but I didn't know why nor did I care why. It really wasn't her business. After they left, Aaron and I went upstairs.

"Thank you for staying with me, baby. I get lonely sometimes," Aaron said.

I was starting to realize that a lot of the things that Aaron said were him flirting with me and he probably wasn't serious. I took most of his one liners with a grain of salt. We were lying in his bed and I said, "How do you get money? And I wanna know what you and Dontez were talking about."

He laughed. "You're just now asking how I make money? That's something that you should have asked out the gate, I know you wanted to ask before. Why didn't you ask Tez? He seems to keep you laced with my business."

I said, "I did. He said he didn't know."

Aaron shook his head and said, "Don't ask that nigga shit about me again. If you wanna know something about me, ask me. That way you can guarantee that it's the truth. And I'm not tellin' you what we talked about, that was between us. Feel me?"

"How do you get money?" I asked again.

"I flip houses with my father."

I said, "So is this really your house?"

He looked at me like I was crazy. "Yes, it's really my house. It's the same shit I told you, baby. I bought it for the low, fixed it up and decided to live in it. I'm a hustler, and just because you see a nigga with some shit don't mean he's on some other shit. All hustles don't have to be illegal. I'm not goin' to jail but I'm not about to starve either. Living around all those white people got you really thinkin' some ol' dumb shit like all black men sell drugs." Aaron shook his head and said, "I bet you think all black fathers are deadbeats too, right?"

I said, "Not all…but most."

Aaron shook his head again and said, "You got a lot to learn. So since your parents broke up, and your father is fucked up, every black father is fucked up too?"

"Aaron, you can't tell me that it's normal for families to be on some happily ever after type shit."

He said, "Maybe not normal for you, but for me it is. My parents have been together since before I was born. They seem pretty normal to me. I mean, my mother owns a beauty shop, my father owns a lawn company, and makes bread on houses too. Neither of them fuck with drugs or no shit like that. I don't know, I guess what's normal for me isn't normal for you. The only thing that's abnormal is that they don't work for no cracker, and they don't honor them either. But it's fucked up to make assumptions just because you come from a fucked up environment. I mean, how would you do better than your parents? If you think the norm is to have a fucked up relationship, then add kids to that fucked up relationship, then break up, then brainwash your kids and make them think the same shit you think makes sense you really are fucked up. That's a fucked up cycle, but trust me, baby girl, it doesn't have to be that way. I can see how you would think that all relationships end up bad because of what you saw, but damn, baby," he paused and said, "I might show you what it's like to be with a real nigga. I might let you have my baby one day." He looked at me and laughed.

I figured he was playing, so I laughed and said, "I don't want kids, so I'm good."

He shrugged and said, "Damn…I tried, oh well. Hopefully one day I'll find me a wife to have my baby." Aaron and his bullshit lines were starting to get old, I wanted to know exactly where he was coming from, but I didn't want to ask how serious he was about all the things he said. I was sure he knew how much I liked him so it bothered me that he said things that could be taken as genuine or bullshit. I didn't respond to his comments. When I got quiet he turned over and said, "Get some sleep."

Chapter 24

You mighta had him once but...

Over the course of the next month, I enjoyed Aaron's company more than I could have ever imagined. I spent time between his house and Danni's mother's house. Most of the time, Danni wasn't home because she was with Dontez. They had become inseparable. Danni's mother gave her a lot of freedom, but not to the extent where she was able to spend the night with him. Sometimes I felt bad because I spent so much time with Aaron, since the whole time, I lied and made Diane think that I was with my mother working on our relationship. The truth was that I hadn't seen my mother since the night my father and Sonya acted like fools at their house. I was cool with never speaking to her again but I felt like it was only right to call my mother from time to time to let her know that her teenage daughter was alive. When we talked I made a point to tell her how great things we were going with my father. I hadn't seen my father either, and I was fine with that. My father had disappointed me to the point where I couldn't imagine being around him. I had even convinced myself that I didn't care that I hadn't seen either of my brothers.

I still hadn't had sex with Aaron and I found that to be weird. I was starting to wonder why he hadn't tried to go to that level. I chose not to ask him because I was afraid of the rejection. He had been true to his word when he said he would buy me underwear because mine were a turn off. We went to the Bannister Mall and he bought me underwear from Victoria's Secret. I didn't know how to act or what to say when Aaron bought me things. I told him thank you, and all he would say was, "It's all good, baby." After we got my underwear, he took me into Dillard's and let me pick out anything I wanted. When I only picked up Tommy Hilfiger clothes, he frowned and asked me why I didn't try to be different.

He said, "It's cool to wear what's in style, but damn, don't you wanna get something that doesn't have Tommy across it? Get some sexy shirts or something." He was right as usual. Once I decided to look around for other clothes, besides the same clothes that everyone else had, I was able to find clothes that actually fit my personality. I kept looking at him when I picked something up that I liked to see if it was too expensive. He insisted that I get whatever I wanted, including a pair of boots and a pair of Air Max from Foot Locker. I kept thinking that he was sure to expect sex from me later that day. He didn't.

After we shopped at the mall we went to Red Lobster to eat. While we rode toward his neighborhood he told me that he wanted me to chill with him for the night. I was fine with staying the night with him since I was sure that he would go down on me again and that was the best feeling that I had ever experienced. Aaron performing oral sex on me had become normal, but I hadn't been returning the favor because I knew he didn't really enjoy it.

The night that he asked me to chill with him for the night, I didn't think anything of it so I agreed. We had just got to his house when he said, "I gotta make a run. I'll be back in a minute. You chillin' with me for the night, right?"

I said, "How long is a minute? I hate being here by myself."

"Not long," he replied. "I need to run by this house and make sure they replaced the toilets today like they said they would."

I told him, "Okay, but don't take long because I'll be bored."

He said, "You'll be cool. Put a movie in, or watch the one I left in there for you."

I looked confused, but all he did was smile and told me, "You know I fuck with you, right?"

I told him, "Yeah, I know."

He said, "I'm probably wrong for saying this but honestly when I met you all I wanted was to fuck. Now I feel different. Don't get me wrong, I knew I liked you, but I wasn't expecting to feel like this. And we haven't even fucked yet. I'm feelin' you for real, I might have to make you my girl. I'm trying to decide what to do with you." He kissed me on the cheek and left out before I could respond.

After Aaron left, I sat on the couch thinking about what he had just said. I was happy that he liked me so much, but at the same time, I was sad. Up until that point I thought I was his girl. We spent a lot of time together, and I thought we both were on the same page where our feelings were concerned. He was always calling me his baby, and picking me up from school when he had time, so I assumed that he was my boyfriend.

I sat in silence for almost an hour until I called Danni. I figured that she wouldn't be home but I called her anyway, luckily she answered. We talked about the news that I wasn't Aaron's girlfriend. I told her, "I'm not worried about another female because we spend so much time together. When he's not with me he's working on houses and I know that because he always comes to get me from school looking tired and dirty from working. I don't know why I'm tripping anyway, that's just a title. He told me how much he likes me and that's what matters."

Danni sighed and said, "Oh my God. Girl, that nigga is playin' you. Have you fucked him? And don't lie." I told her that I hadn't and she said, "Heaven, that nigga is so full of shit. Don't let him play you. He knew damn well that you thought y'all was together. He ain't shit, I swear."

I said, "Danni, a lot of your advice is right, but you're wrong on this." I decided to watch the movie he had ready for me as I talked to Danni. I turned the TV on and pressed play and was shocked and uncomfortable. The first thing I saw was a woman sucking a man's penis as he ejaculated in her mouth.

I paused abruptly and Danni said, "Hello? Finish the bullshit you were about to say, I'm listening."

I said, "Danni, will you shut up? I turned on the TV to watch a move he said he wanted me to watch and it's a fuckin' porno. It's a bitch sucking a man's dick like it ain't shit."

Danni said, "See, that's what I'm talkin' about, he's grooming you or something. Is he a pimp? And where is he right now? Out gettin' pussy?"

I said, "No, he's not a fucking pimp, and he's not grooming me for shit. He left to go check on one of his houses. He had to make sure that some stuff was done to it." I decided as I talked to Danni that I would not to talk to her about my relationship with Aaron. She was a bit too judgmental for my liking.

Danni laughed. "Okay, Heaven. Tez just got here, so go ahead and watch the flick on how to suck dick the right way and I'll get at you later." Danni hung up. I watched the video because I really did want to suck dick the right way so that Aaron would be pleased. I was pissed at Danni for being so negative and hanging up with me in such a rude way. I missed Dontez and I would have liked to say hello to him, but Danni hung up before I had the chance.

I sat watched bit and pieces of the movie but I turned it off because I was aroused. After I turned the movie off I paged Tandra. Talking to Danni had really put a damper on my mood and I regretted calling her. I decided to page Tandra since I hadn't talked to her in what seemed like forever. I knew we had some catching up to do.

Tandra called back five minutes later, after she realized it was me paging her. She said, "Where are you at?"

"Girl, over at my boyfriend's house, bored. What are you doin'?"

She said, "WHAT?! Your *BOYFRIEND?*"

I said, "Yeah, my boyfriend." I laughed casually like I didn't understand why she would be shocked.

"He has his own house? How old is he?" she asked. "I'm about to come over there. I wanna see what he looks like."

I replied, "Yes, he has his own house, he's nineteen. He's not here right now though. Girl, he's always hustling."

Tandra said, "He hustles?"

I replied, "Yep, but it's not what you probably think. Not all hustles are illegal, feel me?"

Tandra laughed. "Okay, well, you need to see if he got any friends!"

I laughed and said, "Girl, I'll see but we really don't be around too many people like that. We just chill at home together."

Tandra became more hype with every fabrication that I told her, it was more fun talking to her than Danni. Danni had too much advice that I didn't want. She said, "Heaven! Y'all live together? Girl, I need to move to the city where the real niggas are!"

I gave her another casual laugh and said, "I don't live here, but I'm always here with him. He gets mad when I leave, so I stay pretty often."

Tandra said, "Girl, YES! Hook me UP! I'm on the way down there; I wanna see what this nigga look like. I'll wait until I know my daddy is sleeping and I'm coming. What's the address?"

I gave her the address and we hung up. I looked at the clock on the wall and realized that Aaron had been gone for longer than he made it seem that he would be gone. I wasn't going to page him because I wanted him to know that I was cool being by myself. Maybe things were taking longer than he expected. After an hour, he finally walked into the house. He didn't look dirty from working or tired. He casually sat next to me and said, "You ready to model for me?"

I said, "I guess."

He said, "You guess? Daddy ain't tryin to hear that." He kissed me on my lips. "You got an attitude?" I told him I didn't but we both knew I did. He said, "If you mad about something you need to say it. Stop actin' like a kid all the time."

I wanted to tell him that my anger came from him being gone so long and offering no explanation whatsoever as to where he was. I also wanted to tell him that I was pissed about him telling me how much he liked me, yet I still wasn't his girl. That title meant something to me. I was also upset about the conversation I had with Danni. She made me feel like I was stupid for falling for Aaron's bullshit. I wondered why I didn't see it as bullshit. Was it because I was gullible, or because Danni didn't like him so anything he did was going to bother her? Instead, I just sat and looked at the TV.

He said, "I'll take that as a 'No'. So did you watch the movie?"

I was getting ready to answer his question when I heard a knock at the door. I jumped up to answer it because I figured it was Tandra.

Aaron looked at me and said in a sarcastic voice, "Are you expecting somebody?"

I said, "Yeah, I told my best friend to come over."

He got up and stepped in front of me to grab the door and said, "Don't be telling people where I live and shit, baby. I don't like a bunch of people knowing where I lay my head. You gotta think about shit like that."

I told him ok, as I opened the door since I was closer. It wasn't Tandra, it was the same girl that came over before, and the same girl that we saw when we were on Prospect hanging out. She had tears in her eyes and one could only assume Aaron had something to do with her tears. Aaron said, "What are you doing here? I thought I told you what was up."

I went and sat on the couch, I was on the verge of tears myself. I didn't want to, but I knew I needed to leave Aaron alone. That night proved Danni's point about Aaron. This time she was visibly upset. I knew things weren't going to go very well when I saw tears in her eyes. Before she responded to Aaron, she looked at me with hate in her eyes and said, "Why are you always here? I guess we take turns fuckin' him, right?"

My heart dropped, and I looked at Aaron. I wanted him to tell me that she was making this up to get to me again. I told her, "I don't have sex with Aaron."

He looked at me and said, "Heaven, why are you telling her our business?"

His friend said, "Heaven?!" with an evil laugh, then she continued her rant, "What kind of dumb ass name is *Heaven*?"

Aaron looked irritated when he looked at his friend and said, "Keisha. Chill. For real."

I got quiet while I watched everything unfold. Keisha started yelling at Aaron, "You got me fucked up! You make it seem like you don't want a girl, but stay fuckin' me when this bitch ain't around! I hate you! You got this bitch programmed don't you? You make her believe that one day you'll be with her too! I know damn well you fuckin' her. You are a fuckin' liar! And don't ever call me again in life! You ain't shit!"

Aaron said, "Girl, get on somewhere with all that shit. I told you from jump that you wouldn't ever be my girl. You wasn't shit to me but a fuck. You knew that." Aaron was standing in front of Keisha with his arms folded across his chest as she talked. He looked heartless, like what she was saying didn't matter at all. I hadn't ever heard him use that tone of voice, and even though it was a very mean tone, I was glad that he chose to talk to her that way. Although there was a part of me that couldn't help but wonder if I would receive the same treatment at some point. The more Keisha yelled at Aaron the harder she cried. I decided to look away because I was crying too. The fact that she cried so hard let me know that she had feelings for him, possibly stronger than mine because she had fucked him. The conversation I had with Aaron about females developing stronger feelings after sex was on my mind as I watched Keisha pour her heart out to Aaron. I had my head in my lap as I listened to everything they said. Keisha was still screaming as Aaron tried to talk over her. He was telling her that she needed to get out.

She yelled, "You had me suckin' and fuckin' you knowin' damn well you didn't fuck with me like that! I hate you! Talkin' about you don't eat pussy! I love you and you know I do! I don't just do that to anybody, it was for *you!*"

I looked up at him and said, "Aaron, take me home, please."

Aaron looked at me like the last thing he expected was for me to be upset. He said, "Heaven, chill out for a minute. I'll take you home, but not until I know you're not mad at me. She's about to leave so we can talk."

I was in a state of disbelief, I thought the reason he hadn't asked me to go down on him, or have sex was because I had learning to do. Not because he was having someone else to do those things.

Keisha said, "I'm not leaving, put me out!"

I was so sick of her and her mouth that I decided to speak up. I stood up and said, "BITCH, WHY DON'T YOU JUST LEAVE?!"

She looked at me and said, "Who are you callin' a BITCH?" She ran toward me, but Aaron grabbed her. He had his arms wrapped around her waist, and was carrying her out of the door as she kicked and scratched him. "Fuck you and this little young ass bitch! Let her suck and fuck you! You're a male whore, Aaron!" she yelled as Aaron carried her out.

Aaron didn't reply as he put her outside. As soon as he put Keisha out Tandra walked in and looked shocked. I had tears in my eyes. Keisha was outside screaming at the top of her lungs that she was going to fuck Aaron's car up. Aaron calmly stood on the porch and said, "Fuck with my shit if you want to." Aaron's tone suggested that he wasn't giving her permission to harm his car; it was more like he was threatening her if she caused any harm to his car. He walked back into the house and closed the door. He said to me, "Let me talk to you for a minute." Aaron didn't bother to acknowledge Tandra who was standing in the living room looking confused.

I said, "No, I don't want to talk to you anymore. We don't have anything to talk about. You are so wrong, Aaron!" I cried even harder and told Tandra, "Come on. Take me to my best friend's house. I'm not staying here."

Tandra said, "What the hell is going on?" She looked at Aaron but he offered no explanation to her. I went upstairs and gathered all the clothes that Aaron bought me, and the clothes that I brought with me when I stayed with him.

Aaron followed me up the stairs and into his room. He grabbed my arm and said, "You don't even know what's going on, Heaven." I told him to let go of my arm and continued to grab my clothes. He said, "She wasn't my girl. We just messed around for a minute."

I ignored him and went back downstairs and told Tandra I was ready. Aaron followed me downstairs and gently pulled my hand before I walked out the door. I pulled my hand away and left.

Chapter 25

Guess the verdicts in, I'm crazy over you…

Danni didn't live far from Aaron so we were at her mother's house in a few minutes. Once we pulled into the driveway, I told Tandra she could come in if she wanted to. We sat in the living room talking as I wiped my tears. Danni wasn't home but Diane was. She came in and I introduced her to Tandra. She looked at her and said, "It's nice to meet you. You are so pretty, Tandra. You have a beautiful skin tone."

I hadn't had the chance to tell Tandra the same thing. The last time I saw her she was what I would have considered just average looking. In the time that we had been apart she had become very pretty. She had colored her long hair an auburn color with blonde highlights. Her skin was no longer dry and blotchy looking either. Tandra and Zandra had always been great at putting cute clothes together so it wasn't a shock that her outfit was cute too. Tandra told Diane thank you and gave her an innocent smile. Diane sat in a chair in the living room and listened to us talking.

Tandra said, "Heaven, you look different. I don't know what it is. I've always thought you were pretty but it's like you're doing something different. You look really pretty."

I said, "I don't feel so pretty right now." I shook my head and wiped tears.

I asked Diane where Danni was, and she told me, "She was with that Dontez earlier. I'm sure she's still with him." I noticed the look on her face when she mentioned Dontez. The way she said his name made it clear that she didn't like him. I wasn't sure why she wouldn't like Dontez and I didn't care. She said, "So, what boy hurt you? At your age that's the only problem you could have."

I told her the truth, while Tandra sat and listened. Tandra laughed out loud. "Why did you lie about all that stuff you told me earlier?"

I replied, "I didn't actually lie to you about everything. I just lied about a few things, but so what? You lie about stupid stuff too." She laughed loud again without saying anything.

Diane said, "Well, that's why you have to make sure that you always know exactly what's going on. Honey, these guys will tell you anything if they think they have a better chance at getting into your pants. And you're so young, I know people will say that you're too young to really be in love, but I don't think that's true. I know it's possible to be in real love because I was in love with my husband when we were in high school. I just think since we know that it's possible to have real feelings, maybe you should try to avoid being involved with anyone until you've graduated from high school at the very least. I feel sorry for you because it sounds like he got in your head more than anything. Saying things to lead you to believe that you two are a couple, but never actually making it official is the oldest trick in the book. Men and love will always be there, so they can wait. The fact that he bought you all those clothes doesn't mean anything except that he has the money to spend."

I didn't agree with everything Diane said because I knew he wasn't the type to spend money on any and everybody, but I did understand her point. Tandra nodded to the point where I thought her head would fall off of her neck. Diane asked Tandra whom she lived with. When Tandra told her that she lived with both of her parents, Diane said, "Be thankful for your mother and especially your father. So many of our little girls have absentee fathers and it makes me so sad. Then guys like Aaron come around and take advantage of them because they don't know any better." I didn't appreciate the way she talked about Aaron because he truly wasn't the guy she described.

Tandra nodded again and said, "Yes, ma'am."

As we finished talking, Tandra said she was getting ready to leave. We stood in the doorway talking.

Diane came and gave me a hug and said, "I love you, Heaven, okay? I don't want to see you upset like this. Always know your worth, even when nobody else does."

I told her I loved her too and she went into her room.

Danni and Dontez were back, I watched them from the doorway where I stood. Danni was in the driver's seat laughing because she was learning how to drive and she was almost in the grass as she tried to pull into the driveway. She was clearly messing up, while Dontez laughed with her as they got out of the car and walked into the house. When Danni saw me she said, "Hey, suga, you mad at me?" She didn't acknowledge Tandra as she playfully pulled my hair.

I said, "No, I'm not mad at you. You might have been right about Aaron." I told her everything that happened.

Dontez said, "Well, what did you expect?"

I looked at him and said, "I wasn't talking to you."

He chuckled and shook his head like I was the biggest dummy he had ever met.

Danni said, "Well, at least you know now. I can't believe that girl was ready to fight you over him."

I introduced Tandra and Danni and they both made it awkward. Danni said, "Hey," as she looked her directly in the eyes.

Tandra gave her a defensive look and said, "Hey," back to her.

Danni said, "Tez, I'm going outside to smoke real quick. You coming?"

Dontez said, "Hell yeah. After riding with you I do need a cigarette." They went outside.

Tandra looked at me and laughed quietly. "Your new friends are so cool, Heaven. They *smoke*?" She was looking like the thought of them smoking grossed her out.

I said, "Yes, they do, and they really are pretty cool. Thanks." I knew she was being sarcastic so I figured that I would match hers with my own.

She laughed because she knew that I was being sarcastic. She said, "Okay, well I need to go, but I was gonna tell you that I don't think you're stupid at all. If I was dealing with somebody that's fine as he is, I would have lost my mind too. How were you supposed to know he was full of shit? And why should you have listened to Tez's ugly self. He probably likes you anyway."

I had forgotten that quickly that I told Tandra and Diane every little detail about Aaron, including Dontez telling me not to talk to him. I stepped outside to walk her to her car. Tandra asked Dontez if he could move his car so she could get out. Danni got up and moved the car and told Tandra it was nice meeting her. After Tandra left, I told Danni that I was afraid that she didn't like Tandra because of the way she looked at her.

She said, "She acts a lot like how you used to when I first met you, but I won't hold that against her. I was checking her out to see if she has good or bad energy, but if you think she's cool, I think she's cool. I wouldn't ever be rude to somebody at my house unless they gave me a reason to." That was why I loved Danni, I noticed a change in Tandra's demeanor from the moment Danni walked in, but Danni still chose to remain cool.

"What do you mean by good or bad energy?" I asked Danni as we stood on the porch talking.

She replied, "It's something my mother taught me. She'll tell you more about it, let's just say it's part of the reason that I knew you were a good person when we first met."

"That's not telling me anything, Danni," I replied.

She said, "My mother wants to tell you about it later, so just wait until then." I didn't care enough to ask any further so I let it go.

We got ready to go into the house when Aaron's car turned onto the street that Danni lived on. He parked in front of the house and walked up and said what's up to everyone. I couldn't believe how bold he was. He was acting as though he hadn't previously had words with Danni, like she wouldn't mind him coming to her house. I stood on the porch looking at him as he stood in front of me. Dontez and Danni went into the house so that we could have privacy.

Aaron said, "I'm not here to beg you to fuck with me, but I do want you to know what's what. I'm not foul like you think I am."

I said, "Oh, you're not?"

He calmly said, "Not at all."

I asked him, "So do you have anything else that you need to say?"

"Yeah, for one thing you wasn't ever my girl, Heaven. I asked you in the beginning what you wanted from me. You said you wanted me to be honest. I haven't lied to you about anything. Just because I didn't volunteer to tell you shit doesn't mean that I'm not honest. I didn't feel like I needed to tell you who I chilled with since you wasn't my girl. Every time I said something about you being my girl you made it seem like that's not what you wanted, or you laughed it off like I was playing with you, right? When I said you was my baby I meant that, but we wasn't actually together."

I said, "You are so full of shit! You also told me that you didn't want anyone else touching me. You went down on me and you were probably doing the same thing to her! You also lied and told me she was calling you daddy to get to me. She was calling you daddy because you were fuckin' her! You knew damn well that I wanted to be with you. Why would I spend all of my time with you? When I wasn't in school I was with you. It's okay, Aaron. I get it. Just leave me alone. I mean, you lied about where you went today, too. You were with her the whole time."

Aaron looked at me like I was crazy. "What?! I wasn't licking that bitch's pussy. What the fuck I look like? Did you not hear her say that I told her I didn't do that shit? That ain't some shit I do to anybody. I did that to you because like I told you, I fuck with you like that. I fucked her a few times. That's it. When I said I didn't want anybody else touching you I was dead serious. I *don't* want another nigga touching you. I knew that you probably would, though. You're still young and in high school, so why wouldn't you? You are my baby, you always will be. That doesn't mean we will always be together. Feel me?"

I shook my head. I could feel myself getting weaker with every word that he spoke to me. He must have been able to sense that I was giving in. He said, "Let this bullshit go, baby. I was wrong, I should have made it clear that I was yours and you were mine. When I left the house earlier, I did go and check on what I said I would, but after I left from doing that, I went by her house. When I told you that I was feelin' you for real, I was serious. I wanted to tell you tonight that it was me and you from now on. I went and told her that I wasn't fuckin' with her and I didn't want her stopping by the house and she flipped out on me. That's when she came by doing all that silly shit. It's that simple, Heaven. Honestly, that's why I hadn't tried to have sex with you. I wanted to make sure that I really wanted to fuck with you like that because I know you're young. You'll be sprung and won't even know it until you start trippin' and shit."

I stared at Aaron without saying a word.

He said, "You wanna be my girl or not? I know you probably don't wanna be with me now. I fucked up, I can admit it."

I told him, "Aaron, let me think about everything, okay?

"What's to think about?" he replied.

"I don't know, Aaron. Just let me think about everything, ok? It's cold out here, I'm going inside."

He said, "Come with me. Please." I looked at Aaron as he looked at me. He was looking genuinely upset as he waited for my answer. It was different seeing him show any real emotion since he spent so much time trying to school me and remind me of how young I was.

"You make me look stupid, Aaron," I said softly.

He replied, "I don't care how anybody else views me or you, baby. I won't ever care. Worry about how we feel about each other, not how others feel about us. This is about me and you."

I agreed with Aaron and told him I would go with him.

He smiled and pulled me into his chest and hugged me. "I love me some you. You just don't know," he said, still smiling.

I replied, "Well, stop calling me young all the time, and making me feel like you're too mature for me."

He said, "Well, you *are* young, but if you want me to stop saying it, I'll try."

Chapter 26

Tonight I need your body…

We walked into the house and Aaron stood with me in the living room as I told Danni that I was leaving with him. Dontez said, "Aaron, let me holler at you for a minute." We all looked from Dontez to Aaron. Aaron told him ok and they stepped outside.

Diane came out of her room and asked me what was going on. I told her that I was leaving to get something to eat with my boyfriend, but I would be right back. It was the best lie that I could come up with at the time. She told me, "Heaven, now listen. I love you a lot, you know that. But you're not welcome here anymore, honey. I know that you've been lying about where you've been. I wasn't born yesterday. I had hoped that you would get things right with your mother, but it looks like that's not going to happen, so you have to go. I can't have you running in and out of here like this."

I looked at Danni but she didn't look back at me, she looked at the ground. I told Diane that I understood. I grabbed my bags that I brought with me and walked out the door. Danni followed me outside and said, "She mentioned it last week too, but I talked her out of it. I'm sorry, Heaven. She doesn't feel comfortable since you haven't been honest. I didn't want to tell you because I was hoping she changed her mind."

I told Danni, "Well, she could have given me a couple of days to figure something out. Now I *have* to go back to my mother's house."

Danni looked like she was shocked by what I said, "Heaven, get serious. You have been in and out since you got here. All you want to do is chill here when Aaron is fuckin' his other girl."

I listened to Danni while I gave her an impatient look, I was sick of her always having only negative things to say about Aaron. She continued, "I love you with your selfish ass, and you better call me when you go back to your mother's house. And promise me one thing…"

I said, "You know I love you too, and I'll always call you. What is it? I owe it to you."

Danni said, "Before you go back to your mother's house have Aaron bring you by here so that my mother can give you a Reiki treatment."

"Danni, what the hell is Reiki?"

Danni said, "She'll basically have you lay on her massage table at her job, then use her hands to transfer positive energy into your body. It makes you feel better than you feel when you smoke a blunt. I'm thinking about quitting cigarettes and weed because Reiki gives me that natural high. I was scared at first too."

This was the first time I had heard of anything called Reiki and I wanted nothing to do with it. I laughed and said, "Girl, please. Y'all better stop messing with that demonic shit. I'm not doing that shit."

Danni laughed and said, "You just said you owe me one and that's what I want you to do. It's not demonic but a lot of black people think that. Anything outside of the norm scares them. It's so stupid that people think like that. My mom always says that people fear what they don't know and that's the realest shit ever. Don't knock it til you try it."

I said, "I'll do it, but tell your mother that it will be a one-time thing and it's only because I feel bad about being with Aaron all the time."

Danni laughed and said, "Okay, I'll tell her that." We walked toward Aaron's car as I told Danni that I understood.

Aaron grabbed my bags and put them in the back seat of his car. I really did understand why Diane felt that way. The only thing was that I knew I would have to go back to my mother's house despite the fact that I hated it there. I didn't have a choice in the matter. This could cause a problem with Aaron because I wouldn't live as close. I knew that I loved Aaron, but I also knew that I couldn't live with him. I would if he asked me, but I was sure that he wouldn't do that, so I had to mentally prepare to go back to hell on earth.

I hugged Danni and told her I would be in touch with her, and I hugged Dontez. He hugged me back and I said, "I'm sorry you think I'm so stupid, I know you hate me."

Dontez looked at me and said, "Heaven, you know I could never hate you, baby girl, and I know you don't have a stupid bone in your body. You just make stupid choices. Make sure you always watch out for yourself. You'll always be my little sis no matter what, alright?"

I got in the car with Aaron and we left. On the way to his house he said, "Tez really does care about you, baby. I don't think he likes you in a sexual way anymore. He just wants what's best for you. He talked to me like a man today and asked me not to hurt you. I told him I wouldn't, and I mean that. I think being with Danni took his focus off of you."

I told him I was glad to hear that because Dontez had me thinking he hated me after all the rude comments he had made to me.

Aaron said, "You should talk to him, though. He's worried about you, but he's fuckin' up out here. For real."

I looked at him and said, "What do you mean?"

He looked at me said, "He thought that since he dropped out of school and sells dope, the money was gonna fall from the sky. When the money didn't come fast enough he started doing silly shit. This nigga was robbing niggas that stay around here and shit like they won't know who he is and come after him."

I was barely listening to Aaron tell me about Dontez because we passed by my dad and Sonya's house and it made me miss Christopher Kyle instantly. As always, I blocked out the feelings I was having and tuned in to what Aaron was saying.

"He bought a gram of coke with money that he borrowed from some nigga he barely knew. He said he was trying to sell it. That was stupid because you only get like seven or eight lines from a gram. That ain't shit to sell and make no real money, but he probably knew that because he was sitting at the crib sniffing powder one night like it wasn't shit. I asked him how much sense it made to start doing the same shit his daddy started out doing, and the same shit that his brother was selling and went to jail for. I don't know, I don't think he gets how he's fuckin' up. That night in the kitchen he was asking to borrow money to take his girl out. I gave it to him, but I told him not to ask me again. I'll always show him love, that's my nigga's baby brother, but I'm not the one fuckin' her. That shit ain't got nothing to do with me."

I said, "He's not having sex with her either, Aaron."

Aaron laughed. "Okay. I don't give a fuck one way or the other. I'm just telling you to talk to him. I tried, and his bro did too when we went to see him last time. He won't listen. I don't want him to get hurt for real."

We were sitting in his driveway and I asked, "Why are you just now telling me this now? I should have known a long time ago. I would have talked to him way before now. Does Danni know?"

He said, "What do I look like telling you what he got going on? I'm telling you now because maybe you can get through that thick skull of his. This nigga is starting to do dumb shit on the daily. He said he looks at you like a sister, so maybe he'll take your advice. He's fuckin' up for real." Aaron paused and then looked at me and said, "But I'm tellin' you to stay away from him. If something happens to you because of that nigga I might kill him myself, feel me? When you talk to him, just page him…don't go to his house. Too many bitch ass niggas around there and anything could happen."

I was flattered that he felt protective of me but I didn't acknowledge his statement about killing Dontez over me. A small part of me wondered if I should make a point to go over to Dontez's house just to see how serious Aaron was. I said, "Does Danni know?"

Aaron got out of the car and I followed him and got out of the car also, he told me as he grabbed my bags out of the backseat, "I don't know and I don't care." We walked into his house and went up to his room. I sat on the bed and watched Aaron carry my bags into his room, and sit them on his bed. He went to his dresser and took his watch off then sat it down. He took the iguana out of the aquarium and let it sit on his hand for a second then put it back. I wondered when he planned to get rid of it like he said he would. He went to the bathroom and washed his hands then came out and said, "Don't be shocked if my Pops comes over here tomorrow. We got some shit to handle tomorrow."

I asked, "What do y'all have to handle?"

Aaron gave me a rude look and said, "You are so nosy," then laughed like he wasn't irritated anymore. He casually went through the Victoria Secret bag and pulled out a hot pink panty and bra set as he talked to me. "He meets me here when we go looking for properties to buy." He tossed them to me and said, "Go take a shower and don't come out unless you're wearing those." He bit his bottom lip while he rubbed his hands together as he looked at me. I told him that I would do as he asked me, and he went downstairs.

I took a shower like Aaron asked me to. I took my time washing my entire body then I shaved my pubic hair again. I couldn't believe how much the hair itched after only a few days of being cut. I knew that Aaron didn't like when I had a bunch of hair on my pussy so I would always keep it hairless for that reason. When I got out of the shower, I dried off with my towel then greased my body with the baby oil that Aaron bought for me when I came over. I had the underwear that Aaron bought me sitting on the toilet seat. I wanted to make sure that I smelled perfect so after I rubbed the oil everywhere except my pussy, I wiped myself with plans to smell the towel as one last measure to be sure I was safe. I had heard horror stories about girls with foul smelling vaginas and I didn't ever want that to happen to me. When I looked at the towel I saw blood. I went into panic mode. I put the beige towel on the toilet seat and sat on it to be sure that I didn't bleed on the toilet seat. I put my head in my lap and cried hysterically as quietly as I could. I knew that both Aaron and I felt like tonight was going to be the night that we made love. I didn't understand why I had to start my menstrual that night of all the nights.

After I stopped crying, I continued to sit on the toilet seat. Aaron eventually came up the stairs and knocked on the door. I didn't open it because I was nervous about what he would say when I told him the bad news. I jumped up and wrapped the towel around my body. I didn't have any pads so I was afraid that I would bleed everywhere. I didn't want to put the pretty satin panties on and possibly ruin them with blood, so I stood in the bathroom with part of the towel pressed against my vagina. I said, "Hold on a second, I'll be out in a minute."

Aaron said, "Girl, what are you doin' in there?" as he opened the door and walked in. I turned around and looked at him. He said, "I want you naked in a minute, but can a nigga see you model first?" He was giving me a flirty grin.

When I said, "No, you can't, Aaron. I didn't know it was that time of the month."

Aaron asked, "*What* time of the month?" His grin had disappeared and he was looking at me like he was upset.

I said, "*THAT* time of the month. What do you think?"

Aaron sighed and said, "That's too bad."

I said, "I didn't know it was time." I wanted sympathy from him but he wasn't giving it to me.

He said, "I mean, how come you didn't know? How old are you? Can't you tell when it's coming if you mark your calendar?"

I said, "Take me to my mother's house, please."

He said, "Awww, look at you, acting like a kid again. Poutin' and shit. I'm not taking you nowhere. Did you watch that movie I told you to watch?" Aaron was grinning at me again.

I said, "Yep."

He said, "Cool, I guess you can give me some head then. It's not the same, but it'll work for tonight."

I said, "I don't think I want to. The last time my jaws were hurting too much, and I wasn't doing it right because you didn't act like that dude in the movie. You seemed bored."

Aaron said, "That's because I *was* bored, but practice makes perfect. Don't ever say what you don't wanna do for your man, that shit is irritating. And really, what you won't do somebody else will."

I didn't know how to respond to what Aaron said to me. It was a slap in the face because I knew that Keisha had shown him how she felt about him by sucking and fucking him often. I said, "Can you go and buy me some pads? I don't have any."

Aaron said, "Damn, that's nasty. But since you decided to be my girl, I will. Just put those panties on or something until I get back then go put some clothes on. I'll be right back."

I put the panties on then put tissue in my panties so that I wouldn't feel wet when more blood came down, then I put the bra on. I wrapped the towel around my body as I walked out of the bathroom after Aaron left and went to the store for my pads. I went into my bags and grabbed a pair of gray sweat pants, and a white tank top. I still couldn't believe that I was bleeding, and the menstrual cramps were slowly, but surely, starting to kick my ass. The fact that the bra I was wearing seemed to accentuate my breast in a way that I never expected was shocking to me. I didn't care much about the bra at the moment because I was focused on the pain in my stomach. The stronger the pain was, the more irritable I became. I stood in front of the mirror on Aaron's dresser and took my hair out of the ponytail that I wore all day. After I put the black rubber band around my wrist I brushed my hair until I felt like it looked pretty again. I didn't take my big gold hoop earrings off because I liked my look and I hoped Aaron would too. I went downstairs and sat on the couch waiting for Aaron. He came back with the pads and a blunt hanging from his mouth. I rolled my eyes at him because he took too long getting back. I told him, "Thanks" and went into the downstairs bathroom to put a pad on.

When I came out of the bathroom Aaron was smoking with his feet kicked up on the coffee table. I sat next to him and he passed the blunt to me. He watched me as I took a pull then released the smoke. He said, "That shit is sexy as hell."

I looked at him and said, "What?"

He leaned over and gave me a kiss and said, "You. Watching you smoke. I love that shit." I didn't say anything in response to him. He said, "So are you ready?"

I said, "Yep, let's get this over with." I scooted closer to him than I already was and tried to unzip his jeans.

He frowned at me and said, "You don't want to?" I was judging, by the look on his face, that he was becoming frustrated, so I got my attitude together.

I said, "Can we turn the lights off?"

Aaron said, "For what?"

I told him, "Because I don't want you to watch me."

He said, "Chill out. You don't have to be shy with me. Let me watch you."

Chapter 27

I used to be scared of the...

I was nervous, but I decided to give it a try despite how bad my cramps bothered me. Aaron continued to smoke as he laid his head back on the couch and said, "Relax, it's only me and you here." I stood in front of him and let him get a good look at me in the underwear that he bought for me. I didn't feel very sexy at all at that moment. I felt overweight and tired but I knew that Aaron would be turned off if I acted how I felt. Aaron shook his head and said, "Damn, you know you are sexy as fuck, don't you?" I squatted down in front of him and finished unzipping his pants. Aaron was looking at me like he was challenging me. I'm sure he didn't think I would know what I was doing.

I said, "You gotta pull your pants down."

He didn't say a word as he stood up and put the blunt in the ashtray, then took his pants off and sat them neatly next to him on the couch. He was wearing a pair of navy blue boxers with the Nautica logo around the waist. He was already hard when he took his pants off so I made sure my mouth was wet in case I wanted to spit on his penis like the girl in the movie. Aaron was still watching me, the look on his face made it clear that he didn't plan to stop watching me anytime soon. I licked from the bottom to the top of his penis as I wrapped my hands around and moved them up and down. I watched for a reaction but I didn't get one from him. I started sucking on the head of his penis while still massaging it with my hands. Aaron leaned his head on the couch and closed his eyes. I knew my jaws would hurt, but I had a point to prove. I scooted as close to his penis as possible and sucked as far down as I could without gagging. As much as my mouth was hurting, I was still able to wrap my lips around him tightly. I kept the same speed while I sucked up and down, not too fast and not too slow. When I realized that he was aroused, I started sucking a little faster. I was no longer rubbing his penis with my hands. They rested on the sides of his thighs. He said, "Damn, baby" as he put his hand on top of my head. Though he wasn't holding my head in a rough manner, it was still uncomfortable for me. I kept the same rhythm while giving him fake seductive looks for what seemed like hours. In reality, it was only about seven minutes. He said, "Don't move….stay…just…like…" Aaron became silent and I noticed that his dick was harder than it was when I first started pleasing him. All of a sudden, Aaron let out a low grunt and released a load of cum into my mouth.

I was livid. I spit the warm salty liquid out on the floor and yelled, "I AM NEVER DOING THAT NASTY SHIT AGAIN. WHY DIDN'T YOU TELL ME THAT YOU WERE ABOUT TO CUM? YOU NASTY ASS NIGGA!" I was still spitting on the floor in between yelling at Aaron. I grabbed his pants and threw them at him, and told him, "I DON'T LIKE YOU! YOU ARE SO FUCKIN' NASTY!"

Aaron got up and put his pants on without zipping them, he was holding them up with one hand. He went to the bathroom near the living room while he laughed hysterically.

I followed him to the bathroom and had to restrain myself from hitting him. I said, "I'm leaving. I don't want to be anywhere near you!"

Aaron was doubled over with laughter while he tried to lean against the wall, he was holding his stomach. He was still laughing as he turned the water in the faucet on. He was still holding his baggy pants up with one hand then he let them fall to the ground while he wiped his penis with a towel. I pushed him aside so that I could rinse my mouth out, because despite spitting it out of my mouth, I thought I could feel sperm in my throat. I was gagging myself with my face in the sink when Aaron finally said, "Chill out, baby, damn. It's not like I don't taste you every time I eat your pussy. You don't hear me crying and shit." He was still fighting laughter but I was still pissed despite him suggesting that he took my cum like a champ.

I said, "That's different, that shit was disgusting."

He said, "What's different? It's all cum."

I said, "Well, for one thing, it's always nastier when a man does it than a woman."

He said, "How would you know? Have you ate pussy before?" Aaron laughed at his comment, I didn't.

I told him, "Get a grip, I don't fuck with bitches. Just don't do that again, I'm not a fuckin' porn star."

Aaron smiled at me and said, "But you know what? You pleased your man like one. That's why I love me some you." He walked out of the bathroom and went through the house and turned off the lights. I followed him upstairs and we went to sleep.

I wasn't in a deep sleep because the menstrual cramps were stronger than earlier. I looked over at Aaron who was sleeping peacefully. I loved watching him sleep because I really got to stare at him and admire how handsome he was. He was lying on his back with one arm on top of his head and the other at his side. His face was relaxed and perfect, his braids looked messy since it was time to have them rebraided, but they still looked nice because of his hair texture. I was lying on my pillow facing Aaron when I heard banging on the front door downstairs. Aaron didn't budge but I sat up in the bed because I went into panic mode. I didn't know what I would do if it was Keisha again, besides cry in an attempt to make Aaron feel guilty. After a couple of minutes of knocking, I heard the door open and a female's voice calling Aaron's name. My heart was beating fast at that point. After she called his name a few more times, she walked up the stairs. I decided to lie back down and pretend like I was asleep. I looked at Aaron to see if he was at least stirring and he wasn't. I could hear her heels on the old hardwood floor as she got closer to Aaron's room. She peeked in the door for a second then walked into the room. She stood on my side of the bed watching me and said, "This is ridiculous" as she slowly leaned in closer to me and pulled the cover off of my head. I opened my eyes slowly in an attempt to make her believe that she woke me up. When she realized I was looking at her she said to me, "Who are you?"

I said, "Aaron's girlfriend."

She said, "Oh, I didn't know Aaron had one of those." She had a thoughtful smile on her face as she stood watching me. She said, "Do you live here, Aaron's girlfriend?"

I sat up and said, "My name is Heaven."

She said, "Oh, Heaven…ok. I'm Gina, Aaron's mother."

I just sat and stared at her because I didn't know what else to say to her. I couldn't help but notice that Gina was very pretty. Her high cheekbones gave her a regal look yet her almond shaped eyes and her olive skin tone made her look exotic. Her long hair was tucked neatly behind her ears showing expensive looking diamond earrings. Her eyebrows were arched to perfection, and her makeup was flawless. Looking at Gina made me wonder if Aaron had a type because she reminded me of Keisha. I didn't see any resemblance between Aaron and his mother whatsoever. I planned to ask Aaron what she was mixed with because of how long her hair was.

Gina said, "You're very pretty, Heaven. How long have you been staying here? You must be what's been keeping my son so busy. He hasn't been coming home for dinner every night like he usually does."

I said, "Thank you, I haven't been staying here often. Just last night."

Gina looked at me like she didn't believe me. She was standing in front of me with her hand on her hip. I wasn't sure what I was doing to offend her but she was obviously irritated. She finally said, "If he's dumb enough to let a girl come in between him and gettin' paper that's his fault. I hope he knows that ain't nobody about to pay his bills but him. You're still young so you might not understand how things go just yet. I keep telling him that females will come later, right now he needs to focus on makin' moves so he doesn't have to struggle when he's older."

I sat in the bed listening to her talk. She had a smooth, calm voice. Gina didn't speak proper, but she didn't speak like she was ghetto either. It wasn't to the point where she sounded ignorant when she talked. Her tone was always even when she talked to me. She never had to raise her voice to make it clear that she had a point to make. I figured she was the reason Aaron was so opinionated. He was probably used to listening to his mother give him the facts of life according to her opinion. Before I could reply, Gina left no room for me to guess that she didn't give a fuck what I had to say back to her. She looked over at Aaron who was starting to make slow movements in the bed. She said, "Aaron, wake up." Her tone wasn't angry, it was calm and direct.

Aaron opened his eyes and looked at his mother then closed them for a second. It took a moment for him to realize that his mother was standing in his room like she owned the place. He sat up and stretched while he yawned. We both watched him, I was curious to see what he would say to her for being so rude and barging in on us. He looked at his mother and said, "Mama, what you doin'? Scaring my girl? You can't just be walkin' up in here like that." His tone with his mother didn't suggest that he was upset, it almost seemed like he was amused by his mother and her boldness. When he glanced from his mother to me I smiled at him, there wasn't a time that he looked at me that I didn't feel butterflies in my stomach.

Gina noticed the way I looked at Aaron, and judging by the look on her face, I was sure she would vomit at any moment. She rolled her eyes at me and spoke to Aaron. She said, "If I had known you had company, I wouldn't have walked in. I'm sorry." She seemed genuine when she told Aaron about her mistake. She sat at the foot of the bed and ignored me as though I wasn't in the room anymore.

Aaron said, "It's all good, beautiful." He got up from the bed and kissed his mother on the cheek then went to his dresser and grabbed a shirt and put it on. Gina still sat and watched me without trying to hide it. I had been trying to cover myself since she pulled the cover from my face and I sat up. Aaron looked at me and tossed me a shirt to put on. Getting dressed in front of Gina was awkward but I knew I had to because I was trying to show her that she didn't intimidate me. I was starting to become frustrated. Gina didn't look like she was leaving any time soon.

Aaron went to use the bathroom, then came out and sat on his bed. He asked, "Where's the old man? I thought he was coming."

His mother said, "He is, he ran to the store but he'll be right back. He loves shootin' the shit with the people he grew up with. You know every time we come back to this part of town he thinks he has to stop." As Gina explained where Aaron's father was we heard him downstairs calling his wife's name. Her tone with me was sassy, and direct. With her husband it became more feminine, and loving. She said, "I'm coming, hold on a second, baby." She got up and walked out of the room to tend to her husband.

When she walked out of the room I got out of the bed. I asked Aaron, "Is that normal? Do your parents always come over unannounced and walk into your house?"

Aaron said, "No, that's the first time."

I said, "It's rude, and your mother makes me uncomfortable. I know she doesn't like me."

Aaron said, "She probably won't like anybody to be honest. She'll be cool, chill out. It's just hard for her because she wants me to focus on making money right now so I can stack it for later." I was listening to Aaron explain his point of view without interrupting him. "I'll always make money, and that's what she wants. Which is cool, but I'm grown. I do what I wanna do. I know females will always be around, but I don't care about them. I'm not trippin' on playing the field."

I sat down next to him and asked, "Is that what she tells you, to play the field?"

He said, "Yeah! Don't knock her, though. She just doesn't want me having kids and settling down until I do all the things I wanna do in life."

I replied, "So how much does what she says to you matter? I mean, if she doesn't like me what happens?"

Aaron gave me the look he always gave me when he thought I said something stupid. He said, "I do what I wanna do. I told you that, baby. Don't ever forget that."

I got up and sat on his lap facing him. After I wrapped my arms around his neck I looked at him and said, "Aaron…I know you probably don't feel the same about me yet, but eventually you will. I know I'm young, but I know that I love you." I looked down at the floor because I was losing my courage and becoming too emotional to get my point across.

Aaron had his arms wrapped around my waist as he sat quietly waiting for me to finish. It wasn't uncommon for me to get choked up when I tried to tell Aaron something regarding my feelings. He always gave me a direct look but it was hard reading how he felt because he had the "keep your game face" technique down to a science. I looked up at him, and he had his eyebrows raised, I knew that meant to continue what I was saying.

I started again, "I just want to know how you feel about me because…I don't think I'll ever feel like this about anyone else. I don't want anything to ever come between us."

Aaron said, "I love you, Heaven, you know that. I wouldn't fuck with you the way I do if I didn't love your ass. You got this ghetto, but at the same time, classy girl thing that is so sexy. You know how to act ghetto if you need to, but you're not like the rest of these ghetto bitches around here. Pretty as hell, you got those long legs too. I can't wait to put them on my shoulders."

I said, "Those things might be true, but you can find that in anybody. What makes you think you *love* me?"

He said, "It's not something I *think*. It's something I *know*. Just trust me on that. The main thing is that you're so sweet, and genuine. You'll love me, and have my back like a chick should. You just got growing to do, and that's ok, I guess." He smiled at me. I leaned in to kiss him on the lips and he moved to the side before I got to kiss him. He laughed and said, "You crazy for real, morning breath having ass."

I laughed too and got up and went into the bathroom to take a shower and brush my teeth. Aaron came in and brushed his teeth and ran a towel over his face. He opened the shower curtain and told me," I'll be back in a lil bit. Hopefully, you'll be done bleeding. How long does that last anyway?"

I said, "Where are you going?" Completely ignoring his question because I knew my menstrual would last about five days and I didn't want to tell him.

He said, "I thought I told you, I gotta go make some moves with my pops." He kissed me and left.

Chapter 28

Dear mama...

I was hoping Aaron's mother was gone, and I was glad that I didn't meet his father. Normally I didn't like being alone in the house, that day it was a welcomed relief. I sat on the edge of Aaron's bed going through my bags looking to find something to put on. My stomach was still bloated, so I wanted something that would be as comfortable as possible. I rubbed baby oil all over my body then put on another of the panty and bra sets that Aaron had bought for me. I wore my gray sweatpants with a white tank top. After I took the black rubber band out of my hair I wrapped it around my wrist and started brushing my hair. I slept in my hoop earrings, so I left them on. I decided that I wanted something to eat so I headed downstairs while still brushing my hair. Aaron rarely went grocery shopping so I figured there wouldn't be much to choose from but I would look anyway. I walked through the hall leading to the living room to make sure that the door was locked and got an unwanted surprise. Aaron's mother was sitting on the couch waiting for me. She had the remote in her hand, but she wasn't channel surfing. Once I realized she was there, I jumped and put my hand on my chest.

She said, "I didn't mean to scare you. Come sit down and talk to me." Gina patted the seat next to her in an effort to make me feel comfortable. I did as she asked and sat next to her without saying a word and looked at her. She started, "I decided to let the fellas go ahead without me, I thought us girls could chat. How old are you? You look awfully young."

I told her, "I'm sixteen." I didn't volunteer any more than she asked, I learned that from Aaron and now I was thankful to have picked that up from him.

She continued, "Oh. Why aren't you in school?" After each question she asked she gave me a look that made me feel like she didn't like me.

I said, "Because I'm about to switch schools when I go to live with my mother."

She raised her eyebrow and said, "Who do you stay with right now?"

I lied and said, "My father, and my stepmother."

Gina replied, "Well, I don't know if you're telling the truth or not, don't really care. You just need to make sure that you're not the downfall of my son. I don't know why you would miss a week from school, but I hope you're not investing all of your stock into Aaron. He's young, and the odds of this lasting are highly unlikely."

I fought tears because her tone was harsh and she didn't care that she was hurting me. I wasn't expecting her to be so evil. I said, "Are you done?"

She looked at me and said, "As a matter of fact, no. I'm not done. Aaron is a good kid. He's not into drugs, he's respectful, and kind hearted. His father and I have really done a good job raising him into a wonderful young man. I just don't want him losing sight of his goals...because of *you*."

I went from being hurt to angry. I wanted Aaron's mother to like me, but I wanted her to respect me also. I knew Aaron would be mad if I called his mother out of her name. So I restrained myself and didn't call her a bitch. I decided to be honest with her instead. "I love Aaron. I'll do whatever he tells me to do. I wouldn't let him lose sight of his goals. Maybe I can even help him reach his goals."

Gina laughed, but we both knew she didn't find anything funny. She said, "You love him. You're a little young to use that word so loosely. Where's your father? *That's* what you want in Aaron, but he can't be that to you, sweetie. *You* can help him meet *his* goals? Child, you got a lot of learning to do. For starters, you're young. Do you have any goals of your own? What can you do to help if you're cool with sitting around wasting your life away to lay up with him? That's not helping him at all, honey. It may be hurting you actually. At some point, he will want someone with goals to match his own. You think because you have a pretty face that it will last forever? You think because he thinks he loves you for now that it'll last forever? Love doesn't pay bills. Never forget that. Aaron is used to being around hustlers, so a lazy woman will never satisfy him in the long run."

The only thing that I heard was that Aaron thinks he loves me. Anything else she said didn't matter, but I still felt like I needed to say something to defend myself regardless. I gave her an evil look and said, "If I'm only here for a short time, what are you so uptight about then? Why are you so worried? You have to sit here and talk clever to me, knowing that I ain't shit and he will get rid of me anyway? Doesn't make a lot of sense, Gina." I purposely called her by her first name, knowing that most adults considered that to be disrespectful.

She said, "Yeah…you gotta go. You are very disrespectful. I'm just glad that I raised my own children to be respectful. Any woman that doesn't respect her man's mother will never work, especially if that man has any respect for his mother. Remember that when he's walkin' your fast tail up out of here."

I rolled my eyes at her and went into the kitchen. There was nothing to eat so I went and sat in the dining room at the table. I no longer had an appetite anyway but I needed to do something to take my mind off of Gina's presence in the house. I refused to be in the same room with Gina, she was a bitch. She sat in the living room on the couch flipping through channels in silence. This went on for over an hour.

Aaron and his father walked into the house laughing and making fun of each other. The first thing Aaron did was look at his mother, then me. Aaron's father who was the spitting image of Aaron looked at his wife like he knew she had said something to me.

Aaron walked over to me and said, "What's wrong?"

I said, "Nothing's wrong. I'm fine."

Aaron's father walked into the dining room and introduced himself to me. He was taller than Aaron and very handsome. He looked exactly how I pictured Aaron to look when he was older. I could see why Gina humbled herself around her husband. The demeanor that he carried demanded respect in a nonthreatening way.

He walked in with confidence that only an alpha male could possess. He said, "What's up, Heaven? I heard all about you. I'm James, nice to meet you." I shook his extended hand. He started talking to me again. "I hope my wife didn't scare you too much. She wants Aaron to stay a baby forever." He looked at Gina, who was watching us, then he smiled at me, but I was too defensive at that point to return his smile. I looked at Aaron's father with no expression whatsoever. I felt like James was feeling me out to see what type of person I was.

I said, "Okay." I wasn't looking in Gina's direction but I knew she was watching me. Aaron pulled up a chair next to me and playfully slapped my thigh.

His father said, "Well, you must be something special, you're all he talked about today." Aaron didn't look ashamed by what his father was saying. He simply watched for my reaction. I looked at his father and nodded without saying a word. I wasn't comfortable with his parents around me and I wanted them to leave. James continued to talk to me. "Aaron showed me where you live. I know your father and your stepmother. Went to school with both of them, they're good people." He had my attention and he knew it. Gina looked up when he told me he knew my family.

I said, "Yes, they are good people."

Gina stood up, and put her Dooney & Burke bag on her shoulder. She was still in the living room. She said, "James, are you ready?" Aaron's dad told her he was ready while walking toward the door.

Aaron said, "I'll be right back, baby." I watched Aaron walk them to the door.

His mother said, "Step outside with me for a second." She glanced in my direction then walked out the door. Aaron's dad said bye to me then left. I was extremely upset because I knew Gina wanted Aaron to step outside because she wanted to talk about me in a negative way.

Aaron came back into the house after a few minutes and asked me to sit on the couch with him. We sat in silence for a few minutes, and it was clear that Aaron had something on his mind. I chose not to say anything at first because I knew that Aaron would talk about what was bothering him when the time was right.

The TV was on, but Aaron wasn't watching it. He was looking in the direction of the TV but he was a million miles away. After sitting and waiting to see what he planned to say for what seemed like eternity I said, "Why are you so quiet? What did I do?"

Aaron looked at me and said, "Who said you did anything?"

I always tried to read his expression, this time I couldn't. I told him, "I was just asking because I know your parents don't like me."

Aaron threw his eyes in the air and said, "You know they don't like you? Actually you don't know, so chill out." I didn't reply to Aaron, so he continued talking to me. "I told you that I do what I wanna do anyway. They don't have to like you, because I love you. Alright?"

I said, "I know, I just…it felt like they didn't like me."

Aaron said, "Heaven, grow up. Who cares if they like you or not? How many times do I have to say that it shouldn't matter what they think? If it does matter then that's your problem. Are you always gonna need me to tell you how much I love you to make you feel comfortable? You really must have daddy issues or something."

That's when I knew that his parents had brainwashed him. He said their opinion didn't matter yet he mentioned daddy issues, which was something that had never come up between us two.

I said, "Daddy issues? What are you saying?"

Aaron said, "Do you look at me as your father figure, not your man? That's some shit that I can't fuck with. You got the wrong nigga if that's what it is. I'm tellin' you that right now."

My voice was weak when I asked him, "So what are you saying?"

Aaron said, "I said what I'm saying. I want you to love me because you do, not because you're missing the father you never had. If you're looking for your father you need to go find him, baby."

My feelings were hurt, and there was nothing I could do about it. Why would he think I was looking for my father in him? I cried hysterically in my lap so that he couldn't see my face. I didn't understand how he could say those things to me, when earlier, he made it seem as though nothing his parents said would matter. I didn't view Aaron as my father, but I would be lying if I said that part of my attraction to him was his ability to tell me what I needed to do without being too pushy with it. I couldn't imagine what I would do if he decided to break up with me.

Aaron said, "Oh my God, Heaven. What the fu…what are you crying for? Look at me." I looked at him but when I tried to hold a stare I cried even more. I thought I knew what was to come; he was going to leave me alone. Aaron said, "Maaaaan…What the hell?" He looked toward the TV again like he was trying to gather all the patience inside of him.

I looked up at him while I tried to stop crying. I still had tears falling from my eyes. I told him, "I don't think you're my daddy. That's so stupid. I love you, that's it."

He said, "Well what are you upset about then?" I was upset because something was different from that day forward. Aaron pulled me close to him and kissed me on the cheek. He told me that he knew how much I loved him. I found comfort in the assurance from him that he loved me just as much. He stared at me for a second then kissed me on my lips. He said, "I love your emotional ass, alright?"

I nodded but didn't say anything.

Chapter 29

Suddenly my sunshine turned to rain...

aron told me that he needed to make a run, and that he would be back later. When I asked where he was going, he told me not to worry about it. I was worried about it, but I decided to play cool and pretend that I wasn't bothered. He put his jacket on and left without telling me when he would be back. My cousin, Misa, had been on my mind a lot, so I decided to page her while Aaron was gone.

After I paged Misa, I sat the cordless phone on the coffee table so that it would be close by in case I dozed off. I was lonely watching television by myself, but I had a lot on my mind. I was trying to mentally prepare myself for life with my mother. I had enjoyed being on my own tremendously. I would be the first to admit that I relied a lot on my friends to help me survive, but they didn't seem to mind. I knew it would be hard to go back to relying solely on my mother for things, and dealing with her temper tantrums, and the overall chaos that living in her house brought. As I sat on the couch deep in thought, the cordless phone rang. I assumed it was Misa but when I checked the caller ID I realized that it was the number to Tandra and Zandra's house. I immediately went into defense mode. Why would anyone from their house call Aaron's house? It dawned on me that I paged her from Aaron's house, and in our last conversation I led Tandra to believe that I spent most of my time over at Aaron's house.

It would only be fair to assume she would call there if she wanted to talk to me.

I answered the phone and the first thing she said was, "Girl. What are you doing?"

I said, "Nothing, what's up Tandra?" I knew that I told her that's where I was, but for some reason, I didn't appreciate her feeling comfortable calling my boyfriends' house.

She said, "I was just calling to see if you still stayed there."

I said, "Tandra I don't live here, I just come chill with him sometimes." I was irritated because I didn't like her keeping tabs on what I did. That was one of the reasons I was never able to hold on to female friends. They seemed to be too focused on what you have going on to focus on what they have going on.

Tandra replied, "Oh, okay, I thought you lived there. Well...I wasn't gonna say anything but you're still my girl even if we don't talk much anymore...Even if you do hang with the chicken heads now."

I said, "Okay...if you have something to tell me you need to spit it out. Don't talk shit on my people, though, alright?" Tandra was starting to work my nerves. I wasn't above saying hurtful things to her if she continued to disrespect me by saying rude things about my friends.

She said, "I was at Ward Parkway today with my sister. Like, we just left right before I called you. So I'm walkin' the mall, headed to buy the new Rich the Factor CD from Sam Goody and I saw Aaron standing in line at Topsy's...with some bitch."

My heart dropped, and I was extremely upset but I refused to let Tandra know. I said, "Are you sure Tandra? Because he told me when he left he was going to his mother's house for a while." I knew I was lying but I couldn't let Tandra know that what she said bothered me.

She said, "I'm sure it was him, Heaven. The nigga was so into this tacky ass bitch that he didn't even look up when I walked past him."

I said, "So he didn't see you?"

Tandra said, "No, he was all in her face! I almost put my clown suit on, but I chilled because Zan told me it wasn't my business."

I replied, "Okay."

Tandra said, "Are you cool? I shouldn't have said anything." I told her I was cool.

I was about to hang up with Tandra when Misa clicked in on the other line. I hung up with Tandra to talk to Misa, she practically cursed me out for not calling her in so long. She filled me in that she was still in contact with Joey's brother Kev, and that Joey always asked about me. I couldn't care less about Joey asking about me. The only thing I wanted from Joey was my virginity back. There was no way I could get that back, so we had nothing to talk about. When I told her all about me and Aaron, Misa laughed and said, "Girl, I can't believe you went and got you a dude, and he's older at that!" I proceeded to tell her all about what Tandra had just told me. I was upset but I wasn't crying. Misa said, "I don't know, cuz, you gotta be careful about what you believe. Bitches are a trip, and they stay on some bullshit. You shouldn't even ask him shit about it. If you come at him with some shit that your homegirl said, he's gone be mad. He might stop fuckin' with you. You should check the numbers in his pager, and call them from his house and hang up when they answer. When they call back just hang up on them, at least you'll know if it's a bitch."

I said, "Misa, I refuse to do that. That sounds more stupid than coming out right and asking him."

Misa said, "I'm tellin' you, you shouldn't ask him anything that came from another female. He's gonna start calling you young and shit. Trust me."

I should have trusted Misa because Aaron was always telling me that I was young and I had yet to come at him with something from a female. The last thing I needed to give him was a reason to believe that I really was young and dumb. I asked Misa if she would come and visit me, I also reminded her not to tell anyone where I was for any reason. Misa told me she was on the way over. When we hung up, I paged Aaron about ten times back to back. When he called back he sounded irritated.

"What's up? You cool? Why you blowin' my shit up, baby? he asked.

I said, "Where you at?"

He said, "Chillin' with my people. Why?"

I said, "Why do you always leave me here like this? I don't have anything to eat! I'm ready to go! You don't even call to check on me."

Aaron sighed. "Alright, I'll be there. Get ready."

I said, "Where are you taking me?" I wasn't ready to go to my mother's house. I wanted to make him upset so that I had a reason to throw the information that Tandra gave me in his face.

He replied, "What you mean 'where am I taking you'? I thought you wanted some food?"

I was tired of dancing around my issue so I said, "Were you at the mall today?"

He said, "Yeah."

My heart started beating fast again. I said, "So you were with some chick and you left me here waiting for your black ass like a fuckin' dummy! I knew you wasn't about shit!"

Aaron said, "I never said I was with a chick. You asked if I was at the mall, and I said I was."

I said, "Were you with a female or not?" The noise in the background was loud so I asked Aaron if he could step outside so I could hear him.

He told me, "No. I can't. We don't have too much more to talk about anyway.

I replied, "We don't? I think we do."

Aaron said, "I told you we don't. You are too fuckin' young for me. You are really that dumb to ask me some shit that your homegirl claims she saw? What part of the game is that?"

I said, "Who said it was my friend?"

Aaron said, "You're the stupid one. Not me. I saw the little bitch walking back and forth staring at me, when I looked at her she started laughing like a fuckin' kid and ran off. This is my last time telling you, you either with me or against me. You let a jealous bitch call and game you up?" I sat and listened to what Aaron said, and got pissed. I didn't know who to believe. Aaron finished talking to me, "So the next time you wanna question somebody it better not be me. You got me fucked up." He hung up without saying bye to me.

Anger isn't the word for how upset I was. Aaron had never talked to me that way before, and based on how mad he seemed, I assumed that he wasn't lying. I was so angry that I was shaking when I dialed Tandra's number. Tandra answered on the first ring, she sounded like she was laughing when she answered the phone. I said," So were you lying when you said you saw Aaron with a girl?"

Tandra laughed out loud and said, "Heaven, tell me you didn't really believe me! You didn't ask him anything, did you? I thought you knew I was just playing with you! You are way too gullible! I thought since you had new best friends from the hood that you would have been smarter than that."

I said, "Gullible? Tandra, you were not playing, you purposely lied to me. I should beat your stank ass when I see you, but I won't. I'm through fuckin' with you. You lyin' ass bitch."

Tandra stopped laughing like she just realized at that moment that what she did wasn't amusing. She hung up in my face. I wasn't done with her and I wouldn't stop until I found a way to make her pay for crossing me. Even though I wasn't going to hurt her physically, I was determined to make her realize that she couldn't just go around making up lies and then laugh like it was nothing. Mentally, would be my best angle. I knew she had no idea how much Aaron meant to me, but the fact that she did what she did was just evil. I had no idea how I would come at Aaron with an apology. The only thing I could think to do was feel him out to decide the best approach. Misa knocked at the door shortly after my conversation with Tandra. When she came in we hugged and she asked where Aaron was. I told her that I wasn't sure but not to be surprised if he was rude when he came in. I knew he would be pissed.

I said, "Where did you come from? I don't know how long I'll be here because he told me to get ready so we can go get some food. I didn't tell him you were coming, and he just told me not too long ago about having people over his house."

Misa said, "What the hell did you have me come over here for then?" She laughed but I knew she was serious.

I told her, "I don't know, I guess I wanted you to meet him. He's cool as hell."

Misa said, "I hope he doesn't act a fool or no shit like that. I hate fightin' niggas."

I laughed at her and said, "He wouldn't hit you, or me. You silly as hell." Misa was sitting on the couch in Aaron's spot filling me in on what had been going on with our family, mainly my mother. She told me that she stopped by to see if I was back yet, and mother told her that I wasn't. When she told me that my mother said she was happy that I hadn't come back because I drove her crazy, it hurt my feelings.

I nodded as I listened to Misa continue telling me everything. She said Angel had moved back in so she was sure that she wouldn't be coming to visit when I moved back in because Angel was too mean to her.

Misa said, "Girl, I think Angel is just as crazy as your mama. I was standing in the living room talking to Aunt Sharon, and Angel's ass was in your old room yelling all types of crazy shit. Aunt Sharon just smoked her cigarette while we talked like wasn't shit happening. That bitch Angel was yelling that she hated her daddy, and she hated her mama. Then I heard shit hitting the door like she was throwing shoes or something."

I sighed and said, "Damn…I didn't know Angel moved back in, and I didn't know her ass was staying in my room. That's just great."

Misa said, "Why you gotta go back?"

I told her, "Because Aaron's mother is a bitch and she came over here on some straight bullshit. Now I don't know where Aaron stands with me to be honest."

She said in a whisper, "His mama wasn't cool?"

I said, "Hell naw. I can't stand that bitch. Tellin' me that he wants a female to match his hustle, and asking me why I'm not in school like she's my mama."

Misa looked at me and said, "Well, why don't you go to school? You don't think she's right?"

I was about to answer her when Aaron walked into the house. I knew he was upset with me, for good reason. That still didn't stop me from getting up and giving him a hug when he walked in.

He hugged me back and said, "What's up, baby," while looking at Misa sitting on the couch.

I looked at Misa and said, "This is my cousin, Misa, Aaron." He went and shook her hand and asked how she was doing. Misa smiled politely and spoke to Aaron. I said, "Is this for me?" I was referring to the bag from a burger joint that he knew I loved.

He said, "Yep, that's you." I told him thanks and sat next to Misa on the couch and ate my burger. He turned his Playstation on then sat on the couch next to me and lit a blunt. After he took a few pulls he made eye contact with me but didn't say a word. Aaron passed the blunt to me then started playing the game. I sat my food down and took a few pulls then passed the blunt to Misa.

She was watching me while she smoked and tilted her head toward Aaron and mouthed, "He's heated" to me as if I didn't know.

Aaron sat up while he played the game and talked loud when something didn't go the way he planned.

Misa tried to make conversation, "Aaron, I like your house. I know you didn't decorate it yourself."

Aaron smiled and said, "Nah, I don't decorate. My mom did that part for me. I just told her what colors I wanted, and she ran with it."

Misa laughed and said, "I knew it. At least it wasn't some chick you mess with."

Aaron looked at her and chuckled. He said, "I only mess with one chick, even though she's young as hell. I love her lil young ass, though." He never stopped playing the game while he talked to Misa. When he told Misa that he only messed with one chick she nudged me in excitement. I still felt uncomfortable because he was calling me young and I asked him not to. I didn't correct him because the stunt that I pulled earlier was something only a young chick would do. I decided to get the issue between us out in the open.

I asked, "Aaron, are you still mad at me?"

He glanced at me then looked back at the game. He said, "We'll talk about it later. It's not something that I'm about to talk about in front of your people. Feel me?"

I told Aaron okay, then I told Misa, "Okay, well I'll call you later."

Misa started laughing, and Aaron said, "You don't have to leave. Damn, your cousin is ill for that." He looked at me and laughed and said, "Chill out, we'll talk."

Misa said she was getting ready to leave anyway and gave me a hug. She told me to page her tomorrow and told Aaron bye and left.

After Aaron locked the door he turned the game off, and came and sat next to me. I said, "I know you're pissed and I'm sorry. It was stupid and I shouldn't have believed her over you."

He said, "Okay."

I said," Is that all you have to say? Okay?"

Aaron said, "You already know how I feel about this type of shit. So I don't need to say shit else. Don't let it happen again, I mean that."

I told him, "It won't. It was so stupid, I should never have believed her. I love you so much, and I know you wouldn't lie to me. I can't believe I fucked up like that."

He said, "I'm tellin' you, it's cool. It's really fucked up, though. When she saw me, I was looking for a present for you. I was happy to see her because I knew she would know what you liked. Then she kept looking at me and laughing. She ran off like she didn't hear me calling her name. I didn't know she had a twin either, but that's beside the point. I ended up calling Tez to get Danni's number but she was with him at his crib. I asked her what she thought I should get you to show you that I fuck with you…"

I looked at him and said, "That's why you were at the mall?"

He said, "Yep," as he reached in his pocket for a jewelry box and handed it to me.

When I opened it I saw that it was a thin gold herringbone chain. The chain was small, but it was real. He watched me as I sat speechless. He said, "You tripped so hard about my parents earlier, so I wanted to get you something to show you that I mean it when I say I love you. When I asked Danni she laughed and said to get you a herringbone."

I said, "Danni told you that?"

He said, "Yeah, I told her nothing too expensive because a nigga ain't rich, but she told me that you would love it, so I got it." I wasn't sure which shocked me the most, the fact that Aaron cared about me enough to buy me something that he knew I would love, or the fact that Danni had once again proved to be a great friend. I was starting to feel bad because I couldn't think of anything that I had done for Danni, yet she was always doing something for me.

I gave Aaron a hug, and told him I loved him. I knew that I loved Aaron more than life itself, and I still didn't understand why God blessed me with him. He was all that I could ask for in a man, and he proved that more and more each day. I was attracted to everything about him physically, but it was the mental aspect that affected me the most. I knew that he had gotten into my head and I was fine with that. Aaron hadn't told me anything wrong, so I had no problem trusting everything he told me. I didn't see why his mother was being such a bitch about it. She was acting like she hadn't ever been in love and felt like she needed someone. I could tell by the way she talked to her husband and looked at him that she was in the same situation I was in. I was sure that all the men in their family had the same charm about them. Regardless of how she felt, Gina was going to have to get used to me. I was determined not to go anywhere.

Chapter 30

The fuck test, you passed it...

I stayed with Aaron the remainder of the week and he was more impatient than ever with my menstrual coming to an end. He was asking me every single day, until Thursday evening I was able to say that I was completely done for the month. The truth was that I was a day before that, but I wanted to make sure I was fresh enough. For some reason, I hated the idea of having sex right after my period. When I told Aaron my menstrual was over, he sat up in the chair in his living room and said, "Damn...finally! Done bleeding...I guess you ready for me then?"

I said, "I guess I am." I gave him a look that I hoped would turn him on and it did. Aaron got up and picked me up off the couch that I was sitting on. I had taken a shower earlier so that I would be prepared if he was ready to have sex right then.

As he carried me up the stairs he asked me, "Don't you need to douche or something?" He had a frown on his face like he thought I was nasty for not douching.

I told him, "No, I don't douche. I don't know who told you that a woman *has* to douche. If a woman washes her pussy like she's supposed to, she doesn't have those problems. Anytime there's an odor there's something wrong. Period. If they're trying to wash away an odor, they need to go see a doctor. Any doctor will tell you that, I asked mine."

Aaron sat me on his bed and said, "Well, I know chicks that do and theirs smell cool, I guess. I won't front, though, not like yours." I gave him a cocky smile because it was the first time that I was sure I was right when I told him something.

I said, "It's so sad how many females run around fuckin' and don't even know the proper way to wash and take care of their own body. It's not safe to douche. It washes away bacteria that we need and the inside of the vagina cleans itself anyway. I make sure I'm clean, don't get it twisted. I just don't stick anything up inside of me." I smiled at him and said, "Do you want to taste me? I want you to see how clean it is."

Aaron smiled at me and said, "And you're smart too. I like that, a woman is supposed to know her body."

I grinned and asked, "You doubted me?"

He said, "Never. You doubted yourself."

Aaron stood in front of me and told me to take my clothes off. I stood up and watched him while I took my sweatshirt off, as well as the baggy sweatpants I was wearing. I had on a purple panty and bra set that he bought for me. I wore an underwire sheer bra that I barely could fit my small breasts into. I wasn't concerned about the size of my breasts because Aaron made me feel sexy. The look on his face was giving me the confidence boost that I needed. I asked him, "Can we turn off the lights?"

He replied, "Yeah…but after you take everything off." Aaron walked over to his stereo and turned the radio on while I took my panties off, then my bra last. He went under his bed and grabbed his tray where he kept his weed. He grabbed half of a blunt from the tray and lit it. I was naked by then, I went and turned the lights off and climbed in the bed with him. He was lying on his back with one hand behind his head and the other holding the blunt. I lay facing him not saying a word but watching his every move. Aaron purposely blew weed smoke in my face as he passed the blunt to me. I giggled and hit the blunt a few times while he played with my pussy.

I said, "Here, I'm cool." I handed the weed to him because I didn't want to be much higher than I already was. I was so relaxed from smoking that I could have fallen asleep. Aaron put the blunt out then took his clothes off and lay on his back.

"Come here," he said. I was already lying next to him but I knew he wanted me on top of him. I was ready to have sex but I wasn't sure if I was ready to ride him. The women in that video made it look easy but it also looked painful. He lifted my body on top of his and kissed me with his tongue. We kissed briefly until he pulled me up by my waist so that I was sitting on his face. He opened my legs wider and gently sucked on my clitoris while I tilted my head back and moaned. Aaron had his hands wrapped around my ass as he guided my movements. He slid his tongue in and out of my pussy while I rode his face like it was a dick. I had my hands on the wall in front of me until I came. As I reached my orgasm I kept one hand on the wall and the other on Aaron's head, I held onto his head for dear life as my body shook. When my orgasm came to an end I got off of Aaron and sat in between his legs. I was prepared to please him the way he pleased me.

He told me "lay down" while he bit his bottom lip. I lay on my back as he told me to do. I was still wiped out from riding his face, and I was still in shock that I had actually rode Aaron's face like that. I had no idea that he could be such a sexual person. I knew I shouldn't have been thinking about it, but I couldn't help but wonder what types of things he'd done with Keisha. I knew he didn't lick her the way he did me, but I did think they were probably nasty together. As Aaron climbed on top of me he said, "I didn't know you could be such a freak." He kissed my cheek, then my neck while he told me to relax.

My heart started beating fast because I had an instant flashback of the night I fucked Joey. It was horrible and I didn't want a repeat of that. I said, "I'm relaxed for you."

Aaron didn't reply, he proceeded to go inside of me. I put my nails into his back while trying to close my legs. He whispered in my ear, "Stop running, baby, let me in."

I replied, "Okay, I'm trying."

He said, "It's gonna hurt a little bit." Aaron kissed me again while he tried to put his penis inside of me. I was shocked by his patience with me, and it further confirmed my love for him. He told me, "Open your legs, baby." I opened my legs as much I as felt I could and his penis went in. I hollered out loud as Aaron slowly pushed deeper inside while telling me that he loved me. He asked me, "Do you love me?" I didn't answer because I was busy grabbing the sheets and turning my head so that he couldn't kiss me anymore. I was starting to think his kisses were distracting me, and I needed to focus on the pain. I was pissed because I wasn't a virgin and it wasn't supposed to hurt the second time, or so I thought. Aaron stopped for a second and asked if I was cool, and I told him I was. He said, "Baby, if you're not cool, don't lie about it."

I said, "Aaron, I'm cool. Come on."

He shook his head and said, "I want your legs around my back." I wrapped my arms around his neck, and my legs around his back. He went in and out while I moaned in his ear. He didn't stop his thrusts until he moved my legs and held them open as wide as he wanted them with his hands. It was starting to feel exactly how I expected sex to feel, but I was afraid to move with Aaron because I thought I would start to feel pain again. Aaron told me, "Don't just lay there. Fuck me back." Joey hadn't asked me to join him so I had no idea what to do. I tried to move with the same rhythm as Aaron. When he pumped me, I pumped him back and that's when we connected. I moaned his name while he asked me, "You about to cum for me?" I didn't answer him because I was in my own zone. Aaron started moving differently, faster and more precise. He held my legs in the air, and it started to hurt like hell because he was going deeper, I didn't stop him because I was turned on. He said, "Oh shit, baby." Then he rested his head on the inside of my neck. I was overcome with emotion after what happened. I held his face in front of mine and kissed him with my tongue, he kissed me back then pulled himself out of me and rolled over. I could feel his semen dripping out of me, and the first thing I thought was that I hoped I wasn't pregnant. It seemed so stupid not to think about it prior to actually having sex.

Aaron lay on his back for a couple of minutes then popped up and jumped in the shower. He didn't ask me to get in with him, but I got in anyway. I stood in front of him and stared at him while he washed his body. He smiled at me and said, "What are you staring at?"

I said, "You." I was more in love with Aaron than ever, and I knew that I would be one of those females that changed after sex. He was mine, and it was that simple.

He grabbed my towel from my hand and washed my body, then he pulled me into his chest and hugged me. He said, "You good?" I told him I was good, but really I was more than good. I was great because I was in love.

After Aaron and I had sex, I felt better leaving him and going back to my mother's house. I figured that he wouldn't need sex often, as long as I made a point to give it to him at least once a week. I had already called my mother and she was expecting me home sometime throughout the weekend. She didn't seem excited but she didn't seem upset either. I was hoping things wouldn't be as bad as they had been before. My mother informed me that I would sleep on the couch in the living room, or the floor in my old room since Angel was using my room. I wasn't happy about it, but I knew that I didn't have a choice in the matter. I asked Aaron to drop me off at Danni's mother's house. I told Danni that before I went back to my mother's that I would have Reiki done. That was my word and I was going to stick to it. I felt it was the least I could do since I was such a liar when I stayed in the house with them. I called Diane and she was happy to hear from me. She told me that she had just got done praying for me and then I called. I asked her about Reiki, and she said she would be glad to.

Aaron asked me if I wanted to stay with him, but I declined. Somehow I knew he was being polite, but as much I felt he cared I knew that I couldn't stay there with him. His mother would have had a fit, and I didn't have the patience to deal with her. He took me to Danni's house and walked me to the door with my bags. I cried when he was about to leave because the realization that I was going to be in no man's land was getting to me. I was concerned that he would forget about me.

Diane walked up to me and put her arm around me while Aaron stood there watching with his hands in his pocket. She told me, "Baby, he will be back, because he loves you. Maybe not when you want him to, but he will be back."

I ignored Diane because she didn't know what she was talking about. Aaron told me to come outside with him and I did. I was crying so hard that he didn't say anything. He just let me rest my head on his chest. After a while he said, "You don't think I'll come see you?"

I told him, "It'll be different, and you know it will."

He replied, "Well, I told you to stay with me, but once again, you think I'm playin' around or something." I told him I couldn't do that because now my mother knew where I was, and she might come looking for me. I didn't want to get him in any trouble. Aaron said, "I doubt she will come looking for you, she hasn't all this time. At some point she will get tired of chasing you anyway, and say fuck it, but that's on you. I'll come see you, that's my word."

I started crying again because of the thought of being without him. He said, "Heaven, you act like you're moving to Africa. Damn, I said I would come see you. All you gotta do is say you're staying with your cousin for the night and you can come spend the night. It's not that serious. Chill out. Now give me a hug, I gotta go." I gave him a hug. He kissed me on the lips and told me, "Don't be giving my pussy away." He told me to call him later and tell him how things were going over at my mother's. I told him I would and he left.

Chapter 31

All I really want is to be happy…

I went back into the house, and Diane was waiting for me. She gave me a hug and said, "Young love…baby, it hurts, but if and when he comes back into your life you'll know it's real. If he doesn't, life goes on." I nodded while thinking that I wanted her to shut up. Diane asked if I was ready for my Reiki Treatment. I told her I was, and asked her what I should expect.

She said, "You should expect to feel relaxed."

I followed her downstairs into her basement and asked her, "What religion is this?"

She said, "I'm glad you asked me that. Reiki isn't religion based, it's more spiritual based than anything." She laughed and said, "Heaven, I'd be afraid if you didn't ask me questions. You never cease to amaze me. I can't wait to see you blossom." I didn't respond because I was taking in everything that I saw. I would never have guessed there was a whole set up downstairs, dedicated to Reiki treatments.

Diane had a massage table with a fleece blanket covering it, and she had beautiful pictures hanging that represented calmness and peace. I also saw crystals, and oils that she told me were a part of the Reiki treatment because they have different vibrations and healing properties. Diane patiently watched me look around the room, as I picked things up. I held up a beige stick that had a string wrapped around it and said, "What's this?" She told me it was called sage, and she used it for smudging. I asked her what smudging was and she told me that it removed negative energy that could otherwise remain in your home. She explained that she was very choosy on who came in and out of her house but sometimes she allowed outsiders in because that was the kind of heart she had. Diane said that was her main reason for keeping sage around at all times. I listened as she told me that she typically smudged her home before and after different people came in and out. I commented, "Is the reason your house always has a welcoming vibe to it? Like, it feels safe."

Diane smiled and told me, "Yes, that has a lot to do with it. That's why I had to ask you to leave. It's my responsibility to be leery of who comes in and out of here since it's my home. Negative energy affects your aura, and it can cause unnecessary stress. I've had enough of that in my lifetime so I try to keep my home the safest place on earth for me. I could continue to cleanse the place, but if I have some idea of the culprit it seems only logical to get rid of it. Does that make sense?" I nodded, and she said, "That's why I don't like Dontez around my baby. He has a negative aura and it's sad because Danielle loves him. It's her life, and I can't control it, but I can control who's in my life. So he's not welcome in my home either."

I asked Diane, "What is an aura?"

She said, "It's something that surrounds you that always tells your true intentions in the form of colors." I was quiet for a second because I was thinking about asking Diane if she saw my aura. She was sitting in a chair watching me.

I finally said, "Diane, do you see my aura or not?" She smiled and told me she did. I said, "What do you see?" She told me that I had a beautiful aura, and that it was full of love. I laughed out loud and told her, "Okay, let's do this Reiki thing before I change my mind. You lost me with the full of love talk, unless we're talking about Aaron."

She shook her head and said, "Not just Aaron, Heaven. Try not to focus your entire life on Aaron. Make some things about Heaven. We're talking about Heaven today. Not Aaron. I see love, not just for Aaron but for everyone." She asked me to lay on the massage table.

I took my Nike Air Max tennis shoes off and sat them next to the table, and then sat on down. I asked Diane, "What made you start doing this anyway?"

She looked at me and told me, "I became really good friends with a lady after I lost my husband." Diane stopped talking then looked down at her wedding ring for a second then she continued. "You wouldn't believe that I met her at church since most people that go to church think Reiki is satanic. If only they knew how much better off they would be. They spend so much time focusing on being religious that they forgot about true spirituality."

I said, "Diane...?"

She laughed and said, "Oh, let me get back to what I was saying. So, the whole church knew what happened to me and they were very kind to me. But Evelyn stood out the most because she was very instrumental in the change that was to come. She was more than careful in her approach, and gave me tons of information before asking me if I was interested in Reiki. Honey, Reiki came at a time when I was depressed, sad, hurt, angry, and anything else you can think of. I really believe I got from Reiki what I needed to keep pushing. I began to pray more, my faith was renewed, I sang louder in the choir, and I had an inner peace that I never had in my life, even when my husband was alive. It's something that you'll have to experience to understand. I was going to church out of guilt, you know that feeling you get when you feel like you *have* to do something? It was not the love of God. Once I started getting Reiki treatments on a regular basis, I had a better understanding of God's love and mercy, but from his standpoint, not from humans'. It's a great feeling to walk in my truth, and not someone else's, Heaven." I smiled at Diane as I listened to her talk. She told me, "Here, take this and read it before we get started." I read through the piece of paper that Diane gave me, and the words were beautiful and simple. The title of the sheet was "Reiki Principles". I read it aloud as Diane watched me.

"Just for today, do not worry. Just for today, do not anger. Just for today, earn your living honestly. Just for today, show gratitude to every living thing. Just for today, honour your parents, teachers, and elders." I looked at Diane and thought that I had figured out the reason she was always so calm and cool. I was sure that if most people lived their lives this way the world would be a better place. I heard Christian people say "Let go and let God" but this was rarely what I saw. I continued my thoughts and laid back so that Diane could begin my Reiki. After

what Diane told me, and the information I had just read, I was curious to see how it would affect me.

Diane had soft music that made me feel calm, and the smell of the room was nice too. It reminded me of the lavender spray that my paternal grandmother sprayed around her house when I was little. I had my eyes closed, and Diane was very quiet aside from occasional heavy breathing like she was meditating. She gently touched the top of my head, the bottom of my head, around my neck, the sides of my face, my stomach, and other parts of my body for a few minutes at a time. She held my feet last, and I could feel her hands pulsating energy into my body through my feet. I wasn't sure how long Diane had been doing the Reiki on me because I was so relaxed. I felt like I was sleeping, yet I could hear the music in the background.

Danni was right when she told me it felt better than and blunt you could ever smoke. I felt more at peace than I had ever felt in my life. Diane mentioned that people that don't know about it assume that it's something bad. If I were being honest I would admit that I thought the same thing. From that day forward, I chose to believe that it was nothing negative. I would take Diane's advice with me forever. I had to learn to walk in my truth, not anyone else's. Common sense told me to be careful about mentioning Reiki to others. For the time being, I would simply enjoy it for myself.

When Diane was done she said my name softly, I didn't budge at first because I felt like I was in a trance. I woke up with a euphoric feeling and I was slightly sad because I wanted it to last longer. Diane asked me how I was and I told her I couldn't have been better. She told me to drink plenty of water and take it easy because it would help me release toxins from my system. I got up and asked her if I could lay down. Diane laughed and said, "Absolutely." We went upstairs, and I relaxed on the couch. I wasn't as sleepy as I previously thought I was. I ended up in the privacy of my own thoughts and that made me happy. It gave me the chance to figure things out. I knew I was going back to stay in my mother's house, but I also knew that I wasn't going back to deal with her bullshit. I felt the same for Angel, I wasn't putting up with her shit either. As I thought out my plan of action in dealing with my family, Danni walked in. The first thing she did was laugh out loud like she knew why I was so tired.

She asked me, "Did you come to get your Reiki?" I told her I did and she laughed again. I told her I wasn't expecting her to come over. She said, "I know, mama told me you were here when I called to check on her.

I asked, "So do you live with Dontez? Why is Diane so cool with you being there?"

Danni said, "It's not that she's cool with me being there, she's cool with him not being here. She really hates him, Heaven. She thinks he's bad news or something, but I wonder if her little aura readin' ass thinks she's perfect sometimes. You know Tez is cool."

I frowned at Danni and whispered, "Why are you talking about your mother like that? She's right in the next room!"

Danni smiled at me and said, "She can't hear me, crazy girl. Come here. I wanna tell you something." I got up to go upstairs with Danni. I was irritated with Danni and I wasn't sure about the new her. I wouldn't tell her that I didn't like the fact that she was so different since she had been with Dontez. She peeked her head into her mother's room and said hello to her.

I said, "What do you want to tell me? You fucked Dontez, right?"

She looked confused and said, "How did you know that?"

I said, "Danni, I'm not stupid. You spend too much time with him not to. Nobody had to tell me that. What changed?"

Danni looked defensive and said, "No, I bet Aaron's black ass told you!"

"Danni, watch it," I said. I didn't want to be rude to Danni but she had to know that she couldn't talk about Aaron to me like that. "If Aaron did tell me, which he didn't, he could only have found out from two people. If you didn't tell him, who did? That's who you need to be mad at."

Danni said, "Anyway, I love him, Heaven. Now I wonder if this is why you seem so stupid over Aaron. It has to be the sex."

I said with a smirk, "Danni, No. I don't see what makes me so stupid over Aaron. I was already crazy about him before we fucked. That was just the icing on the cake." I sat on Danni's bed and looked at her, but my mind was on Aaron. I hated even talking about him because I started feeling like I needed to see him at that moment. I decided to put it back on Danni. "What changed? I thought you were planning to wait until you got married." Danni always had an answer, and she was rarely uncomfortable. It was weird seeing her facial expression change showing me a lack of confidence in whatever her logic was. I said, "Well, you have to have a reason. You go from little miss tight pussy to this and not have an answer." I laughed to make light of the subject.

Danni looked serious, she told me, "I don't know, I guess I did it because I wanted to. He said he loved me and I believe him. He does all the things for me that my dad used to do for me and it makes me feel loved again. I don't have to ask him for anything and I miss that. He told me that he didn't even know that I was so mature until he got to know me; I think that's why we're so close. We both act older than our age."

I smiled and said, "So you fucked him." Danni threw her pillow at me and laughed. I said, "Are you on birth control?"

She said, "No..." Danni looked away while I sat on her bed staring at her. When she looked up at me I watched her in silence. She said, "Why are you looking at me like that?"

I said, "Danni, your mother has to know you're fucking him. Come on now, ask her to get you some pills before your ass gets pregnant."

Danni insisted that her mother didn't have any idea about her and Dontez having sex. She told me, "Trust me. My mama would ask me, and besides that..."

I looked at her and cut her off. "Besides what?"

"One day he asked me to have his baby, and I might do it. I hope I'm pregnant right now."

I said, "Bitch, are you crazy for real? I love Aaron so much, you just don't know. But I don't want a baby with him yet. Not until I get some shit out of life."

Danni nodded, but she really wasn't hearing me. She said, "So what are you about to do? You should come with us, ain't like you have a ton of options." I wasn't done with our conversation but Danni was, her decision had already been made. We laughed as we got ready to leave. I told Diane that I was leaving with Danni, and gave her a hug. I wasn't sure when Danni became so distant with her mother but I thought it was sad. I would have given anything to have a normal mother that loved me. Danni had that and yet she rejected it. Danni gave her mother an impersonal kiss on her cheek and told her she would see her later. We waited outside for Dontez, I had my bags with me once again.

I asked Danni, "So is there any reason we're standing outside? Do you know when he's coming?"

"I told him I would page him when I was ready. He said he was stopping by Aaron's house," she said, giving me a weird look.

"Oh," I replied.

Chapter 32

I've been around enough to know enough...

Dontez pulled up a few minutes later and jumped out of his old car. He had on a Kansas City Royals baseball hat to the back and a white t-shirt. His black jeans were starched heavily which made it to where you couldn't miss the crease in them, he even had a crease down the front of his t-shirt. I stood on the porch and watched in shock because every time I saw Dontez he was shining more and more. He had gold rope earrings in his ears and a thick herringbone chain around his neck. I liked the thin chain that Aaron bought me a lot more than Dontez's chain. He walked up to Danni and said, "Let's ride, baby girl."

Danni looked at him the same way I looked at Aaron and went to get in the car. Dontez was slowly starting to come up, but I still couldn't see what Danni saw in him. I said, "What's up, Dontez?"

He gave me a hug and said, "What you been up to?"

I said, "Nothing, now help me with my bags, I'm coming with you and your girl."

He said, "Does Aaron know?" Dontez grabbed a few of my bags, and I grabbed the rest as we walked toward his car.

I told him, "It doesn't matter if he knows or not. You act like he's my daddy or something."

Dontez said, "I'm tellin' you, I'm not getting mixed up with y'all's bullshit. I just left the nigga's crib and he told me not to have you over my house. That nigga is scared something might happen to you over my house."

I rolled my eyes at Dontez and said, "Damn, is he your master or something? Okay…he told me the same thing. So what? I'm not staying here by myself, and I don't wanna go to my mama's house yet."

Dontez shook his head and said, "Man…you are so fuckin' hard headed." We got in his car and he sped off as he lit a cigarette. He took a few pulls then passed it to Danni.

She turned her nose up and said, "No, Tez, you know I'm trying to quit." Dontez chuckled like he thought she was talking bullshit.

I was sitting in the back seat thinking that I was proud of Danni when we rode past my father's house. My heart skipped a beat when I saw my father and Christopher Kyle sitting outside. I yelled, "Dontez, back up! I need to go see my brother!"

Dontez said okay and turned around. He parked in front of the house and got out so that I could climb out of his back seat. My father stood up when he saw me. Christopher Kyle ran as fast as his little legs would carry him. I immediately let tears fall from my eyes as I grabbed my brother and hugged him. He was bigger than he was the last time that I had seen him. I told him, "I missed you so much!" I kissed him on the cheek while he hugged my neck. Dontez and Danni sat in the car waiting patiently for me while I reunited with my family.

Christopher Kyle asked me, "What took you so long to come home, Heaven? I wanted to go back to the store." I walked to the porch where my dad was standing and watching me.

I told my brother, "I was trying to get back to you, but I had a lot of stuff to take care of." My dad was looking as calm as ever as I approached him. I said to him," I know you're mad that I didn't call you, but…" I was prepared to apologize while at the same time tell him that living in their house was driving me crazy.

He cut me off, "Offer no apologies, you handled everything how you saw fit. I knew you were okay because you're a survivor. If you want to act like a grown up, I'll treat you like one. I had to focus on getting my shit together anyway, Heaven. I'm trying to stay clean and I can't stress about a rebellious teenager." I wasn't sure that I agreed with being labeled rebellious and his words hurt my feelings. My dad smiled at me while I put my brother down to give him a hug. I held him tightly for at least two minutes. He continued talking to me after we hugged. "I've only stopped using for a month, but it's progress. Your brother needs me more now than ever. His mother is one crazy bitch; I should never have married her."

I asked, "Where is Sonya? I thought y'all would have broken up after everything that happened."

He said, "She's staying in a crazy house downtown for now. That silly bitch tried to kill her fuckin' self."

I wasn't shocked at all. I asked him, "So you stay here with Christopher Kyle?"

My dad answered in a rude tone. "Who else do you think is going to stay here with him?"

Ignoring his rudeness, I said, "I was asking because Sonya said she was done with you when she told me to get out, so I didn't think she would let you stay here. Did you know she kicked me out and I had to figure out where I was going to live? That's one of the reasons I didn't call you or try to come back."

My father looked at me like I was crazy and said, "Well, there's nothing I can do about it now. I could stand here and say sorry, but what good would that do? It's not going to change anything. The fact will still remain. I hope you know now that in life, all you ultimately have is yourself. Let that be a lesson to you. It'll make you stronger and more independent to think that way. What do you want me to do? Baby you? Tell you that daddy will make it better? I can't. This is the real world, Heaven."

I stood staring at my father in disbelief. Was I wrong for thinking that the things he mentioned were exactly what I wanted? I needed to hear from someone that everything would be okay, and I needed to hear that somebody had my back. I hated feeling like I was all alone in the world, but I already knew it before he said it. It bothered me that my father was so fucked up in the head that he really thought of the relationship with his only daughter as a real world situation, instead of an opportunity to gain my trust back and have a decent relationship. I told my father I was leaving. I hugged Christopher Kyle and told him that I would be back to see him soon. He cried and tried to leave with me, but my father grabbed him and gave him a look that told him to get his emotions together.

My father hugged me again and said, "Don't be a stranger, call me sometime." I told him that I would and I meant it. As I walked away, I turned around and blew Christopher Kyle a kiss. Watching him cry broke my heart, but I had to leave. The thought of Christopher Kyle being alone with my father and his temper concerned me. What bothered me more than anything was the fact that I couldn't do anything about it. He didn't mention the money that Aaron had given to him and I didn't either. My father said he was drug free and I wanted to believe him, but I wouldn't be able to live with myself if he hurt Christopher Kyle over twenty dollars.

Chapter 33

I got no time for fake niggas...

Once I was back in the car with Dontez and Danni I was calm and quiet. Danni asked if I was okay as Dontez drove and chained smoked cigarettes. I watched my surroundings like Aaron told me to do when I was in a foreign place. I didn't feel safe at all when I saw where Dontez lived. My first instinct was to call Aaron, but I knew I couldn't because he would be upset that I chose not to listen to him. Dontez and Danni got out the car like they were completely comfortable. I followed them but I was uncomfortable.

When we walked into the house there were people everywhere. It looked to me like the standard uniform was white t-shirts and jeans. I saw at least six males and a few females. I followed Danni through the smoky, dirty house and into a back room where she told me to put my things. My bags were still in the car and that was where I planned to leave them. I told her thanks, but no thanks.

After I looked around for a few minutes, I said, "What the hell is going on? Niggas shootin' craps in his house? Bitches braiding hair and looking mean as hell. This place is dirty and whose baby is that running around with a diaper hanging off his ass?"

Danni said, "Girl, this is normal, it'll calm down in the middle of the night. Don't be judging people like you used to, that's not cool. Everybody here is cool, they don't fight unless they get drunk and they always forget about it the next day. The baby is the chick braiding hair, we all watch him for her when she's making bread. She braids Aaron's hair sometimes too."

I wasn't concerned that she braided my boyfriend's hair at all. I wondered why nobody had changed her baby's diaper, since Danni claimed that they all jumped in to help out. I said, "I'm ready to go." I couldn't believe Danni was hanging out with these types of people.

Danni said, "Come on, let's go to Tez's room."

I followed her and said, "I thought Tez had his own house, looks like he's staying in a dope house."

Danni said, "I mean, they do hustle out of here but it's not like it's a real dope house. It's all of their house, really."

I said, "You let him fuck you here? What if someone walks in?"

Danni sighed and said to me, "Just relax here. I'll get you something to smoke on."

I said, "No thanks. They probably put coke in their shit." I laughed.

Danni said, "No they don't, well not Tez. I asked him to stop doing that so you're cool smoking his if you want it. He said it didn't make him any higher anyway, just made the weed taste funny."

I tried not to look as shocked as I was and I chose not to acknowledge Danni saying that Dontez added coke to his weed. There wasn't any point in mentioning it to Danni anyway. She seemed to be impressed with everything Dontez did. I told Danni, "I'm cool. I don't want to smoke anyway." Danni was standing in front of me biting her lip and in deep thought. I asked her, "What's wrong with you?"

She sighed," I need to go ahead and tell you..." I didn't respond to her, I just looked at her. She said, "Remember when I told you that I want to have Tez's baby?"

I asked her, "How could I forget?" Now it was Danni's turn not to respond. My eyes got big and I said, "Oh my God. Please don't tell me you got pregnant by him."

Danni said, "Yep...I'm pregnant. I know you think I'm stupid, but I don't care. We both wanted a baby, he wants a girl, and I want a boy."

I said, "Danni..."

She cut me off. "I don't want to hear it. It doesn't matter. I love him, and he loves me." The air was thick in the room because Danni was defensive and I was upset with her. I knew she was missing love, I was too. I just didn't think it was serious enough to get pregnant on purpose with or without Dontez wanting a baby.

I sat on Dontez's twin bed with Danni while we listened to music that was louder than it needed to be. I wasn't sure what else to say to Danni but she was ready to defend herself when or if I decided to say something.

Dontez and his friend walked in, Dontez was holding a red cup in one hand and a bottle with a sip of liquor left in it. Dontez said, "Y'all cool? Why y'all sittin' in here being all antisocial?" He looked at me like it was me that caused us to be secluded from the crowd.

I said, "I don't mind going in there with everybody else."

Dontez said, "Yeah right, you ain't tryin' to go in there with them. I saw the types of bitches you hang with. The prissy stuck up type." I chose not to dignify Dontez with a response.

His friend said to me, "What's up with you, I'm Pooh." Pooh held his hand out for me to shake it so I did.

I said, "I'm cool."

Dontez laughed and said, "Ol' stuck up ass."

I turned around and looked at Danni and she was just as offended as I was by her facial expression. I looked at him and said, "Don't tell people that please."

He replied, "My fault, Heaven. I'm drinkin' and shit. I'm trippin'."

Danni told him, "Drinkin' or not, that shit ain't cool. You do that shit every time y'all get around people. That's not cool, Tez." Dontez shot her an evil look and she matched his stare. I didn't want to cause problems with Dontez and Danni, especially with her being pregnant now.

Pooh said, "Stuck up or not, you are pretty as hell to be so dark. Yeah, I'm feelin' you." If there was one thing I hated it was to be told that I'm pretty to be dark skinned, it wasn't a compliment. It was a statement that suggested that typically girls with dark skin were unattractive, so I should be extremely flattered that I'm unlucky enough to be dark skinned, but lucky enough to be considered pretty. I looked Pooh up and down and decided to ignore him because I didn't know how rowdy he could become. He was short and stocky with a big head. His hands were big and I didn't want to get knocked out trying to defend myself. Pooh was persistent, "So shit, what I gotta do to get with you? Can I call you?"

Before I could respond, Dontez spoke up and said, "Bro...that's Aaron."

Pooh never took his eyes off of me and said, "Aw shit...well, that's cool. I'm not a player hater. It's all good."

Dontez continued, "Bro, I don't know what she did to that nigga...but he's looney over her. He was pussy whipped before he even got the pussy."

I was done with Dontez's mouth. I said, "How the fuck would *you* know? You need to watch your mouth because you're talking reckless right now. You don't know what the fuck you're talking about."

Dontez looked like he was embarrassed but he kept talking. "I know what I'm talking about, you had that nigga open the first time he saw you. I shouldn't have told him anything about you."

Danni spoke up and said, "Why wouldn't you tell her anything? Why would that be cool?" Dontez ignored Danni's question.

Pooh said, "Damn, nigga...do you want her or something? If that's his girl then that's what's up. You can't be talkin' about the nigga to his girl, what the fuck?"

Dontez started talking louder than necessary, "I'ma put it to y'all like this..." Before he finished his sentence he held his red cup in the air and grooved to the music for about five seconds while we all watched him make a fool of himself. He continued, "It's hella niggas out here right now that wanna kill me. I robbed niggas, fucked the bitch they love, man, I even sold a fiend some bad dope one night. I don't give a *fuck*. Y'all can add Aaron to the list. You feel me? I ain't running from none of these hoe ass niggas out here. Now what?"

I said, "Aaron's not dumb enough to stoop to your sorry ass level. You're the worst kind to have around, I don't fuck with you. I feel sorry for Danni. I don't know what the hell she sees in your ugly ass."

Danni said, "Heaven...chill. He's drunk. This shit is about to go too far."

Dontez said, "You chill! I'm not near faded. She got me fucked up. I'm not Aaron, talkin' clever to me will get her fucked up."

I stood up. "What? I'll get fucked up? Really? Nigga I would *never* talk to Aaron the way I talk to you. You should know that by now."

Pooh stood in between us, Dontez was trying to move around Pooh so that I could see him. Pooh was holding him back while he yelled, "Yeah, bitch. You'll get fucked up." Dontez lifted his red cup and tried to throw it in my face. The look in his eyes was full of hatred toward me. His aim was off so the cup and the brown alcohol flew against the wall.

Danni jumped up and yelled at Dontez, "Are you crazy?"

Dontez told Danni, "You defendin' this ho? Oh, it's like that! You can take care of your own baby. Fuck both of y'all bitches." I looked at Danni who didn't say a word to Dontez, she narrowed her eyes at him like she was trying to see through him. Pooh pushed Dontez against the wall that he was standing in front of. Dontez looked disoriented as he tried to throw a punch at Pooh and missed.

Pooh told him, "Calm down, nigga, before I have to hurt you for real. You trippin' because you want the nigga's girl. Bitch ass nigga." Dontez was still yelling obscenities at me while wrestling with Pooh as I walked out of his room and asked one of the girls for a phone.

The house was loud from the banging that Dontez and Pooh were doing, and the music that played nonstop. I stood in the living room with Danni right next to me. As I paged Aaron I told Danni, "I don't know what you're going to do. You need to have an abortion. What if the baby comes out like him? That would be horrible." I asked Danni for the number to the house and put the number in and hung up the phone.

Danni said, "Heaven, I would never have no abortion. I think he was just drunk and talkin' shit though. We'll be cool."

"Danni, what he said was unforgivable. I wouldn't even let him see my baby."

Danni snapped at me. "Well, it's not your baby, it's mine. I'll forgive him if I want to. He's my baby daddy, and he'll always be in my life."

I shrugged. "I wish you hadn't ever met his dusty ass." The phone rang as Danni was preparing to defend her relationship.

Aaron's number came up as Dontez walked into the living room yelling. "You can get the fuck out! Both of y'all can!" I ignored his request as I asked Aaron to pick me up as soon as possible. Pooh was behind him threatening to hit him if he tried to hit me.

Aaron said, "What are you doing over there?"

I told him, "Dontez was taking me to my mother's house, and he stopped over here first. He is trippin' right now. Please come get me."

Aaron said, "Who's that yelling?" I told him it was Dontez, and he asked, "Who is he yelling at?"

I told him, "He's yelling at me! He's drunk and saying all types of shit. He tried to throw a cup of Paul Masson at me!"

Dontez was in the background yelling, "Fuckin' right I did! Bitches talk shit they get fucked up where I come from. It's nothing."

Aaron calmly said, "I'll be there. Go sit on the porch or something."

I walked outside to Dontez's car to get my bags. Danni followed me quietly. I said, "Are you staying here?"

She told me, "I might as well, he'll mess around and get hurt. I'll look out for him. Him and Pooh fight like this every time he drinks. Everybody else knows how to walk away but you and Pooh." I rolled my eyes at Danni because I didn't understand her logic. She made it seem as though we were wrong for not walking away when Dontez was disrespectful.

I sat on the porch as I listened to Dontez in the house talking loud. "She wants a nigga that ain't about shit. Feel me? A nigga that eat off his daddy's money and shit. Just cuz his daddy fuck wit houses, he wanna fuck with houses. Nigga, do you, you doin' what yo pops want you to do. The fuck? What type of bitch would fuck with a nigga like that? She scared to fuck with a nigga that move with the gritters. The niggas that don't fear no nigga, you dig?"

Pooh came outside with a blunt in his hand. He was shaking his head and said, "Let me get this straight. Tez like you, but she's his baby mama…and y'all friends. Is that right?" He took a drag off the blunt while I looked at Danni. She was looking hurt and it was clear why she would be.

I said, "Danni, I don't know what his problem is with me, but I would never mess with him knowing how you feel about him."

Danni sighed and said, "Don't you think I know that, Heaven?"

Pooh said, "I see y'all got some shit y'all need to talk about," and went in the house and shut the door. We could hear him yelling and telling Dontez to shut the fuck up when he walked in the house.

I asked Danni, "Why are you acting funny with me?"

She told me that she wasn't trying to act any differently toward me but she couldn't help it because it frustrated her knowing that Dontez would never feel for her the way she felt for him. She told me that she knew that he liked me before I even realized it, but she thought his feelings would change. It hurt me to know that Danni had heard all the things Dontez said that night, yet she chose to stay with him. The very thought of the man I love telling me to take care of our child by myself would be too much to bear. I hugged Danni and told her that I loved her regardless of anything.

Chapter 34

And his name is Mitchell Bade...

Aaron pulled up and got out of the car wearing a red Kansas City Chief's skully cap and a long sleeved t-shirt with a pair of blue jeans. The Jordan XIII shoes he wore looked brand new. When he got to the porch I stood up and he kissed me on the cheek. He said, "What's up, baby? You good?" Danni rolled her eyes and I knew it was because she thought I would become more helpless than I was previously.

I hugged him and said, "I'm cool, let's just go." Aaron took my bags and put them in his car then told me to go wait in the car while he went to holler at Dontez. I begged him not to go into the house but he insisted and walked in the house. I stood next to Aaron's car with Danni and waited for whatever was to come. Dontez came out of the house first and he wore a nervous look on his face. Aaron looked evil as he walked behind Dontez, Pooh walked behind Aaron as well as the gang of others that were in the house and felt the need to investigate what was going on. Aaron looked like he was waiting for Dontez to do something stupid so he would have a reason to hit him. Dontez stood in front of me with his head to the side. Aaron roughly puts his hand around the back of Dontez's neck and pushed him closer to me.

Aaron said, "You got something to say to her, bro."

Danni had tears in her eyes and ran in the house without saying anything.

Dontez said, "My fault, I fucked up." He tried to walk away, and that's when Aaron became more offended than he already was. He walked up on Dontez and said, "You think you can talk clever to my girl, then throw a fuckin' drink in her face?" Aaron shrugged his shoulders and said, "That apology ain't enough." I hadn't ever seen Aaron so angry, and as mad as I was at Dontez, I didn't want to see him get beat up.

I said, "It's okay, Aaron, he apologized. Let's just go now." Aaron glanced at me but didn't respond to my request.

Dontez said, "So what now, nigga? We 'bout to fight over your bi—"

Before Dontez could finish his question, Aaron punched him in his face so hard that he stumbled and fell onto the ground. Pooh saw me about to run and try to hold Aaron back and grabbed me.

He said, "I don't want you to get hurt, baby. Stay right here and don't move." I stood where I was in front of Aaron's car, and yelled at Aaron to leave Dontez alone. Though Dontez was wrong for the things he did, I knew that it was coming from a hurt place, so I did have some sympathy for him. I couldn't believe that nobody broke the fight up. Dontez was lying on the ground holding his jaw, while Aaron told him to get up. Dontez wouldn't get up and it seemed to make Aaron more upset.

Dontez tried to give a real apology but it was too late. "Heaven, I'm sorry…you know I love you like a sister, you know that. Get these niggas, they trippin' like we don't always do that shit."

Aaron ignored the apology from Dontez and said, "Nigga, I said get the fuck up." Dontez tried to get up and lay back on the ground with his hands up.

Pooh said, "That bitch ass nigga just want somebody to feel sorry for his ass." Pooh walked to where Dontez was laying and kicked him repeatedly all over his body. Dontez started coughing and begging for mercy.

By that time I was so scared I was shaking, I said, "Aaron, please, I don't want y'all to kill him. Let's go, I'm begging you." Aaron told me to get in the car and I did. He got in the car after I did and drove to his house. I looked out the window the entire ride to his house because I didn't want Aaron to know that I was crying. The thought of running away in tears really got under my skin. I would never have expected Danni to be the crying type and I figured she didn't want to be my friend anymore, I had brought a lot of trouble to her life and I don't think I would want to be my friend either.

Chapter 35

I can feel your water...

I sat in Aaron's living room on the couch watching him play his PlayStation. He noticed I was quiet and said, "It's over now, baby. Relax."

I said, "Aaron, I didn't know you could get upset like that."

He said, "Why would you have known that? Blame your bro, Tez, for lettin' his nuts hang tonight. You had to know that I had to handle it when you paged me to come get you. As long as I call you my girl, when a man disrespects you, he disrespects me. Feel me? If I let that bitch shit ride, he'll think it's cool to talk greasy to you and other shit all the time. Fuck that. This nigga is mad at you for not fuckin' with him." As Aaron talked I listened to him and understood everything he said. He paused and smiled at me then said, "You must have that fire...you got niggas trippin' *before* they get the pussy."

I giggled and said, "I see Pooh told you what he said."

He smiled and said, "My lil nigga filled me in as soon as I walked in. That nigga Tez went in his room and shut the door like that was supposed to stop me from hollering at him."

I was glad to know that he had my back. I knew I didn't have Aaron's full attention because he was sitting up on the couch focused on playing the game. I stood in front of the TV and looked at him with a grin on my face.

He said, "Girl, move before you make me lose." I didn't move, I stood in front of him while taking all of my clothes off. Once I was completely naked I stood in front of him with one leg in front of the other while biting my lip the way he did to let me know that he wanted me. Aaron sat back and got comfortable so I sat in front of him and unzipped his pants. He told me, "Give me a minute while I finish this game." I decided to ignore his request and suck his dick while he played the game. Eventually, he sat the controller down and relaxed his head against the couch while I drove him crazy. He stopped me before he came and stood up. He took everything he was wearing off and sat them on the chair across from his couch. He told me to bend over and spread my legs. I put my hands on the couch to keep my balance and arched my back for him. The thought of wearing a condom hadn't crossed my mind but I heard him unwrapping one. After he put the condom on he put one hand on my waist and the other hand was used to rub my pussy. He told me, "Put it in." I still had my back arched while I took his penis and guided it inside of me.

As Aaron pushed himself inside of me I closed my eyes and rested my face on his couch. The thought of the doggy style position had never crossed my mind because it didn't seem exciting to me. I would never have expected to feel so much pleasure. Aaron was able to go deeper than he would have been in the missionary position. While I moaned, Aaron said, "Throw it back to me." I started throwing my ass back as he pumped me. When he asked me, "How you want it, baby?"

I said quietly, "Like that."

Aaron gently slapped my ass and said, "I can't hear you, tell me how you want it."

I knew he wanted to hear me talk shit back to him. Even though I was uncomfortable, I replied, "Don't stop, daddy…I want it just like…that." My tone turned me on as well as Aaron. We climaxed at the same time. I followed Aaron into the bathroom and we washed our private parts and got dressed. I dosed off in Aaron's lap watching him play his game.

I woke up in Aaron's bed the next day. I sat up and looked at Aaron. He was showered and fully dressed. I said, "I don't remember coming up here."

He said, "No shit, I carried you up here."

"Why didn't you wake me up? You look like you have somewhere to go."

Aaron said, "I just got back. I just took the iguana to my sister's for my nephew." He grinned at me and said, "You're a heavy sleeper. Get dressed; I'm taking you to my parents' house to eat breakfast." My heart skipped a beat. I told him I didn't want to, but he told me that he really wanted me to get to know his family. He went and grabbed clothes for me out of his car while I got dressed. I wore a white t-shirt under a thin pink jacket that stopped at my waist with yellow sleeves and a pair of blue jeans. The only shoes I had that would look halfway decent were my black Doc Martens. I didn't feel like taking the time to deal with my hair, so I brushed it into a ponytail.

When I was finished getting dressed Aaron said, "You look cool, baby, but don't you ever do anything else with your hair? You should let moms fuck with it." I rolled my eyes at Aaron and told him that I would never let his mother touch my hair because she would probably burn it on purpose. He laughed and said, "I don't think you believe that."

Chapter 36

I'm head over heels in love, and I need to know...

I didn't bother to ask where Aaron's parents lived because I assumed they lived somewhere near Aaron. We drove forever, at least it seemed that way to me. On the way to his parents' house I told Aaron that he had to take me to my mother's after we left his parents'. I knew my mother was expecting me, she told me when I talked to her that she had enrolled me in school in case I was still interested in going. Aaron told me that he would take me after we spent the day together. I said, "It can't be too late, you don't know how my mother is. It won't be pretty if it's late."

He asked me, "What's late?" I told him that I honestly didn't know because it seemed like anytime was too late. I was hoping things had changed since I had been gone. Aaron casually said, "She'll be alright. I mean, she gotta be, right? If she says it's too late all you can do is say sorry and be done with it. What's the worst that can happen? I doubt she'll punish you. If anything she'll put you out...if she does that, just call me. It's been too long since you been there and honestly two women can only stay in the house together for so long. That's why my sister moved out when she was eighteen. She was ready to get on my mother's head but she knew she couldn't."

I looked at Aaron and asked him, "How come she couldn't?"

Aaron frowned at me and replied, "What do you mean how come she couldn't? Because that's her *mother, that's why.*" I got quiet. Aaron noticed instantly and asked me if I would ever hit my mother. I told him that I wouldn't do it again, but that I had before. He was turned off by what I told him.

I said, "Aaron, I know it's wrong to hit your mother. But you don't know my mother. She was making me want to do more than that to her. I was sick of her bothering me all the time."

He still wasn't impressed with my answer. "I don't ever wanna see you disrespecting her around me. That shit ain't cool." I nodded but didn't give him a definite answer because being in my mother's house could cause things to go either way.

I checked out the area we were in and I wondered why anyone would want to live in a place that literally had dirt roads. I saw a bank, a McDonald's, a high school and not much else besides houses that were about the same size and style as my mother's. I asked Aaron where we were, as he parked in front of a neat well-kept house.

He said, "It's Lees Summit, you have never been here? It's not that far from your hood." I told him that I had heard of Lees Summit but I had never been. I never had a reason to. I thought the neighborhood my mother lived in was full of white people. Aaron's parents were surrounded by white people.

We walked up to the door and I asked Aaron why he lived in such a bad area and his parents lived in a nicer area. He said, "What makes where I live bad? That's just your opinion. I feel better being around my people, so I'll always stay in the hood. They feel better out here, for whatever reason. I do me and they do them. It's that simple." Aaron knocked at the door like a visitor and I found that to be weird too. When Angel moved out she was able to keep the key to my mother's house.

I said, "You don't have a key?"

Aaron shook his head at me and said, "Why would I need a key to their house? I don't live here. This is their house, not mine."

I told him, "But they have a key to yours."

He smiled and said, "True. I live by myself though. If I lose a key, my mother will always have it."

Gina opened the door and said hello to us. She seemed to be in a pleasant mood, and that made me relax a little more. Aaron held the door so that I could walk in and his mother gave me a hug. It was awkward, but I hugged her back. Aaron's father James came and hugged me as well. Aaron left me in the walkway making conversation with his parents while he went into the kitchen to comment on how good everything looked. Gina told me I could go and have a seat while she finished setting up.

I looked around the house and it was decorated beautifully. The furniture was large and plush. There were gold chandeliers in the living room and the family room. I saw a painting of an African American woman wearing a white dress with ballerina shoes hanging over the fireplace as I walked past the living room. I noticed that nobody walked in the all white living room that was right off the walkway. Aaron sat next to me on the love seat in the family room. James sat across from us watching the big screen TV. Aaron poked me in my side and asked if I was cool. I was cool, and comfortable much to my surprise. I told Aaron that I loved the house, and James cut in. "I'm glad you like it, Gina spends so much money decorating that I'm almost in the poor house."

I laughed and said, "It's money well spent."

James jokingly said to Aaron, "Watch out, son, your future wife likes to spend money!"

I laughed and said, "I'll take good care of him, he won't mind it."

Aaron looked at me and laughed. "Yeah, right! You better learn how to ball on a budget," he replied.

James looked at me and said, "You noticed I said *future* wife, didn't you?"

Aaron said, "She is my future wife, if she acts right."

I felt like I had butterflies in my stomach. I noticed his father said future wife, but I wasn't sure why he said it. I knew that I only wanted to be with Aaron so the fact that he felt the same was refreshing. I gave Aaron a look that only a girl in love could give. His father said, "Y'all are young. It's cool to have feelings for each other. I met my wife when she was your age, Heaven. You two gotta still take care of business. Love is cool, but it's not enough to make a relationship work. Y'all both have growing up to do so just enjoy each other's company for now. Aaron, do you know exactly where you would like to be in five years? Heaven, do you?"

Aaron said, "Dad. Come on now, we talked about this. You know I know where I wanna be. That's what I'm saving for now."

James continued as Gina walked in and sat on her husband's lap. "Does Heaven know what your plans are?"

I spoke up and said, "I don't know what my plans are for next week, let alone the next five years. But I know that I love Aaron, and whatever his plans are I'll go with. He's smart, so I know whatever he wants to do will work for both of us." James looked at Aaron like he needed to tell me something.

Gina looked at me with sympathy and said, "Heaven, I know I was harsh to you the first time we met, and I sincerely apologize for that. I do need to tell you that you gotta come up with plans for yourself, baby. At some point, if you and Aaron do actually work, you'll see that your happiness shouldn't be waivered for his. A man will always do what makes him happy. It's in their nature. You have to figure out what to do to make you happy. I know he's my son, but I'm telling you this woman to woman."

Aaron looked annoyed with his parents. He said, "Is the food ready?"

Gina said, "It sure is, but go ahead and tell Heaven what your plans are." I looked at Aaron because his parents made me curious about what his plans were and the fact that he was trying to change the subject was alarming.

Aaron looked at me and said, "It's not even that big of a deal. My uncle owns a barber shop in Indiana and he's retiring so I'm thinking about buying it from him. I'm going to look at it and go over exactly what needs to be done to run it. If it sounds cool then I'll break bread with him."

My heart dropped, I was in a state of disbelief.

Aaron said, "Why are you looking like that? You act like I can't come back and take you with me."

I nodded but didn't say anything to Aaron. I couldn't believe he didn't tell me his plans were to move out of town yet he claimed that he planned to be with me forever. I felt sick to my stomach and I didn't have an appetite anymore.

Gina told Aaron and James to go ahead and eat without us, and she took me into her room to talk.

Aaron said, "Heaven. It's not that big of a deal."

I ignored Aaron and followed Gina down the hall. My heart was beating rapidly and I was fighting tears. There was no way I was moving out of town without knowing anything or anybody there but Aaron. Why would he assume that I was willing to go *that* far with him?

Gina told me to go sit down, so I pulled the chair from her vanity that sat against the wall. I looked down at the ground shaking my head. Gina sat on the king-sized bed watching me. Gina said, "Heaven…that's what I meant about men. They always know what they want. You have to always know what you want or at least have some idea." I didn't respond so she kept talking. "I asked Aaron as much about you as I could and he told me as much as he knew. My heart has really softened where you're concerned. I asked Aaron to bring you over today because I wanted to talk to you. It's funny because he went and found a girl that is like is mother in more ways than one…."

I looked up at her and asked her, "What does that mean, Gina?"

She told me, "Well, for starters…I come from a troubled background myself. Both my mother and father were alcoholics. When they weren't abusing each other, they were abusing all four of their children, including me. I met James at a time when I was just about done with life, and I was only fourteen. I know to you this doesn't sound crazy, but I knew instantly that I wanted him forever. That feeling has yet to leave me. It was more than him being handsome, it was the fact that he was protective of me, and he never hurt me the way others did. He *loved* me. I was drawn to him in a way that nobody understood. I felt like I needed him. I remember telling my mother, God rest her soul, that I needed James. She sat in her filthy living room holding a bottle of Canadian Mist whiskey and laughed until she practically choked. She told me that a woman shouldn't ever need a man. I felt stupid and small, but I couldn't shake the feeling of needing James, and I was okay with that. He told me he needed me too, just in different ways than I needed him. I chose to believe him. What he needed was for me to be his backbone through thick and thin. I found that it's okay for a woman to need her man, and vice versa. We were both afraid of losing the other so that made us constantly work at making each other happy. From the time I was fourteen, and he was eighteen we stuck by each other's side. Though James came from great parents, he understood that it was me and him against the world. He never judged me based on my upbringing. He always tried to make me better. He opened my eyes to so many different aspects of life that I taught our children based on what he taught me, not my parents. I probably shouldn't be telling this but I'm saying all this to say that it's okay to love your man, but you have to have a clear idea of where the other wants to go with everything. I believe you do love Aaron, and you need to tell him that he owed it to you to tell you his plans if he's that serious about you. Make sure that he needs you, and make sure that he loves you as much, if not more, than you love him."

I listened to what Gina said, and I couldn't believe what she told me. I assumed by looking at her that she would have come from a perfect family, but that wasn't the case. She told me that there had been problems along the way with her husband, but overall they had a strong relationship. Gina got up and gave me a hug and said, "Take your time, Heaven. I'm not saying break up with Aaron, but I am saying live your life while loving Aaron. I don't have any regrets because I've done all the things I wanted to do and the whole time I had a husband."

I told her, "I understand. I just can't believe he didn't tell me his plans. I can't move away, I don't want to. But I know I want him and only him."

Aaron walked in on our conversation and said, "I was gonna tell you today, so stop crying like that. It shouldn't matter if you love me like you say you do anyway."

I said, "Aaron, leave me alone. I don't have anything to say to you right now."

He spoke loud to me, "You don't have anything to say to me? Whatever."

Gina told Aaron to leave while we finished talking. After he left she said, "He'll be fine, he gets that from his father. They don't know how to let things go until it goes their way. I know that you mean something to him because I haven't seen him with one girl since he was in high school." I told her that I knew I meant something to him too, just because I knew. No other explanation needed. Gina stood up and said, "Okay, the next thing is your hair. Now I don't know if you've ever heard this but there are no ugly women, just lazy women. We gotta do something with your hair one of these days. You can't be running around looking like a chicken head." We both laughed, and walked out of the room.

I walked into the kitchen after Gina who had started making me a plate. I still felt sick so I didn't want to eat the plate of eggs, bacon, pancakes, and potatoes that Gina sat in front of me at the table.

James said, "Everything ok?"

Gina said, "Just fine." James and Gina walked out of the room and left me with Aaron watching me at the table. I tried to ignore him but his stare was bothering me.

He asked, "What's wrong with your food? Is it nasty?" I told him it wasn't nasty but that I just wasn't hungry. I asked him if we could leave and he said, "Not unless you tell me you love me."

"Do you think I stopped?" I asked. He told me he knew that I couldn't stop loving him. He just wanted to hear me say it. I said, "I love you, Aaron."

He came and sat next to me and said, "I love you too. I know I got you fucked up right now, but I wasn't about to leave without you." I shook my head and asked again if we could go. Aaron got up and threw my food in the trash, we told his parents bye and left. I felt good leaving Aaron's parents' house because of my new friendship with Gina. I never expected her to be so open and honest with me. I gave Aaron directions to my mother's house while we smoked a blunt. I told Aaron that I was done smoking because I couldn't shake the nauseous feeling that I had.

When we pulled in the driveway I got that depressed feeling that I always felt when I went home. Aaron looked at me and asked if I was cool. I told him, "Yeah, I'm fine. Why?" He said I looked flushed in the face, I did feel hot but I told him I was cool. Aaron got out of the car to help me with my bags and I said, "You're coming in?"

He said, "How else do you think these bags will get in the house?"

I said, "I'll grab them, don't worry about it."

Aaron said, "Girl, step aside. Ain't nobody worried about your house."

Chapter 37

Don't be afraid....

As we got closer to the front door we heard yelling. Aaron walked in front of me with a few bags. I opened the door since it was unlocked as usual and he walked in. He stood in shock at what he saw, I was numb to it. My mother was standing in the living room throwing plates against the wall and yelling, "Fuck you! I wish I never met you! You fat, black son of a BITCH!" In between throwing plates she would pick up anything that she could find and throw it with the intention of breaking it.

When my mother realized Aaron was watching her she said, "Leave it to Heaven to just pop up without calling some damn body." Then she looked directly at me, "You went and found you a black ass boy, didn't you? Two blackies together, how sweet."

Normally, I would have reacted to her comments, but I was trying to be respectful. And for some reason, I felt calmer than I did before.

Aaron looked amused by her behavior. He asked me, "Where do you want these bags, baby?"

My mother repeated what Aaron said in a mocking tone. I ignored her and said, "We can take them to my room."

My mother ran up to me and got in my face. She said, "I don't want his black ass running all over my damn house! He might steal something!"

Aaron said, "Alright, I'm about to slide out, Heaven. Call me later." I took my bags from Aaron and walked him outside. He looked at me and said, "Is this normal? That shit is crazy as hell."

My mother was in the house screaming at the top of her lungs again. I knew that she didn't mind behaving any certain way when just our family was home. I was extremely mad because I felt that she could have shown some restraint when people came over. It was like she knew that she was embarrassing me yet she continued to do so because she needed the attention. She was saying that she hated her life and that she would be glad when she died. I told Aaron that it was normal, but I would just go and listen to music and go to sleep like I always did.

He hugged me and said, "Why do you want to stay here? Just come with me. I didn't know she was silly like *that*. I haven't seen this type of shit in my life." I told him that I wouldn't come with him. At first I wouldn't come to stay with him because it just didn't seem right to me being that we were so young. After I thought about a little more I decided that it shouldn't make a difference because we were going to be together anyway. Then I found out he planned to move to Indiana and that changed my whole mindset where Aaron was concerned. I had to decide if I wanted to do something like that. I had never thought about moving out of town, and he didn't even give me a clue that he wanted to move or buy a barber shop.

After Aaron left, I walked around the house because it had been so long since I had been there. Nothing had changed. Dale was laid across the bed looking fat and lazy, Leonard and Angel weren't home but I didn't bother to ask my mother where they were. I went into my room and began unpacking my clothes. My room didn't feel like my room anymore. There was shit everywhere that belonged to Angel. It was a total mess and unorganized which made me feel panicky and anxious. I was hanging my clothes up when my mother finally stopped her tantrum and walked into my room. If there was one thing that I learned once I came back it would have been to ignore my mother and she would stop. Sometimes I wondered if she was on alert waiting for people to come around so that she would be prepared to put on a show for them. I didn't close the door to my room because I didn't feel like dealing with the disrespectful behavior from my mother when she barged in.

She stood in the doorway and watched me saying, "I guess you think your shit don't stink. You got you an ugly boyfriend now, huh? Well if you think you gonna lay around here fuckin' all day you got another thing coming."

I said, "I would never have sex in your house." I had my back to her and I spoke as calmly as I possibly could.

My mother gave me the updates on everything negative that she could think of. "Well, ain't shit changed over here. We still broke, I still hate my job, I'll always hate this thing called life, your brother is failing everything in school, and Angel's dumb ass got kicked out of her place for letting some nigga sell drugs out of there. I swear, I gave birth to some real losers."

I still had my back to her while I organized my closet the way I liked it. I said, "It must suck to be you."

She got closer to me and said, "What the fuck did you say to me?"

I turned around and looked at my mother. Her eyes were bulging and wild looking. She was waiting for me to say something so that she could react violently. I asked her, "What do you want me to say, mama? There's nothing I can do for you. I'm asking you to let me stay here until I figure things out. Is that okay?"

My mother walked out of my room and hit the door on the way out, then said to Dale, "Dale, you better get that little smart mouth motherfucker in there! I'ma hurt her little ass, I swear to God!" I listened to my mother talk about me and I expected Dale to defend her. While I realized that I wasn't going to provoke her in any way, I was more than prepared to defend myself if she put her hands on me.

Dale said, "Sharon, leave that damn girl alone, she ain't did shit to you. Go sit yo ass down somewhere."

My mother slammed the door in their room and yelled at him about not being on her side.

I decided to give Tandra a call to let her know I was coming back to school in our neighborhood. I also needed to make her think that we were cool so that she would be shocked when I paid her back for lying to me about Aaron being with a girl at the mall. When I called the house, Zandra answered and was happy to hear from me. She said, "Tandra is never here anymore since she started messing with KD all the time." Tandra hadn't told me that she was dating KD and I found that to be weird since we were supposed to be friends.

I said to Zandra, "I know, she's brand new. She's been messing with him for like...how many months has it even been?" My tone suggested that I knew how long it had been but that it had slipped my mind.

Zandra said, "RIGHT! She really has been brand new for the past three months!" I thought to myself that she had been with him for a while, and hadn't mentioned a word to me at all. I asked Zandra not to tell her that I was coming back, because I wanted to surprise her. That was true. I did want to surprise her.

After I hung up with Zandra I called Danni's mother's house, and she picked up on the first ring. I asked her if she had seen Danni. She told me she hadn't since earlier. I said, "Is she gonna come back to your house? I can't keep up with her anymore, she's always with Dontez."

Diane paused for a second and said, "When's the last time you talked to her?" I told her it was Saturday night. She said, "Oh my goodness, Heaven. You don't know do you?"

I said, "Know what?"

Diane told me, "Dontez had been shot and killed by one of his friends at about two this morning. They were at his house." I dropped the phone and sat still for I don't know how long. When I picked the phone back up Diane was saying my name. I told her I had to go and hung up without waiting for a goodbye. I paged Aaron first then Danni and waited impatiently for someone to call me back. I knew that Dontez and I had a rocky relationship, but underneath all that I would always love him. For whatever reason, I truly believed that we would talk everything out and go from there. Now I would never have the chance. Aaron called back first and I asked him. He told me that he had just heard the same thing himself. One of his friends was over his house telling him that Pooh had been arrested and taken to jail for questioning.

Aaron asked me how I was doing and if I needed him to come chill with me. I told him I didn't need anything except for him to ask Danni to call me if he saw her in the neighborhood. He told me that he loved me and hung up. The odd thing was that I didn't shed a single tear when I got the news that Dontez had been killed. It wasn't that I wasn't sad, it was just that it felt unreal at the moment. I had to make myself realize that it was true.

In the process of me gathering my thoughts Angel walked in without saying a word to me. I didn't say anything to her either because I wasn't in the mood to entertain her. She started tossing my bags around and throwing my clothes around the room. When she saw me looking at her like she was crazy she said, "Why did you have to come back here? You're in the way. You should have stayed with that crack head."

I shook my head at Angel and asked her, "Where's *your* father at? You seem to know a lot about mine but not enough about your own." She was shocked that I talked to her that way. I was waiting for her next move because I was sick of her shit and I would beat her ass if I needed to. I wasn't sure why I hadn't acknowledged it before but she wasn't any bigger than me. The fear and intimidation that I once had was no longer there.

She said, "Well, I know where he's *not* at, and that's the crack house. Your father is probably sucking dick for a rock as we speak."

I laughed out loud at Angel and said, "And you're sure that's where my father is? Angel, just stop before you get your feelings hurt. When are you leaving anyway? I still can't believe you were stupid enough to let a nigga sell dope out of your house. Are you supposed to be his *ride or die*? Did you know that there are plenty of niggas out here that have money without selling dope?" I looked at her while shaking my head. "You didn't know that, did you? You're so dumb, I swear."

Angel was livid and it was all over her face. "I'm dumb, and you're a black ugly bitch. I look better than you, and everybody knows it. I don't care if I got kicked out of that shitty apartment, I'll find a hustler to give me the money to get another. Fuck you thought? That I was gonna be here? Broke? Like you?"

I was amused to say the least, the days of my mother and Angel suggesting that I wasn't good enough was over. They couldn't say anything to me that would make me love myself any less. In the time that I had been gone from the madhouse that belonged to my mother, I had met great people that taught me a lot about myself and life. I think the Reiki helped me develop inner peace and understanding. I wasn't perfect, but I was better off than I was before I left my mother's house. I told Angel, "You better pull it together, Angel. Your pretty face will only get you so far in life. Soon, nobody will give a fuck about your light skin, and okay-at-best face. You're really not very pretty. I never understood why light-skinned girls always think they're prettier simply because they're light-skinned." I had my arms folded across my chest as I talked to my sister.

She looked at me and said, "Why are you so evil?! You always hated me, Heaven!" Angel had tears in her eyes as she talked to me. I chose not to deal with her dramatics and walked out of our room. Before I walked out, I told her, "If you throw any more of my clothes I'm gonna beat your ass. I put that on my life."

Chapter 38

Can it be that you're the one and I am too blind to see?

Not much had changed about the school I attended. In fact, it was me that had changed. Everyone seemed so clueless and immature. They walked the halls without a care in the world. I purposely kept my distance from the kids I went to school with because I simply couldn't relate. I was quiet all day in most of my classes unless I had a question for the teacher. I was quiet all evening at home as well because I couldn't relate to anyone there either. Leonard was always in and out of the house. One day I was coming in from school and Leonard pulled in front of the house driving. Boomer was in the passenger seat grinning proudly. Leonard jumped out and said, "Heaven, did you know I knew how to drive? That nigga Boomer showed me how to drive when we started gettin' tilt's all the time." A stolen car was called a "tilt".

I said, "No, I didn't know you knew how to drive." I walked into the depressing house and did my homework in the room that I shared with Angel. I heard Leonard and Boomer speed down the street.

I didn't see Tandra around school at all, but she had to have known that I was back because I had a level of popularity that I didn't have before. The thing that was different this time was my confidence and the way I dressed. There was also the fact that I was aloof and it made people curious about me. For a while people didn't even realize that I wasn't technically a new student until they heard my name. I was sure that people had been talking, especially since I walked the halls with Zandra daily, yet Tandra hadn't shown her face. When I asked Zandra about her sister she didn't say much of anything except that she didn't see her much either. Common sense told me that she had talked to Tandra about me because she wasn't quick to volunteer information.

I sat by myself every day during lunch, and I was fine with that. It was entertaining to watch from a distance without being a part of the action. I was starting to get worried since the nauseous feeling hadn't left my stomach. The thought of me being pregnant crossed my mind, but I threw that out because there was no way I could deal with a baby at that point. I was sitting at my normal table writing Aaron a letter that I planned to mail him since he wasn't returning my pages, or calling me. I needed to know what I did to make him not want to be bothered with me. I called his phone every chance I got and he never answered. If I had the number to his parents' house, I would have called his mom too but I didn't.

When KD walked up to me and sat down I looked up at him to let him know that it wasn't cool for him to be there. His best friend, Kendall, watched from their table with a grin on his face.

I said, "May I help you?" I wasn't sure what it was about him before, but now he wasn't doing anything for me but getting on my nerves. He had that same smile that he had before but it seemed generic to me, like he was trying to come off more confident than what he was.

He said, "What's wrong with you? Why are you so mean?" He looked confused while he waited for my answer.

I told him, "Sweetie, I am not mean at all. You don't even know me."

KD said, "Let me get to know you, Heaven. You seem so…I don't know…grown or something. Like you're above this high school shit. You weren't like that before. You used to look sad all the time. What happened? Where did you go?"

I asked him, "Why are you watching me so closely? Don't worry about where I went. Worry about yourself and your girl. Not me." There was nothing about him that I liked, he seemed corny and irritating.

KD told me, "I used to watch you because I had a crush on you." He laughed after he said it, like it embarrassed him to admit it. He continued, "I didn't know how to come at you because I wasn't sure if you'd like me or not. I used to have my brother mess with you so I could see what type of female you were."

If I had known that KD liked me the whole time that I liked him, I probably wouldn't have left. It taught me that you never know how insecure a person is regardless of what they look like. KD was handsome by anyone's standards, yet he was afraid to approach me. I told him, "That's so sweet, KD. It really is, but you have a girl now, so what do you want with me?"

KD replied speaking proper like he always did. "That's the second time that you said I have a girlfriend, who is it? Because I don't know."

I said, "You really are gonna sit here and tell me that Tandra isn't your girl?"

He said, "Tandra is cool, and that's it. We chilled a few times but that's it. She told you that?" I told him that she hadn't told me that but somebody close to her told me. He assured me that they were cool, not as close as I thought.

It didn't matter to me either way because I had to figure out what was going on with Aaron. I didn't have a car so I couldn't drive to his house and see if he was okay. I said, "Well, okay KD…"

He laughed and said, "Oh, okay…that's my cue?"

I didn't respond. I gave him a look that told him his answer. I watched him walk over to Kendall who was laughing hysterically at him. I wasn't sure how Kendall knew that KD hadn't been successful at getting my attention but he did. KD looked back at me and I sat in the same position watching him.

I could never date someone like him, and I didn't know what I was thinking before. The fact that his best friend was white bothered me. What could they really have in common? Didn't KD know that they were the enemy? In a perfect world we could all get along and live happily ever after. In the real world I felt like white people were sneaky, evil back stabbing liars. I thought most of them were ugly too. I wouldn't go as far as saying Kendall was ugly because he wasn't, but it was rare that I saw a decent looking white person. He looked like he belonged in a Tommy Hilfiger modeling ad.

In all honesty, I didn't know Kendall so it wouldn't be fair to say how he acted, but I hoped he was able to be himself even though he hung around mostly black people. I couldn't decide which was worse, the type of White person that tried to act like a Black person stereotypically acted, or the type that acted like a stereotypical White person. I found both to be annoying, I wondered why people couldn't simply be themselves. It bothered me a lot that it seemed like a lot of black people strived to be like white people. White people set the standard for what was good, bad, or anything else. And the black community was always ready to adapt to their standards or lack thereof. My hope was that I would marry Aaron, but if I didn't, I would always date and marry a dark-skinned man. They looked better than light-skinned guys to me, and when I thought about it, I was bitter about Joey in a way that I hadn't been previously. I understood why those white women were always in our men's faces. Everyone seemed to see the beauty in the black man, but the black man himself. White men saw it too, why else would the prisons be packed with mostly black men? My father told me years ago that when a white boy got into trouble with the law, he was more likely to get a lecture from the judge and sent on his way. On the other hand, it was typical for a black boy to be given by-the-book consequences. That's why it bothered me to see my brother doing such stupid things with Boomer. He clearly didn't know any better because my mother was always bailing him out. He thought that was how life went. The rules that we had to live by were different from their rules, so I didn't understand how KD and Kendall could connect.

I recall telling my mother that I would not relax my hair anymore because it was breaking my hair off. I had been home for a month at that point and I noticed that my hair was thinner than it had ever been. I read in a black hair magazine years before that stress caused breakage, so that could have played a part too. The conversation that I had with Gina about my hair stuck with me and I wanted it to always be healthy looking and pretty. When I wore it to school all back in a headband my mother looked at me like I had lost my mind. She called me stupid for not putting the chemicals in my hair. I told her that I didn't feel I needed to straighten my hair to be pretty but that I would when I wanted a different look.

My mother laughed and said, "I guess I kinda understand what you mean, we're ugly anyway. We're too dark to be pretty. It's sad, ain't it?" I chose not to respond to such ignorance. Meanwhile, my hair grew faster than ever without the harsh chemicals from relaxing it. My mother said, "What are the white people at school going to say?" For the first time I honestly felt like my mother was asking me a question out of genuine concern.

I told her, "I don't care what they think about me, mama. You shouldn't either."

She said, "I hate those bastards too, but we gotta work with them and go to school with them so we better at least act like we got some sense." I told my mother to look at my hair, I wanted her to see that there was nothing unreasonable about the way I wore my hair. It was soft and curly when it wasn't straight and I liked it either way. She said, "Well, it's not bad."

If that was the only compliment I would get from my mother, I would take it. What else could I do? I told her, "Mama, I can wear my hair however I want to. It doesn't define who I am. If white people or anyone thinks that I'm a weirdo for the way I wear my hair they can kiss me where the sun don't shine."

My mother went back to her old self. "While you runnin' around lookin' like a runaway slave don't be mad when you can't get a job."

Chapter 39

So you're having my baby...

I was forced to go and take a home pregnancy test since I couldn't recall the last time I had a period. I asked my mother to take me to the Osco up the street from our house. I told her it was because I needed maxi pads. I asked her for money to get them, but I walked in the store, stole the test and pocketed the money. My mother gave me the money but gave me a funny look at the same time. When I stood at the register paying for my drink, I acted as casual as I would have if I had paid for it. I asked the clerk for a bag to put my pop in. Once I was out of the store, I put the test in the bag and got in the car.

My mother watched my every move and said, "Let me see what kind of pads you got." She snatched the bag out of my hand before I could grab it. When she saw the test she practically went into convulsions. She screamed, "YOUR DUMB ASS DONE FUCKED AROUND AND GOT KNOCKED UP AND YOU AIN'T SEEN THE NIGGA SINCE! THAT SORRY BLACK SON OF A BITCH AIN'T CALLED OR CAME BY SINCE HE FUCKED YOU!"

I sat in silence as my mother drove back to our house. I was quiet because she was right. Aaron hadn't called me one time since I had been home. I still had the letter that I wrote him at lunch but I didn't have the courage to mail it. If he didn't respond to the letter I would be devastated, but if I didn't mail it I could blame myself and say that he didn't know how I felt about him because I hadn't told him. My mother was still yelling at me the whole time. "I THOUGHT YOU WERE SMARTER THAN THAT…BUT NO. YOU'RE JUST AS DUMB AS ANGEL! YOU TAKE THAT TEST AS SOON AS YOU GET YOUR FAST ASS IN THAT HOUSE. YOU HEAR ME?"

I was pregnant. I had no idea where Aaron was, my mother was so upset that she had stopped even talking to me. The norm for her was to walk in after work and go off on all of us, the new norm was for her to walk in and go straight to her room. I didn't understand why she was so disappointed in me. It was like she had high expectations for me to go and become something great in life. I paged Danni for what I told myself was the last time because I was done with her and Aaron. I hadn't even talked to her since Dontez had been murdered weeks ago. She called me back within ten minutes.

I picked up the phone and said, "I know you've been getting my pages." She told me that she had been, but that she had been really upset about Dontez dying so she wasn't talking to anyone. I said, "Danni, I'm so sorry that you lost your baby's father. I don't even know what to say." She cried on the phone while I listened to her. I didn't say a word. I just sat there because I wanted her to know that I was there but not to talk about myself. It was her time.

Between sniffling she said, "This is the second time that I've lost somebody that I love, it's like I'm cursed. Why would my baby daddy have to die? I mean, I knew him and Pooh was always talkin' shit to each other but I didn't think it was ever that serious to kill him." Danni started crying ever harder. At that point I didn't know what to say. She noticed the awkward silence and said with a laugh, "I'm sorry, Heaven. How are you doing? How are things at your mom's house?"

I sighed and said, "Things couldn't be better. Let's see…" I started crying too.

Danni said, "Heaven, what's wrong? Why are you crying?"

I said, "For one thing, I'm fucked up about Dontez. I know we weren't cool but I loved him. The other thing is that Aaron ain't fuckin' with me…He won't return my calls or pages at all. But the fucked up thing is that I'm pregnant. I can't have no fuckin' baby right now. I'm sorry, I can't."

Danni said, "Oh my God…PREGNANT?" I sat there while she continued, "What do you mean you can't have a baby? What are you planning to do?" I told her that I needed to get some money to have an abortion.

She said, "Heaven! Please don't do that. I'm begging you."

I told Danni, "If I can get some money I'm having an abortion. You have your baby, if that's what you want to do. I don't want a baby right now. I already called Planned Parenthood and I need a little over three hundred dollars."

Danni sighed and said, "Our babies would be raised together. It would be so fun, Heaven." I told Danni that she wasn't thinking about this enough. There was no way that I was ever going to struggle because of having kids then hate them for it. I fucked up and got pregnant and I wondered if my mother had felt the same way I did but chose not to have an abortion. She knew she didn't want kids, but she knew she wanted to fuck. Instead of getting herself birth control, she continued to have sex then got pregnant and took it out on her children because she never wanted them. That wouldn't be me. I was going to find a way to get an abortion and start my sex life over, using birth control.

I sat at my usual table, I was more angry than usual that day because I knew I needed money. When I looked up and saw KD and Kendall staring at me a light bulb went off. I smiled at KD and waved at him. He pointed to his chest to show that he was asking if I was talking to him. I gave him a seemingly genuine smile and nodded like only a teenage girl would. He walked toward me like he was feeling confident. His brother KeAndre walked into the cafeteria and spotted us. I wasn't worried about him, and I was prepared to embarrass him if he got in the way.

KD sat down and asked me why I was being so nice to him all of a sudden.

I told him, "I don't know…to be honest, I felt bad for being so mean to you. It wasn't called for, especially since I liked you a long time ago too." The way I saw it was that I could kill two birds with one stone. I could pay Tandra back like I planned, and fuck KD and tell him I was pregnant by him. Then get abortion money and live happily ever after.

He said, "Okay, well give me your number so I can call you sometime."

I wrote my number in his hand, and closed his hand back then looked up at him with all the innocence that I had in me.

KeAndre walked over to us and said, "What's up, Heaven? I heard you came back."

I said, "Hey, KeAndre. Did you miss me?" I laughed at the uncomfortable look on his face.

KD said, "No, he didn't miss you, but I did." He smiled at me and I smiled back at him.

KeAndre blushed and said, "I just wanted to see what was up with you, Heaven. I'll get at you later, K." He walked off leaving me and KD alone. He asked me if he could take me out to a movie so we planned on hooking up over the weekend.

KD and I hung out for two weeks straight and I was amazed at how cool he was once I gave him a chance. I'd previously decided that he was corny and too proper for me. While he did speak proper, it wasn't something that made him less black acting or more white acting than anyone else was. It donned on me that when I went to a different school I was made fun of for speaking proper also, and I knew that I didn't want to be white.

One afternoon when school let out, we were riding in his banged up Nissan and I asked him why his best friend was white. He laughed and said, "Why not?"

I told him, "Because they're not even cool people. I don't trust them. I wouldn't ever be able to be that cool with them. They're snakes."

He said, "Yeah, but that could be the case with anybody. My mom always taught me that there are good people and bad people in life. It's not cool to say that just because a person is black they're good, or just because they're white they're bad. You'll limit the amount of good people around you if you think only black people are good, Heaven. And to be honest, I've been snaked by more black people than white people anyway. But I won't stop loving a whole race of people because of that."

I said, "I don't think only black people are good, but I do think most whites are bad."

KD said, "You're too pretty to be so negative. You really think Kendall is foul? Without ever giving him a real chance? You're smarter than that. Who taught you to think like that?"

I told KD to shut up talking to me because I would always feel how I felt. However, the truth was that what KD said did make sense. I was offended that he called me negative since that was what I always called my mother behind her back. But in all honesty, what I said really was negative so he was simply being honest.

What I loved most about KD was the fact that he was opinionated. He came off initially like he was more timid than what he was. I had great times with him because he was a typical teenager. He had a car, he had a curfew, he played on the basketball team, and anything else that you could think of that would make it easy for him to fit in. We spent hours sitting over at the house he shared with his mother and KeAndre. We would laugh at silly movies, play cards and get upset when we lost, or wrestle like kids around the house. Most of the time when his mother came home from work, I would stand at the front door like I hadn't been there since school let out. I knew his mother didn't like me and I didn't care because as much as I was enjoying myself with KD I knew I was on a mission. We sat in his room playing cards like we usually did when I stood up and took my shirt off. KD's eyes got big and said, "Heaven, are crazy?! Put your fucking clothes back on before my mother comes home."

I smiled and said, "She won't be home until five-thirty. It's only three-thirty now." I took my skirt off that I wore also. KD was speechless. I said, "Is your dick hard now?" I looked at him as casually as I would have if I would have asked for a glass of water.

He tried to cover himself with a blanket on his bed and said, "I'm not going to answer that." I told him that he didn't need to because I could tell. I knelt in front of him and sucked his dick until he came in about a minute flat. When he was about to cum he moaned loud like I did when I was with Aaron. After I was done sucking his dick, I told him to lie back so that I could ride him. I knew I would be able to ride his dick with no problem because his penis was small. I was able to swallow it entirely without gagging, and that would never have happened with Aaron. I climbed on top of KD and he asked if I had a condom in a weak voice.

I sat on his dick and moved just a little so that he wouldn't want me to stop and asked innocently, "Do you want me to get up since we don't have a condom?"

He said, "You can stop in a minute." I laughed in my head because I knew that he would cum much sooner than a minute. I could hardly feel anything as I rode his dick and that pissed me off. I couldn't show how frustrated I was because I had to pretend I was turned on by KD. He started grabbing my waist and squirming and making weird faces while moaning in a high pitched voice. The more into it he was, the more I pretended I was. After his orgasm he was drained and looking at me like we were in love. He said, "Heaven…when I met you I wouldn't have thought that we would lose our virginity with each other."

I looked confused at first, then I realized that he thought I was a virgin. I knew that I planned to forget about Joey and that made me a virgin, but I wasn't ever going to forget about Aaron. I didn't even appreciate having to lie about that part of me. I replied, "Yeah, I'm shocked too." I got up and got my clothes on and asked him to take me home because I was sick of him for the day. Sex with him made me miss making love with Aaron.

I followed through on my plan to fuck KD so that I could make him think we had a baby on the way. I became distant with him because the truth was that he was genuinely getting on my nerves. When I saw him in school he was always in my face asking me what was wrong. When I would snap at him for no apparent reason he looked like a sad puppy dog. I couldn't think of any excuse to break up with him so I continued to distance myself. I skipped lunch every other day because I didn't want to see KD. No matter how hard I tried, I couldn't shake the feelings that I had for Aaron. I walked down the hall one afternoon after skipping lunch again and was shocked to see KD and Tandra in the hallway kissing. I stood and watched them and it made me very upset. I knew that I didn't want KD but I didn't want Tandra to have him either. When they realized I was standing in front of them watching their kiss they abruptly stopped. I didn't bother to speak to Tandra, I looked directly at KD and said, "I thought you didn't fuck with her like that? Why are you all up in her face and kissing her stank ass?"

Tandra said, "Heaven, why are you so worried about what he does? Don't tell me you're still mad about that Aaron shit. It was a fucking *joke*, damn."

KD said, "Who is Aaron?" He looked at me like he had the right to an answer from me.

I told him, "Don't worry about it. You need to worry about lying to me. You said you didn't fuck with her."

Tandra said, "Wait…." She looked down at the ground like she was trying to put the situation together in her head then she looked up at me, "Are you supposed to be fuckin' with him?!"

I stared at her without answering her.

Chapter 40

So I call you my best friend...

"**A**re you fuckin' with her, KD?" Tandra asked.

He said, "I don't have a girl, everybody is cool. That's it."

I looked at KD and said, "Just cool? So we were just cool when you fucked me?"

Tandra's eyes got big and she yelled, "YOU FUCKED THIS BITCH WHILE YOU WERE FUCKING ME TOO?!"

KD said, "I'm done with this."

As KD walked off I said, "You ain't shit with your little ass dick, you pussy!" I couldn't believe he lied to me about being a virgin. He kept walking as if he hadn't heard a word I said.

I had my back to Tandra so I wasn't prepared when she pushed me and said, "You stupid bitch!" I fell onto the floor and got up holding my stomach because it started hurting immediately. I pushed her back into a locker and grabbed her by her hair while punching her in her stomach. I wasn't sure how I was able to fight Tandra because the pain in my stomach was excruciating. It felt like menstrual cramps to the one hundredth power. Tandra and I fought until we were broken up by a teacher. Tandra was taken into the principal's office and I was taken into the nurse's office. People that saw the fight were cheering me on because very few people liked Tandra, people that didn't see the fight said I lost because they saw me going to the nurse's office to be treated. I was in tears because of the pain I was in. The nurse asked me if I was pregnant and I told her I was. She informed me that since I couldn't have been very far along it wouldn't make sense that I could be going through a miscarriage. She told me to lay down and try to relax so that I wouldn't stress my baby any more than I already had. I listened to her tell me that it could be likely that I could miscarry if I was a drinker or smoker. The nurse explained that young mothers were more likely to miscarry than older mothers and a poor diet could play a huge part in that as well. I didn't tell her that I hadn't been eating much since I had been home because there was never much food. I left out the fact that I never ate lunch because the food was nasty. I wasn't sad about the fact that I may have been losing my unborn child. I didn't want it anyway.

After I had the miscarriage I was ready to swear off males altogether. I was glad that I didn't have to lie to KD and get abortion money. I had started to believe that I got what I deserved when I had the miscarriage. The pain was something that I would never forget as long as I lived. I took a week off from school to allow my body to heal, and to hide from the world for a while. My mother didn't bother to ask when I planned to go back to school. When Angel caught wind of everything that happened she came into our room and grabbed some clothes. She slept in the living room on the couch to keep her distance. I was lying in the bed on a Friday evening, it was the week I had the miscarriage. I heard a knock at the door and ignored it because I figured it was Boomer for Leonard. Angel came and told me, "It's somebody named KD at the door for you, Heaven."

I jumped up and threw my hair into a ponytail and rinsed my face off. I went to the living room and said, "What do you want?" He asked if he could talk to me outside for a second since Angel wasn't shy about the fact that she was in our conversation.

I followed him outside, and he said, "Heaven...I can't stop thinking about you. I feel like I love you. Even if you don't want me, I wanted to come tell you that I don't fuck with Tandra. She's not...you. She doesn't know what a man wants. I'll do anything to be your man." I was surprised by what KD said because I thought we were done after everything that happened between us. I told him there was nothing I wanted from him because he hurt me so much. He seemed to melt when I told him how I supposedly felt. He said,

"Can I take you out to eat? Please? I just want to talk to you." I couldn't deny that I was feeling something for KD and I figured since Aaron clearly wasn't messing with me that I might as well be KD's girlfriend. Maybe he could help me get over Aaron. I told him to wait a second while I got dressed. He told me, "I don't care what you look like. I just want to be with you."

I went into the house and changed my clothes so that I looked decent and we left for Red Lobster. It was the same place that Aaron and I went together but I was ready to create new memories. It was a Friday night so I expected the place to be packed, but not as packed as it was. We walked in and were told that the wait would be an hour and a half. KD asked if I was cool with that and I was. I put my hand in KD's hand to show him affection. He didn't say anything about my gesture. He just looked at me to acknowledge it. I rested my head on his shoulder and told him I was glad that he came to my house to talk to me. When he said he was nervous but he knew what he had to do I was flattered. Hopefully, one day, I could get the feeling with KD that I got with Aaron. KD was very nice to me and I knew that he would be nice to any girl he messed with. I chose to forgive him lying to me and saying that we lost our virginity to each other. I had been full of shit myself so there wasn't a lot of room for me to be upset. Though I truly felt like his penis was smaller than I preferred, I was ashamed of myself for becoming angry and reacting that way. They called KD's name for us to be seated right at an hour of waiting. KD allowed me to follow behind the hostess and he followed behind me looking as handsome as ever. I walked through the restaurant looking at each table simply for the sake of being nosy and was shocked to see Aaron sitting at a table with a girl that I had never seen before.

Chapter 41

I never wanna be without you…

My eyes got big from the shock, while he didn't bat an eye. Aaron looked as cool and calm as he always did. I went from being in a good mood to a foul mood. I walked to our table that was one table away from the table that Aaron and his date were on. Aaron had his back to me but I had a clear view of the girl. I was watching her laugh and giggle at whatever Aaron said to her. I wanted to go and strangle her, but I kept my composure. KD watched me and asked if I was cool. He said that something was different between now and the walk to our seats. He turned around then quickly turned back to face me. I told him, "I'm cool. Do you know what you're getting?"

The truth was that I had lost my appetite, but I was planning to fake it so that KD wouldn't suspect anything. Aaron's date only had eyes for him. She was oblivious to the fact that I hadn't taken my eyes off of her. When she leaned in for a kiss I lost control of the situation. I jumped up and prepared to walk over to their table. KD asked where I was going. I told him, "I'm so sorry, I have to say something to them." I was about to embarrass Aaron because he deserved it. I was going to tell him everything he did to piss me off in front of the entire restaurant. When I approached the table and looked in his eyes my heart started beating fast. My eyes started watering and I said, "You can't even say hi to me, Aaron? Really, it's like that?" All of the feelings I had for Aaron were still there and I didn't have the heart to say anything mean or hateful to him. I couldn't stop the tears from rolling down my face, so I walked off looking for the restroom. I turned around and glanced at KD who was standing up watching the whole ordeal. I told a random waiter to show me to the restroom. Once I was inside I went into the stall and cried harder than I had ever cried before. I was mad at myself for not being able to hold my tears in. I showed him that I still cared and that bothered me because there were other things that I needed to say to Aaron besides asking why he didn't speak to me. I didn't know how I was going to expect KD not to hate me, and I didn't care.

I wiped my tears and walked outside of the restroom to find Aaron standing against the wall waiting for me. I tried to turn around and go back into the restroom, but he grabbed my arm and told me that he wanted to talk to me. I cried more and told him, "No, you don't Aaron, because if you did you wouldn't have ignored my calls and my pages."

Aaron said, "I'm sorry, Heaven. I was gonna call you, I swear I was. After I left your mother's house that day I didn't know if I wanted to deal with all that shit. I started wondering if you would be crazy like that. I love you so much, baby. I'm here right now trying to get over you. I can't shake…you. When I saw you walk in tonight I wanted to knock that nigga out, but I didn't because I knew that I fucked up with you. What I gotta do? Just tell me."

I shook my head and told him that we both were out with other people so there was no point in doing anything tonight. Aaron told me, "I don't give a fuck about that. Is that the only thing stopping you from being with me? I mean, tonight, and here on out. I don't want you to leave my side."

I asked Aaron, "What about you moving away? You didn't tell me."

Aaron replied, "Because I haven't decided yet. If I do decide to leave, just come with me. You don't have shit to lose. I only care about being with you, that's all I want right now." He wiped my tears while I told him that I wanted to be with him too. I asked him to let me go and apologize to KD and I would call him later.

I said, "If you return my page I'll know you're serious."

Aaron said, "Did you fuck him or something? Why do you care about his feelings and shit?" I explained that it just wasn't right to leave someone with no explanation whatsoever. I felt I owed KD that much.

Aaron said, "Okay, well, I won't leave this part of town then. I'll wait for you to page me then I'll meet you at your mom's house." He hugged me and told me that he loved me again.

I walked back to the table and noticed that Aaron's date was boiling as she sat and watched me. I would be upset too if I were her, so I didn't get mad or defensive.

KD said, "Let me guess…that was Aaron?"

I nodded and said, "I am so sorry, KD. Please don't hate me…I didn't mean to…"

As I was finishing my speech Aaron walked up and said, "What's up, man?" He had his hand out for KD to shake it but KD refused. Aaron shrugged and said to me, "You ready, baby? I'm about to run her home but I want you to go with me." Aaron totally disregarded our initial plan.

I looked at KD and he said, "Heaven, just go. Damn, it's not that serious anyway. You don't have to feel bad at all." Though what KD said was rude, I was happy that he didn't seem to care because I didn't want to feel bad about anything. I followed Aaron to the table he was sitting at and stood by him. He told his date, "Did you want a to-go box? I'm about to take you home and chill with my girl." His tone wasn't rude or demanding. He was talking to her as if she shouldn't be upset.

She told him, "Just take me home, and don't ever call me again."

Aaron replied, "Okay, I won't."

I rode in the front seat of Aaron's car and his date rode in the back seat as we headed down the highway to take her home. I watched Aaron drive with a genuine look of love. I would always appreciate the boyish charm that KD had, but Aaron was the man for me. The few lessons I learned from KD were valid, but I knew my heart would always belong to Aaron because he loved me unconditionally. I didn't care how far I had to travel to be with him, as long I was with him.

Who am I? I was given the first and middle name Abeni Kahmila at birth. However, my name does not define who I am. I am a Mother, Author, and above all else I am a Woman.

I've always had a story to tell, I just didn't know how or where to start. I remember writing my first book when I was in third grade. I don't recall what the book was about. I just knew that I wanted to write stories. Time passed and I insisted on pushing my God given talent away. I chose to tap into my talent after many years of living my life with the feeling that there was more to my life than what I felt others considered normal. Though I went through many road blocks, I'm still standing. I gave birth to my son Jordan when I was a teenage girl, and by the grace of God he's a wonderful young man that I am very thankful for. I didn't go through all of what the character in my debut novel A Piece of Heaven went through, but our story is very similar. I believe that the things we go through in life can either make or break us. My strength comes from the obstacles I've endured. I was blessed three years ago with a little girl, we named her Ayah. She is just as feisty as her mother and we truly enjoy watching her grow.

I love listening to music, but reading is by far my favorite past time. I don't get much time to read anymore since I'm almost always writing. I find myself writing notes down, or making mental notes because inspiration is everywhere. Most authors will agree that words are as powerful as the air we breathe, and the water we drink. I listen carefully to people's stories, because we all have one. I pay special attention to colors, and shapes and sizes as well. I hope to inspire, and encourage anyone that I come into contact with. Since I am a new author, I am eager to meet other authors. Feel free to email me, or go to my Facebook page, even if it's just to say hey.

I enjoy reading almost anything, but I will drop what I'm doing when I get word that Mary Monroe or Sister Souljah have released new books. My favorite book of all time would have to be No Disrespect, by Sister Souljah. I read that book for the first time at a very young age but the truth in the book is what touched me. I truly believe that my novels will touch others in the same way.